Praise for the works o

Being Emily

Winner - 2013 Moonbeam Children's Book Award
in Young Adult Fiction – Mature Issues
Winner - 2013 Golden Crown Literary Award
in Dramatic / General Fiction
Finalist - 2013 Lambda Literary Award
in Young Adult

Engrossed... Enchanted... Rachel Gold has crafted an extraordinarily poignant novel in *Being Emily*... The unique mechanism of depicting Emily's speech as computer code is striking, defining the character distinctively. The careful and deliberate spacing of Claire's chapters are extraordinary; resulting is a pacing of action that is gripping. There is definitely gold to be found in this well-constructed novel.

-Lambda Literary Review

It's rare to read a novel that's involving, tender, thought-provoking and informative... What's impressive is Gold's delicacy in handling the physicality of Emily's story. She smoothly navigates the more intimate parts of Emily's transformation. And the author can bring you to tears as you read about Emily's struggle with gender identity.

-TwinCities.com

I couldn't put it down... It's not a sad or angst-ridden story at all. Instead it feels incredibly honest, and there are moments of joy, anger, and sorrow, laced together in a way that will make you cry and laugh along with the characters. It doesn't shy away from the hardship but it also doesn't make the claim that this hard stuff is all a trans person's life is ever... All in all, I think this is an excellent book that captures an honest, painful, but ultimately hopeful and joyful story of a young trans teen.

-YAPride.org

Just Girls

Winner 2015 Golden Crown Literary Award
in Young Adult

The novel covers all manner of sex, sexuality and gender identities and is an excellent educational tool, as well as a very good read... This book sits particularly well in the teen / young adult audience category, but can be enjoyed and appreciated by a much older audience as well, especially those who are keen to expand their knowledge and try to understand a little more about what it means to be trans*.

-Curve Magazine

Brilliant, brilliant, and all kinds of brilliant... Written with a sure-footed and almost magical lightness... Like a great wine: a beautiful blend of different emotions and different people told with depth, and complexity. It is a richly layered novel, which leaves the reader enthralled and wanting more of this exquisite concoction.

-Lambda Literary Review

As I said for *Being Emily*, this is an excellent book for any young person to read as it is a story about people like them and unlike them, which is always the basis for a good tale... What comes across strongly is that, to use my favourite quote from that great woman philosopher Marge Simpson, "our differences are only skin deep but our sames go down to the bone." This is also another fine read for any age – we were all young once and as I always maintain, still changing, still evolving.

-Glasgow Women's Library

My Year Zero

Winner 2016 Golden Crown Literary Award
in Young Adult

Gold has skillfully written a story with timely topics for navigating the slippery approach to adulthood, ranging from sex and sexuality, relationships, self-discovery, overcoming difficulties with authority figures, parental bullying and neglect, and bipolar disorder. *My Year Zero*...will appeal to both young and more experienced adults, meeting difficult topics head-on with a compelling story (and a masterful story-within-a-story) written to both inform and entertain.

-Lambda Literary Review

In the Silences

Winner 2019 Moonbeam Children's Book Award silver medal in Pre-Teen Fiction – Mature Issues
Winner 2020 Golden Crown Literary Award in Young Adult

Rachel Gold has crafted a story that is both a sweet coming of age romance, but is also a treatise on societal issues that impact everyone. ... *In the Silences* is something I think could be and should be required reading for a number of people and could be used in a classroom setting. I absolutely loved this book and found myself learning new things. This book will leave you thinking and that is something that only great books can do.

-The Nerdy Girl Express

As many white people are starting a long-overdue education in whiteness and anti-racism, *In the Silences* is a great book to turn to. This is a YA novel equally about Kaz's exploration of their nonbinary identity and their awakening to how racism affects their best friend (and love interest), Aisha, who is Black and bisexual. I loved how both Aisha and Kaz educate themselves to be better allies to each other—they support each other while recognizing that their struggles are different. ... For both the nonbinary rep and the exploration of whiteness, this is a perfect addition to any high school library or teen's bookshelf.

-BookRiot

synclair

Other Bella Books by Rachel Gold

Being Emily
Just Girls
My Year Zero
Nico & Tucker
In the Silences

About the Author

Raised on world mythology, fantasy novels, comic books, and magic, Rachel Gold is the author of multiple award-winning queer & trans young adult novels. Her novel *Being Emily* was the first young adult novel to tell the story of a trans girl from her perspective. Rachel is a nonbinary lesbian, all-around geek and avid gamer, in addition to being a Visiting Assistant Professor of English at Macalester College. For more information visit: www.rachelgold.com.

synclair

rachel gold

BELLA
BOOKS

2020

Bella Books, Inc.
P.O. Box 10543
Tallahassee, FL 32302

Printed in the United States of America on acid-free paper.

First Bella Books Edition 2020

Editor: Katherine V. Forrest
Cover Designer: Kristin Smith

ISBN: 978-1-64247-174-8

Acknowledgments

I want to thank God, of course, with immense gratitude, awe and love—plus the mundane sense of "Thank God," that happens every time I send the final version of a novel to my publisher. I've been blessed to have an experience of the sacred that is full of humor and joy. I hope this comes through to you in these pages and, if you want, in your life.

Heartfelt thank-yous also go to:

• My editor, Katherine V. Forrest, whose intelligence and encouragement is always so welcome! I learn more from you with every novel.

• My dear friend and alpha reader Stephanie Burt who ignores barriers and believes in magic.

• My family who has always supported my spiritual journey.

• My aunts Rachel Pollack and Kate Bornstein who are still teaching me so much and whose support has been life-giving.

• The keen beta reading insights of Patrice James, Kirstin Cronn-Mills, Raikha Patel, and Alia Whipple. Special thanks to Raikha for helping me understand teen perspectives on religion and atheism.

• Joann Bell for sharing her thoughts and her sermons with me and helping me get a sense for LGBTQ-affirming Christian community.

• Todne Thomas, Assistant Professor of African American Religions at Harvard Divinity School, for her help with Camden's religion, especially pointing me toward Monica Coleman's remarkable *Making A Way Out Of No Way*. (Also for nerding out with me!)

As always, much love to the members of my household, who support me through all my wild endeavors.

For my teachers and the generations of queer and trans ancestors who make me possible.

CHAPTER ONE

My best friend and her girlfriend pretend to clear dishes from the patio table but don't return from the kitchen. This means they're making out in my bed. Yes, I have feelings about that. If you have a spare weekend and a psychology degree, I'll tell you all of them.

Kinz and I have been friends since eighth grade and I made it all the way through ninth before recognizing my profound crush on her. Timing and courage aligned during junior year, last winter, but Camden got there first. Camden who we didn't even know was into girls.

Kinz has told her parents she's queer plenty of times. Her father refuses to believe her and if he did—if she tried to bring Camden home in a making-out way—they'd ban Camden from the house. And ground Kinz forever. They can't do girlfriend stuff at Camden's house either, because she's not out. That leaves Kinz's car, but she'd begged me for the comfort of a real bed and I'd agreed that as long as they stayed on top of my comforter, they could make out a little.

I had not realized this would leave my bed scented with a combination of girls I liked who I was not dating. There aren't enough swear words to express that degree of shitcrappery.

This is not how I intended to begin my beautifully quiet summer. I'd planned to have a spiritual quest in the fortunate absence of parents, especially my mom.

I knock on my bedroom door and say, "Kinz? Get decent."

"I am," she insists.

I crack the door open and slip through without peeking at the bed. I don't want to see if either of them had to hastily throw their shirt on. I will not think about that any more than I already am. I grab the bag looped over the back of my desk chair and the meditation book I'd found in my box of religious and spiritual treasures.

"Going for a walk," I say, my back to the bed.

"You sure?" Kinz asks. She knows I'm not the walking type.

"Yeah, have fun. But not too much fun, okay?"

Camden's laugh propels me out of the room—because of its clear surprise and joy—and then out of my house.

As soon as I leave my front yard, I'm under the cover of trees. This neighborhood has so much greenery. We used to live a couple of miles north, within walking distance of Kinz. Three years ago, the tech company where my parents work got acquired by a bigger company and they made a bunch of money. We moved from that suburb of Minneapolis to one south with expensive houses bordering big lakes. I still go to the same school, but now my house is a lot bigger than Kinz's and that's not even counting the outdoor kitchen. I can't walk over to see her anymore. I could borrow Dad's trusty Toyota and drive, but not this summer because my brother has dibs and my folks don't want me driving by myself while they're out of the country. Like I'd get in an accident when I'm a much safer driver than Kinz. Not that I'd tell them that.

Two blocks from my house, a hiking trail intersects the sidewalk. The official paved trail winds through the trees for a half mile and then around a small lake, but there's a spot a hundred paces from the sidewalk where a dirt footpath leads into the trees and down to the river. I duck onto that cooler, shaded path. It's almost nine, but the sun hasn't set fully so under the trees is dusky without being dark.

The stream that made the ravine behind my house feeds into this river, making it wide and deep enough that it's tricky to cross in the middle. Over the years, people have rolled large stones into the water. It's possible to hop across if you have longish legs and good balance.

The space under the trees grows darker from the density of branches and trunks. Past the stones, I sit in a flat area, carpeted with old, dry leaves, beside the river. Of course now it's too dark to see the pages of the book and figure out how this meditation thing works.

I shine my phone's flashlight on the cover. Below the title, *The Posture of Meditation*, there's a statue of an Asian guy with his legs crossed and his hands together elegantly. His facial expression is serene or slightly annoyed or puzzled and dealing with it, I can't decide. I want to be able to be puzzled and annoyed without freaking out. I open the book and turn to the first page.

"Oh!" a girl's voice says from across the river. "Is that really you?"

Squinting into the darkness, I see a person kneeling by the far bank. Maybe my height. Slender if those are her shoulders. I can't tell much from the few syllables I've heard, but I feel that she's probably my age, maybe from my school.

"I'm sorry," I say. "Who are you looking for?"

She leans forward, hands on the river sand, as if she could crawl across the water to me. Then she stands up and asks, "Emma?"

That *is* my first name. I haven't used it in a few years and most of my teachers call me Synclair, but she could've heard one use it.

She asks, "Emma Synclair?" so she must go to my school. Someone I haven't heard speak often? A girl in one of my classes maybe or a friend of a friend.

"Who's there?"

"Stay there," she says and moves to the rocks in the river. She's between my average height and Kinz's tallness with long, straight, dark hair. She's wearing a sleeveless shirt and loose pants, barefoot. The search engine in my brain is throwing all kinds of errors because she resembles no one I know. And I would remember a girl like *this*.

She dances across the rocks and strides down the bank to crouch in front of me. Her fingers find the edge of my phone and turn it so the light shines on her face: very black hair and eyebrows stark against warm, pale skin, a long nose, beautiful cheekbones, all-around beautiful. How could I have missed her at school? Except…she tosses her hair out of her face and smiles at me. One dark brown eye, one blue. I've only ever known one person with heterochromia; she's the reason I know the word.

"Avery!" I lunge forward and hug her. Her arms close around me just as hard. This body is so much bigger than I remember, but she still smells of deep sandalwood, soft rose, and bright jasmine—especially her hair, which is significantly longer than six years ago.

I let go and slide back out of the hug. She might not even like hugs now. But she's grinning.

"Are you real?" I ask her.

Her laugh is a richer version of the bell-like laugh I remember from when we were eleven and best friends. From second through fifth grade, we'd lived three blocks apart. At first we'd played at each other's houses every day out of convenience, but in fourth grade when everyone was acquiring more friends, we stayed best friends.

I'd cried so much when she and her mom suddenly moved out of state before sixth grade. Her mom hadn't left any information about where they went. My parents helped me search for her online but we didn't find her and eventually my mom said we should stop. I'd written letters to her for a while, imagining that someday I'd have a place to send them. I still had them on a flash drive in the box with my action figures and dolls.

Back when we were little, Avery had been a twiggy kid with a mop of black hair that her mom kept short because Avery tended to get things stuck in it. Now her hair falls to mid-boob and she has boobs! (Which I am absolutely *not* looking at under her thin shirt.) This is superbly not the Avery I remember from fifth grade; my lungs have forgotten their main job and are busy squeezing my heart.

"I'm real," she insists. "Here for the summer. Staying at my grandparents'. Wow." She touches the shaved side of my head that I can flop my hair over or not as I want. "I like this." Her fingers brush the frame of my nerdy-hip square glasses with rounded edges. "And these."

"You grew up," I say.

"Working on it. You too. I might not have recognized you except for your smile."

I must've been smiling at the meditation guy on the book cover. My smile is dorky and lopsided, especially when it's big. It's off-center; the first two-thirds of my smile happen only on the right side of my face.

"Where did you go?" I ask. "You disappeared. You didn't write me or anything. I looked for you."

"Oh. Yeah." She sits back on her heels and watches the river flowing by us, her mouth twisting with a scowl. "We had to hide from my dad for a while."

I scoot forward, crunching old leaves, and hug her again. She holds onto me. I remember being scared of her dad and I didn't even have to live with him.

She pulls out of the hug and tucks her hair behind one ear, twists her fingers together. "He moved," she says. "Now I can visit my grandparents. I'm staying with them for the summer."

"They live around here?"

"North a ways. You didn't used to live here either. I went by your old house, just to see. I wasn't sure." She stops and watches the water again. "I was afraid you'd be mad at me. That you'd think I ditched you."

"I'm not mad," I say. I am extremely not mad. "This is all kinds of amazing."

"What are you doing out here?"

"All my really good friends love to cook and they took over my house since I've got the best kitchen. Plus my brother has friends over so it's super loud. I figured I'd hide in the woods and learn to meditate," I tell her, not having the presence of mind to come up with anything cool.

"And because it's the solstice," Avery says.

"The what?"

"Summer solstice? Isn't that why you picked tonight?"

"No, it just seemed like a good time."

"You *accidentally* picked the summer solstice to learn to meditate? Good instincts. I can teach you, the basics at least," she says. "There's a solstice bonfire. Do you want to come see it? We don't have to dance or anything, we can stay at the edge, but I should let my cousin know where I am."

"Yes," I say before most of the words have registered. I bought in at "do you want," because no way can I let seventeen-year-old Avery vanish into the woods now that I've found her. Or she's found me.

I have a lot of questions, like: how is there a solstice bonfire in my boring neighborhood and why don't I know about it? But that can wait.

"Oh good, come on!"

I drop my phone and the book into my bag and loop it over my shoulder. Avery takes my hand as if a day hasn't passed since the last time we hung out and draws me up the bank to the rocks. With my hand in hers, I cross well enough. My foot slips once and my toes get wet. She's barefoot, her long toes curling over the edges of the rocks. She's gotten so much longer as she grew up, not only her toes but her feet and legs and waist and fingers and neck. And that hair! Pure black and loose, shifting and shimmering in the fading glow of the sky.

On her side of the river, her sandals sit next to a pile of loose dirt. She slips her feet into them, points at the dirt and says, "Planting my prayers."

"Sure."

She flashes a grin at me, pulls me down a path I've never used before as she says, "You have no idea what I'm talking about do you? I thought your parents sent you to get some religious education."

"Yeah, to churches and temples, I don't remember anyone planting prayers."

"Wicca? Paganism? Witchcraft?"

"Seen it on TV."

"That'll do," she says. "It's so good to see you. I can't believe you were just there. I saw the flash of light and looked up and you had that smile. I thought I'd made you up."

"I'm not completely sure you didn't," I say. This fast walk along the narrow dark path feels too dreamlike and she still has my hand. How long can I hold her hand before it becomes deeply weird?

She laughs and we scramble down a slope of dirt to exit the trees at the edge of one of the bigger lakes in my neighborhood. We stand at the crescent tip of a beach. At its widest point, maybe a hundred feet away, a bonfire burns orange-red. Low drumbeats play and a half-dozen people dance while another dozen sit around the fire talking. This is my neighborhood?

"You don't have to meet them," Avery says. "Wait here and I'll tell my cousin and get us something to drink."

"I don't drink alcohol," I tell her.

"I wasn't offering," she says, grins at me, kicks off her sandals and runs down the beach.

The seating options are sand or dirt. I choose sand and put my bag next to Avery's sandals. She returns with two bottles of water and a small bag of pretzels.

"Are they symbolic?" I ask. "We're going to bury our pretzels later to signify puzzles in our lives?"

"That's a great idea."

I open a water and take a sip, collect a small handful of pretzels and watch tiny waves lick the lakeshore. Avery sits next to me, so close the tiny hairs on her arm might be touching the tiny hairs on mine. Mine are standing up, for sure, raised toward that possible contact. There's enough light to see the crisscross lines on her dark pants and the swirls on her loose V-neck shirt.

"Cool shirt," I say. "And pants."

"They're pajama bottoms. Summer weight. Super light. Better than shorts for running through the woods and stuff."

"There's stuff? What stuff?" I ask chuckling, then add, "You always did love pajamas. Weren't there some weekends you never changed out of them?"

"I tried, but Dad wouldn't let me," she says. "You used to have the best Lego collection of anyone. Do you still?"

"No, I gave them away a few years ago. I have some action figures and dolls but I don't really set up scenes for them the way we used to with the Legos."

"You sound like you want to," she says. "We're not too old, you know."

I laugh because as the youngest of three kids, I'm never considered too old for anything. Maybe I should set up a scene with my awesome Jesus action figure and my *Prince of Egypt* dolls. Of course then my brother would take a photo and send it to our parents, so maybe not.

"You know how to meditate?" I ask her. "Since when?"

She shrugs one shoulder and her arm brushes mine. "Mom got into Buddhism after we moved. More than the Wicca she'd been into. I stayed with Wicca and added Buddhist meditation techniques. Why'd you pick meditation?"

"My brain is kind of a jerk most of the time. And I feel like…I lost something and it's out there waiting for me. Remember when you gave me that statue and my mom freaked out and made me give it back?"

"The triple goddess, Hecate. I still have her," Avery says softly.

"You do?"

"I took her with me when we left, because I knew I was going to miss you so much. She's on my altar at home. I used to ask her to watch over you, to make sure you were having fun."

"I missed you too," I whisper.

She leans her shoulder into mine.

"When did you stop asking Hecate to watch out for me?" I ask.

"I had a dream about you," she says and is quiet for an awkwardly long time. I assume she's figuring out how to tell me the dream, but instead she says, "And I realized you were okay. You'd make other friends."

"Eventually," I tell her. "How about you?"

She shrugs. "Why meditation instead of a church, temple or mosque, or rituals?"

"Meditation I can do by myself. I don't know any Muslims or Wiccans, until now. My life is too weird for a church or temple and I'd have to find a gay-affirming one." I stop and hold my breath, realizing I outed myself.

"Oh," Avery says and we sit in silence for an excruciatingly long time, maybe even a minute.

"You can't be Wiccan and not cool with gay people, can you?" I finally ask.

She takes a long breath and says, "Emma, you were my first crush. I date girls."

"Whoa! Shizzle sticks, what?"

Laughing, catching her breath, she sips from her water bottle and settles back next to me in that almost-touching way. "I came out to myself two years ago. And when I looked back I could see how smitten with you I was. I followed you around everywhere."

"I thought you didn't have anything better to do."

"No, you were the coolest nerd. You made up the best games and make-believe. I cried so much when we moved away."

"Me too," I admit, feeling like we're a thousand years old. As if we're vampires sitting around talking about that time we were human in centuries past. "Also everyone calls me Synclair now."

"Nice. Why?"

"My friend Kinzey and I decided when we started high school that it'd be cool to go by our last names and it stuck. And I don't know if I feel like an Emma."

"Synclair," she says my name slowly, drawn out, soft. "Are you ready for me to teach you to meditate?"

"Yes please."

"You can sit in a chair or on the ground and just cross your legs. There's also full or half lotus, or this cool Burmese way."

Avery crawls across the sand until she's in front of me. She sits with her heels pulled in toward her crotch. My knees don't approve of that, so I sit cross-legged.

"Put your hands on your thighs wherever it's comfortable," she says. "You'll adjust them in a bit. And imagine somebody's pulling up on a string that's attached to the back of your head, so the back of your neck is long but your chin is down a smidge."

I try to do all of this while watching Avery do it, which means watching Avery and contemplating what color the moonlight makes her hair because "black" is not enough words to describe what I'm seeing.

She tells me, "Now pay attention to your spine. Imagine there's a channel that's the width of a bubble tea straw running up the inside of your spine from the bottom of your pelvis to the back of your head. Move around however you need to and make sure that the channel is open, not pinched or closed anywhere. That'll show you how to sit. If you only focus on how your legs are or where your hands are, you can end up with the channel all smooshed and you want it open."

I nod but she has her eyes closed, so I say, "Okay."

"Imagine there's a balloon in your lower belly and feel it get bigger when you inhale and deflate when you exhale."

As I try this, I wonder what color the balloon is and what Avery has been doing the last six years and if she dated anyone. How did she know to come out to herself? Was there a girl? Or did she crush out on some actress? When did she realize I was her first crush? And, omg, what does that even mean?

I remember playing with her almost every day after school, even when other girls were getting into boys and people started practice dating each other—as if it was a big deal to say you were dating some boy in fifth grade. We had *both* ignored that foolishness. I'd assumed that was because we were both smart—hadn't figured it would mean we were also quite thoroughly lesbian. Though she could be bi or queer or another identity. "Dating girls" includes a lot of identities and she hadn't specified. I want to ask but I'm supposed to be meditating.

"How's it going?" she asks, the sound of laughter in her voice. How badly have I been fidgeting?

"I'm thinking. Aren't I supposed to stop thinking?"

"That's probably not going to happen anytime in the next few years. I've been meditating most days for two years and I still think all sorts of things."

"Like what?" I ask.

She opens her eyes. Her blue eye, the left one, is in shadow, deep sapphire. Her brown eye is a lustrous black pearl. "When did you come out?" she asks.

"A couple years ago, but it wasn't a surprise really. My..." I stop before I can say "best friend," because it seems mean to say that to my former best friend. "A really good friend came out and I was super envious for a few months. I realized that I wanted to be a lesbian too because I already did like girls so, wish granted, I was one. How about you?"

"I kissed a girl at a party," Avery says and I'm instantly jealous. "She was joking around but I wasn't. Then when I thought about it, I've always had a girl friend who I wished was a girlfriend. Do you?" She pauses, brushes her hair out of her face. "Have a girlfriend?"

"Not at the moment, I mean, not for a while, I mean, no."

Meditation is clearly not working. I am *not* calmer than I was when we sat down with our knees almost touching.

I ask, "So I'm supposed to imagine this balloon and sit for a while and that's it?"

"That's the first step," she says.

"And you don't tell me the next one until I've mastered this like some *Karate Kid* business?"

She laughs. "No, silly. I can tell you, it won't make the kind of sense that it will after you practice for a while. And there are so many ways to meditate. You should read your book and try other ways and see what works best for you."

"But this is what you do?"

"Yes, I sit and feel the inner channel and let my body relax around it and breathe low in my belly. Mom and I first learned in the Hindu context, with Shiva and Shakti creating the world, and the kundalini energy inside our bodies echoing their love for each other. The kundalini is that energy you feel in the bubble tea straw. But you can have different divine beings who make the world and aren't gendered as a woman and a man. I mean, our gods switch gender all the time—and they're divine, they're beyond that. So I can have two women if I want. It's a way to put a relatable story on a reality we can't define."

"So God is a woman in your version?" I ask. "Or two women?"

"Yes." She's beaming now and sitting still, her body upright and loose, head balanced, eyes level with mine. I see the rise and fall of her chest in the V exposed by her shirt; it's moving a lot slower than mine. She says, "In my creation story, there are two goddesses Inanna and Gaia. Out of her eternal love for Inanna, Gaia makes the whole universe for them to play in. Gaia is the universe. But it can be hard for Inanna to fully connect with Gaia because there's so much stuff going on in the universe. When I sit to meditate, I feel the energy of Gaia under me and Inanna above me. Their energies can meet inside of me."

"That's...kind of hot," I say.

"Makes it easier to want to meditate," she tells me, eyes shining. "Try it?"

I close my eyes but I don't know what Gaia looks like or Inanna. Gaia is Greek and if I were guessing, based on knowing Avery, Inanna's from somewhere in the Middle East. Now I'm wondering which one of them would be me and which one Avery and how we'd make a universe together—and I am certain that I am not meditating one iota.

"Where's Inanna from?" I ask, opening my eyes.

"Sumer," she says and tells me a story about a goddess who travels into the underworld and then escapes. I'm not so much listening as watching her lips.

Not quite meditating—except then I am. My eyes unfocus and my attention goes to the night around us, the distant drumming and laughter, the crackling of the fire and subaudible licks of the waves on the shore, the air warming my skin as my skin also warms the air. Energy moves within me. Rising? Perhaps. Moving, certainly, with my breath in and out and in again.

The love Avery describes between the two goddesses is there, holding me. As if a hand is reaching up from deep in the earth with me seated in the palm, energy rising through me, the fingers curled up, loose, outside of my body. Another hand reaches down from the sky, touching the fingertips of the hand cradling me.

EMANATION ONE:

Consciousness

Vastness arcs outside of time, connecting other ages when I've felt this presence. I see the painting of Jesus that hung in the classroom where I attended Christian Sunday School when I was seven and eight. It showed the classic white guy Jesus with wavy, light brown hair and pale skin. He wore a flowing white robe with a blue sash over it and sat on a rock with his shepherd's staff propped next to him. Sheep surrounded him, some eating, others napping, and he held a tiny ewe in his lap.

I *loved* that painting. If I got bored, I'd stare at it and think about sitting on that rock with Jesus. When I gazed at it for a while something greater connected to me.

At the time I said, "I like Jesus. He's nice."

But what I meant was: I feel loved. I understand that there's a force in the world that knows me and loves me no matter what.

* * *

By the end of seventh grade, after knowing my best guy friend Duke for most of the school year, I started going to temple with him. I didn't miss Jesus. Duke's temple has beautiful art of holy cities and fruit trees, but my favorite was the Hebrew calligraphy, especially the aleph. The shape of the letter looks to me like the world opening, like two hands reaching each other through that space.

I'd stare at it in the prayer book until it blurred and reformed—and I felt that the force that made these letters, and all letters, had made this world.

* * *

The third place I routinely found God—or was found by God—happened in my mind, in my bed, falling asleep, slipping into the place between waking and dreaming, in the possibilities of my imagining. I never felt alone there. There's always been someone with me.

Sitting on the beach with Avery, I feel that presence again, more strongly than I have in the last few years. Are these Goddesses reaching for each other—or are they reaching for me?

CHAPTER TWO

A log cracks, making a distant person yelp while others laugh. The loudest voice grows louder, yelling, "Avery! Hey, Ave, get over here!"

Avery opens her eyes. My mouth curls up, right side first, crooked smile, and she beams back at me, as if we are two goddesses on the shore of the world sharing a private joke.

"I like this," I tell her.

"Good! You have to practice. It gets easier."

She twists around, toward the fire in the distance. There's a tiny person waving her arms, yelling, "Time to go!"

Avery stands up and yells back, "Five minutes!" then, more quietly, asks me, "Do you want us to drive you home?"

"Yeah," I say, but I'm sinking inside, wanting to stay near her. I'd spend the whole night out here with her if I could. I stand up and she hugs me, hard, same as we did by the river, but now the whole front of my body is pressed to hers and there's no question that she's a lot taller than when we were little kids. And boobs.

From way too close, a girl says, "Ave, come on! Granddad's freaking out that it's way late and we said we'd be home."

I step back from the hug too fast and wobble on the sand. Avery catches my arm and says, "This is my friend Synclair, from when I was a kid and lived here. This is my cousin, Nadiya."

Nadiya has Avery's same long, dark hair, but bigger eyes and a smaller mouth. She's hopping in place as she says, "Who is about to get grounded. Which would destroy my summer plans. Let's go."

"We should drop Synclair at her house."

Nadiya walks fast to the bonfire. We hurry to catch up. She's talking to a middle-aged white woman with classic short lesbian hair, and has arranged me a ride.

"Come on," she says to Avery as she heads into the parking lot.

Avery gives me one more fast, tight hug and says, "I'll call you," before sprinting after Nadiya.

The ride home takes a few minutes around the edge of the park and up the main street of my neighborhood. I learn that my driver's name is Jo and she's both Wiccan and Christian, which I didn't know was a thing. She gives sermons at a local church. That sounds cool but I'm only half listening because so much of my brain is about Avery right now.

Lights blaze from the living room as we pull into my driveway. I hope everyone's not being too loud, my bedroom isn't that far away. When I unlock the front door, I hear silence. The living room is empty of furniture because our house is being remodeled. Pillows and blankets create a comfy place to sit in front of the Xbox and TV but no one's there.

I'm halfway across the room when Camden says, "You're back" and I yelp.

She's sitting against the wall reading Karen Armstrong's *Twelve Steps to a Compassionate Life*. How is she reading the same book I am? Oh right, she was in my bed; she borrowed it from my desk. I should be mad, but I'm super curious why she picked that one.

Camden's frilly white T-shirt makes her brown skin luminous in the golden light from two lamps. Her blue denim overall-shorts exude fashion rather than carpentry. Her wide glasses have round cats-eye frames in black with gold etched sides. I've seen her in other styles; she owns at least three pairs of glasses. I only have one because if I had two, I'd lose them both.

Her fashion sense is one reason people assume she's straight, even though she hangs out with Kinz. Even though Kinz has three braids the exact diameter of Camden's braids like even their braids are dating. Also she's my height and curvy while Kinz is tall and curvy, leaving not enough curvy girls for the rest of us to cuddle—incredibly unfair. The other reasons people assume Camden's straight are: she's religious, femme, Black and cute. As if those aren't compatible with queerness.

"Where is everyone?" I ask.

"Kinz and Mac are looking for you. Everyone else went home. I stayed to make sure you'd let them know you're back."

Mac is my brother—formally Maddox, but no one calls him that—and if he's looking for me, I am in trouble. I fumble my phone out of my bag and see six messages from him and about sixty from Kinz. It's after midnight. I'd thought it was ten or ten thirty.

I call Mac. "Hey, I'm home"

"Where the shitballs were you?" he spits back. "I'm driving around worried that you got serial killed."

"I could really only be killed once," I say.

He hangs up on me.

I call Kinz. "I'm back. Sorry, I wasn't checking my phone."

"Do you have a really good reason?" she asks.

"Actually yes. There's this girl."

"Oh! I am turning my car around right the flood now. Be there in five."

"Flood" is her substitution for "the f-word" as she puts it. She learned strict non-swearing when she was too young to break the habit now.

Mac returns first and boxes me into the kitchen, which is open to the living room and not at all private.

"I did a lot of stupid shit at seventeen, but I left my damned phone on," he tells me at a volume between speaking and yelling.

Mac is twenty-four and back for the summer while our folks vacation in Europe. Apparently, although I'm nearly a high school senior, I can't be trusted. To be fair, contractors arrive on Monday to start working on the house. Mac will be able to answer their questions and won't lose his mind in the mess and noise; he nerds out on remodeling.

He and I have the same very dark hair, pale, creamy skin and pretty faces. He's a foot taller, so his kind of pretty makes people drool over him. I'm routinely compared to a doll—not a life's vocation I've ever wanted. The tips of his hair stand up, wild and tangled, because he'd been rubbing his head while he drove around mad.

I tell him, "My phone was on, I just didn't feel it vibrate because I was meditating."

He pushes around me to grab an orange sports drink from the fridge. "I'm responsible for you. Next time you go out, turn on the Find My Ass app."

I press my lips together to not laugh; that would screw up my ability to protest. Before I can, Kinz beelines from the front door to the kitchen archway, where she leans and folds her arms.

She's in a sleeveless blue shirt that makes her shoulders seem broader and tanner than usual. Kinz's long brown hair is growing out of the purple she'd dyed it last summer, halfway down it's now blond tinged with lavender. This year she's added the braids: three thick cornrows on the right side. The rest of her hair is loose curls.

Kinz demands, "Where were you? What happened? You never wander off for…"

"Four hours," Mac says. He's dramatizing, it was barely three.

"I ran into an old friend," I explain.

"We're too young to have old friends," Kinz points out.

"Who?" Mac asks.

"Avery, my friend from grade school. Remember the little kid with the really black hair and one blue eye?"

"Oh yeah, everyone thought she was a witch."

"Well now she is." Since her eclectic spiritual practice includes Wicca, that counts—plus this answer confounds Mac.

He dismisses my words with a wave and heads for the basement door. He's sleeping down there, since the second floor bedrooms are all draped with drop cloths and his old first-floor bedroom will be torn up this week.

He says, "Night, sleep tight and don't freakin' leave the house before morning."

Kinz moves around me to retrieve the plate with mini-eclairs from the fridge. She hands one across the counter to Camden, then leans against fridge and says, "Spill."

"Hot chocolate first," I insist.

Camden winces because we've hit that point in Minnesota, three weeks into June, where the weather gets truly hot. I make hers lukewarm. Camden got a ride from Kinz, so she's stuck here until Kinz is ready to go.

Not wanting to sit on the floor, I carry my mug and eclair into my bedroom. If I sit on my bed, Camden has nowhere to sit. I settle in my desk chair while Kinz flops out on my bed. Camden perches carefully on the foot of it. Very much not how she was a few hours ago, but I appreciate her not rubbing that in.

I tell them, "Avery used to be this funny, skinny kid and now she's beautiful and queer and amazing."

"Oooh! Did you ask her out?" Kinz asks.

"No, she taught me to meditate."

"You have the strangest dates," Kinz says.

"Where did you meet her?" Camden asks.

"By the river."

Kinz flips her hair behind her shoulder and stares at me. "Wait, roll that back. You just rando happened onto this hottie from fifth grade *by the river*?"

"Yep. And then there was a whole solstice bonfire. How did we not know about that?"

"How would we have found out about it?" Kinz asks. "Do either of us hang out with the solstice people? Where would that even be? Does Avery live around here?"

"No, she's here visiting her grandparents."

"Summer fling! Yes! When are you going out again?"

I should text her right now and find out, except...I stare at Kinz as a lurch of dread wobbles through my gut. "I didn't get her number."

Kinz has her eyebrows way up with a thousand questions, so I keep talking. "When we were in elementary school, she was Avery Liakos, but that's her dad's last name. Her folks got divorced and she moved with her mom. Her dad's some kind of bad, so she probably switched to using her mom's last name, which starts with an H. And that's all I remember because I was eleven and it's not like we talked about our parents' maiden names: Avery Ha—something."

She said she'd call me, but does she have my number? Can she look me up? It's not as if I have the strangest last name and officially it's still Sinclair with an "i" like everyone else. I go by Synclair with a "y" because it's cooler, but my family's name is Sinclair and she knows that. Right? Does she remember my parents' names? Will she be able to find me? She didn't drive me home, so she doesn't know where I live now.

"Oh wow, I've got to make every social media profile I've ever made public in case she's looking for me," I say and spin around to open my laptop.

CHAPTER THREE

All week I search for Avery online whenever I get time to myself. Mac drags me to hardware stores, as if I care about bathroom tile, fixtures, and basement paint colors. Mom calls every day from Greece to make sure I'm helping Mac move delicate things, art and boxes, to the basement. She says that she trusts me with the breakables and pricey art way more than she trusts him.

Kinz keeps texting me about a fight she's having with Camden. She wants me mad on her behalf every time Camden talks to her about ancestors and theodicy. At least she typed that so I could look it up. The last time she said it out loud I'd thought she'd said "the Odyssey" and been monstrously perplexed for weeks. Theodicy is about why a good God permits evil in the world. Apparently there are a lot of answers and Kinz doesn't believe any of them. I'd like to hear some, but I can't tell Kinz that.

Why are they fighting now, when there's finally another cute, queer girl in my life? If she really is in my life—because

Avery hasn't hit me up on any social sites. Granted, I was only on three. I make profiles on a few others, but that feels desperate so I delete all of the new profiles except one.

On Saturday, I escape Mac by volunteering to run to the plant store with Kinz to get ground cover for the strip of land between the patio and the trees that border our yard. Before we can possibly look at plants—especially me, Kinz loves plants—we need to be thoroughly fortified, so Kinz drives us downtown for brunch.

My suburb used to be a small town and that part still exists as the old downtown, which is three blocks long and has lots of brick. The new downtown is more than twice as long and twice as wide with gleaming white, glass and metal storefronts. I prefer the old downtown but so does most of our burb, so we go to the new one and the expensive brunch place because it'll for sure have seats open on a weekend. The host gives us the side-eye because we're scruffy kids and then it takes me forever to figure out my order. Everything on the menu is tweaked from regular brunch food. Chicken and waffles with Cornish game hen, who does that?

"How's the house?" Kinz asks.

"They've started taking down walls and it's weird. The whole time I've lived there, the living room had four walls and now it doesn't. I get why Mom and Dad bailed and went to Greece. It's going to be a huge mess. Plus the contractors show up at seven and get *loud*."

"Rough life," she snorts. "Found Avery?"

I stab a spoon into my coffee cup and stir the creamer that's already been mixed in. "It's been eight days and nothing. After this can we drive to her old neighborhood and look around? Maybe there's a neighbor who remembers her mom's maiden name."

"Sure," Kinz says. "Did you already Google her old house and thoroughly online stalk her?"

"As much as I dared. What she said about her dad—I think he's terrible. I don't know if he was abusive to her mom or her or both, but her mom hid them from him after they moved away.

That's why I couldn't find her when I was a kid. So what if the online stalking leads to him?"

"Don't call him, that's for sure," Kinz says. "But her grandparents—"

"Are going to have the same name as her mom, which I don't remember. And there are a ton of Averys in New York. I don't even know if she lives in the city itself or someplace like Brooklyn."

Our food arrives: a bulging omelet and a stack of blueberry pancakes. I cut the omelet in half, slide the cheesier section onto a side plate and push that over to Kinz, then take the top pancake. After folding the pancake in half next to my half omelet, I drench it with syrup.

"You're gross," Kinz tells me. "You're getting syrup all over your eggs."

"You're ridiculous. Sweet eggs aren't bad."

She rolls her eyes at me and puts an entirely reasonable amount of syrup on her remaining pancakes. "And you wonder why Duke and I can taste flavors you can't?"

This is well-established in the history of our school's Culinary Club, so I ignore it and return to my plan to find Avery. "Mom's supposed to be calling her old friends from that neighborhood to see if anyone has info about Avery's family. She hasn't called in two days, so she's due. If she has nothing, I'm going to call some New Agey stores and see who had a flier about the solstice bonfire. If they saw anyone who fits Avery's description, maybe she bought something and they'd have a record. I don't know. What am I missing?"

Kinz doesn't answer. She has peeked at her phone twice while I talked and now she's frowning, so I ask, "Camden?"

"Yeah. Distract me. How was the meditation teaching Avery gave you? Was it sexy?"

"She said one way to think about the world is that one Goddess made it for another." I paused, not sure if I should name the Goddesses. That seemed like a personal thing. "One creates the universe so they can play in it together. And we're part of that—I'm not sure how, but I love the idea—and sometimes our everyday stuff gets in the way of the Goddesses interacting with us, so meditation brings them back together."

Kinz's eyebrows are way up. "Oh yeah, she was *definitely* hitting on you. We've got to find her." Her eyes flick to her phone and darken. "Maybe you should pray about it," she says with a snort, but then perks up. "Oh hey, you could at least write down your intentions so you can law-of-attraction her or whatever."

Kinz's dad has a fundamentalist Christian version of the Law of Attraction, which is this idea that positive thinking and feelings attract good stuff into your life. His version relies heavily on using intentions with prayer. Kinz has a lot of issues with her Dad's belief that God rewards people in general—and even more with his belief that God picked him out to be special and get rewarded. I'm pretty sure that egotism is very far from holiness, not closer to it, but don't know how to say that to Kinz, who'll flinch from anything about holiness.

Instead I say, "I thought you said the law of attraction was white people reveling in their privilege."

"Well, we're white. And focusing your mind to help you find your summer hottie is so queer that it handles that privilege thing."

I find a pen in my bag but no notebook. Kinz pulls the printed sheet of daily specials off the front of the menu and folds it in half so the two blank sides face out.

"What *is* my intention?" I ask.

"To get her pants off? That for sure includes finding her. And it implies kissing because she'll want that before any pants are removed."

That's where Kinz starts? Has she gotten Camden's pants off? Yeah, probably—but, how often? And where? Not in my bed. Maybe in my bed? Wow, I should not be thinking about this!

I write "pants off?" on the sheet and scoop up more of my overly sweet eggs. I add, "kiss Avery" and "find Avery—hang out with her." Now I'm paranoid that I haven't left space for consent in these intentions, so I fill out the first phrase to say, "Someone takes their pants off?"

Kinz taps the top of the sheet. "You know, if you're making a list, you could assign each intention to a different god, pray a bunch and see which one gets answered. Then you'll have handled your summer religion search too."

I blow on my coffee, which is already lukewarm, and take a sip. Yes, Kinz is mocking my most important summer project ever, but more than that she's mocking religion in general and right now, in her life, she needs to.

Now I get why Kinz and Camden are fighting. Kinz is prickly at best about all things religion—and Camden hasn't known Kinz as long as I have, so she probably doesn't get how hurt Kinz has been for so long by her family using religion as a weapon. She doesn't see how Kinz is always looking for the next hurt in any conversation about religion, so of course she's going to find it some of the time and feel attacked and strike back.

"Who gets to be in charge of 'pants off?'" I ask.

"Avery's goddesses, natch."

"Kinz, what are you going to do if Avery shows up and takes off her pants? Are you going to freak out? What happens to you if this is real?"

Her head jerks back, eyes fixed on my face. "It can't be," she says.

"Because then we're all going to hell?"

"Flood this, change the topic," Kinz insists.

"Ice cream or gelato?" I ask. It's a mainstay of our Culinary Club to default to food choice questions whenever things get too tense or awkward.

She grins. "You know that's an unfair question because it breaks down by flavor. Berry flavors are ice cream except raspberry. Most chocolates are gelato unless it's a double chocolate. Vanilla ice cream, pistachio gelato."

"Mango?"

"Sorbet. All citrus flavors are sorbet."

"Almond?"

"Gelato."

I let Kinz tell me her complex theory of dessert flavors until we're both done eating. Then I pick up the folded menu with the list of intentions. I've added "talk about everything" and "learn more meditation and other stuff." On the riverbank, Avery had said she was planting her prayers. Is that what I do with this? Maybe under the new plants we're buying next? The idea is exciting; I'm breaking out of this aggravating spin of not finding Avery. I tuck the sheet into my bag and pay for brunch.

* * *

Driving around Avery's old neighborhood is a bust. Kinz is brash enough to ring the doorbells of the neighbors on both sides of the old house and two across the street. Nobody's home in two of them, the third has a family that moved in a year ago. The most promising is an older couple who tells us that Avery's mom always seemed so sad and they were glad she left, but they have no details.

"I guess intentions don't work that fast. Or at all," Kinz says when we get back in her old Mazda wagon. The backseat is full of bags of bird seed and rodent food, horse blankets, and tack.

"Maybe we should've started less ambitiously than pants off."

"We?" Kinz asks.

"It was your idea," I protest. "I guess I'll start calling New Age stores. That feels so weird."

"Is she worth it?" Kinz asks. The answer is so obvious I don't bother to say it out loud.

Garden centers are number nine on Kinz's list of places she loves to go, after four kinds of outdoors, the wildlife center, my house, Duke's house, the stables. She gushes about plant-related things and drifts farther into the greenhouse area, talking with one of the green-vested experts. I stare around at the plants and wonder if I could grow some herbs in the backyard so we've got freshness for our salads. I did once successfully start an avocado tree, until I transplanted it outside and winter killed it.

A bright column of purple, blue, and green cloth flows between the plants: a tall woman walking slowly, unevenly but with a shoulders-back, head-high grace that makes her loose clothing resemble the sails of a tall ship. My feet move toward her, hesitantly, until I see the strap of her shoulder bag with its double woman sign symbol and a rainbow pin and one that's pink-white-blue for trans. Then I follow her outright. I want to see her face. There are not enough queer adults in my life. She flows through the shrubs and small trees section, pauses by herbs and goes left toward shelves stacked with small pots. Her legs are a lot longer than mine and I'm jogging to catch up.

She lifts a pot and turns with it in her hands, bright eyes focusing on me as I stop.

"What are you looking for?" she asks. The corners of her mouth turn up, crow's feet by her eyes deeply crinkling.

"Groundcover," I say, because anything else isn't going to make sense in a garden store, right? "Maybe hostas. Did you find what you needed?"

"The secret to finding what you need is to need what you've already found," she says and then laughs, a throaty chuckle. "I'm joking. That's not the secret at all."

"Your buttons are great," I tell her. "I don't…" This is going to be weirder if I don't say it, no matter how dorky I feel. "I don't know any adults like me."

"None?"

"They're on TV and there's a gay teacher at my school but he's super mainstream." I don't mean to say any more out loud, but she's considering me with blue-gold eyes that seem to already know everything. I say, "You look like magic. Are you gay magic? Is that a thing?"

"Lesbian magic, you mean? Or do the kids say 'gay' for everything these days?"

"We kind of do. But yeah, I mean lesbian or queer, any of it. Inclusively lesbian, bi, queer women magic?"

I expect her to laugh. Instead she cups the clay pot in one hand and rubs her finger over a small, verdant leaf. "Yes."

"For real? Because I wrote down my intentions an hour ago and does it work that fast? Can you teach me stuff? Meditation maybe?"

"My wife teaches most of the meditation." She pulls a card out of her bag. "I'm Miri, she's Jo. You are?"

"Synclair."

"Come see us." She nods her chin over my shoulder. "Your friend is waving from the hostas. Those will do, but you might look into some phlox. I'll be seeing you."

I walk back to Kinz with the card between my fingers. "I found queer magic already," I tell her.

She looks confused and then worried.

"Never mind," I say. "Load up the cart. Oh, can we get some phlox, whatever those are? Let's get these back to the house so I can resume my online stalking. This intention thing is working."

Kinz signals the green-vest guy and they load the cart with plants while I read the card in my hands: *Tree of Life Meditation Center, Miri and Jo*. The woman who drove me back from the bonfire was named Jo, but that can't be the same woman. That would be too weird. And Miri, is that short for Miriam?

There's one avenue to find Avery that I haven't tried yet and now I'm burning to get home and try it.

EMANATION TWO:

Wisdom

I may not be hot stuff about meditating, but I have another way to get some answers, or at least better questions. When I was in junior high, still miserable that I didn't have Avery around, spending more time alone than I wanted, I learned that I could go to bed early and start dreaming before I fell asleep.

I don't know what to call that mix of daydreaming and night dreaming. I traversed a persistent world inhabited by characters from stories I'd watched or read. They kept me company while my parents were out having adventures again now that us kids were all old enough. Mac was at college and my sister Tracy didn't want much to do with an eleven-year-old kid. She kept telling me I was old enough to play by myself, but I didn't want to. So I went from making up elaborate stories with my action figures and dolls to lying in bed and imagining stories with the people they represented.

I'd been trying to give that up. It felt super kid-like. But sometimes all I wanted was to hang out with my dream friends in that imagined, enduring space.

I haven't tried it in the middle of the day before, but why not? When I lie down, I can't easily feel the bubble tea straw up my spine. Instead I try a relaxation exercise Duke recommended: starting at my toes and relaxing one body part at a time until my whole body is relaxed. I try to feel all my toes, but they're a mass of chaos, so I start with the big toes. When I can feel those pretty well, I add the next two and so on until I get to the pinky toes on both feet. This I boring, so I go up the rest of my body quickly.

Dozing now, I feel a long, purple bubble tea straw inside my spine. Gold sparks travel up and down along a flow of silvery energy. The flow is thicker and brighter in some places, darker in others.

In the past—by which I mean up to last week—I entered my dream world by imagining walking through the back of my closet. Yeah, kind of ridiculous in terms of going back into the closet, and super symbolic since I hid my dolls and action figures there, but it worked. This time I don't picture myself getting up and walking, I relax into the flowing energy in my body, moving like the stream in the woods, and let it carry me across the room and through the Narnia-wardrobe-style magic door in the back of my closet.

I'm in a dim passage, dirt on all sides, roots reaching down through the dirt, fingering out in places. This isn't the usual way I go, but it has the flowy dream logic that tells me to keep going. I follow the passage down until it turns up, toward light. I climb out from the tangled roots of an old broad tree into a forest. I think this is a part of my world that I've never explored before. It has to be, doesn't it?

Dreaming-awake has most of the same rules as the sleeping kind—I'm supposed to go with whatever shows up and not think about it too hard or I'll come fully awake.

Standing amid the trees is Miriam from *The Prince of Egypt*. I've always imagined her as a young, more Semitic-looking Sandra Bullock, since that's who voiced her in the movie. She has two winged horses with her. Kinz would know what kind, assuming winged horses are the same breeds as regular horses.

One is tan, the other bay with a white star on his face. I remember him from Kinz's horse-crazy years. He was the one she'd picked out for me and I rode him a few times at the stable where she went for lessons. His name was either Luke or Geppetto.

"I'm supposed to get on one of those?" I ask, because they look terrifying to ride.

"We've been working on teleportation, but the results are unpredictable," Miriam tells me.

I'm used to this world going on without me. I always assumed that was my subconscious. At least that's what I tell myself.

"Oh, you've got jokes," I say. "I thought Tzipporah was the funny one."

She grins. "I *was* being serious. Do you want to try it? I think I can get you on the same continent but I can't promise we'll be in present time."

"Why is my dream world so snarky?" I ask as I walk toward Geppetto.

"We're not only yours. You don't usually visit midday, what's up?"

"I'm trying to find a friend of mine. Can we go through my memories?"

"I have a better idea," she says.

I walk to Geppetto's side and put a hand on his warm flank. Paying attention to the sense details of my awake dream helps me stay in it. "How does that work? Aren't you just my brain?"

"Whatever you say," she answers. "Let's go find your friend."

I climb on and learn that riding a winged horse is totally different from riding a regular horse. His wing muscles shove me back and forth as he flies, and he's still moving up and down like we're on the ground. I grab handfuls of mane and wish I'd taken more riding lessons.

Peeking through my mostly closed eyes, I see trees and more trees: a whole world of forest. A strange forest in which the redwoods are the smallest of the trees, dwarfed by massive fir and ash. These give way to a tree I don't recognize, very tall with bushy canopies, and we descend through a break in them to land on a wooden platform.

There's a whole city in these trees.

A girl stands on the platform, black hair shimmering. I hop off Geppetto and run up to her. I might be fully dreaming at this point and I want to talk to her before I wake up.

"Avery!"

She turns around; she's a more Avery version of herself than in real life.

"Are you really here?" I ask. "Is this real?"

"You don't know what real is yet," she says, her smile dense with meaning.

"Can you tell me?"

"I don't know either," she answers. "Probably couldn't tell you if I did."

"Why not?"

"You're asking for answers you don't have the capacity to hear. Remember when you were a little kid and your mom told you other people are as afraid of you as you are of them, and you didn't understand?"

I nod.

"And now that you're older you've begun to understand. When you pause inside yourself and look without judgment, you can see it in their bodies, their faces, the way they hold themselves, you can see that fear. It was always there, but when you were a child you couldn't see it because you didn't know how to look. Now it's like that again only it's not your mom talking and you can barely hear the words and even if you did, you couldn't see it."

"Who's talking? Goddesses?"

"Yes," she says. "Everything."

"If you're the real Avery, would you call me?"

She catches my hand and squeezes it. "If I'm the real Avery, I don't have your phone number."

"Can I give it to you now? We're having a party, July fifth. I want to invite you."

She's already fading into a shimmer of sunlight on leaves. "I'm looking for you too. We'll find each other. Trust."

I grab for her and wake myself up, sitting up in bed, my open closet just a closet. My *Prince of Egypt* doll who represents Miriam is sitting up in a box of my treasures, her arms open toward me.

This can be totally explained by the fact that I must've set her on top when I pulled out the meditation book. I'm being silly about all of this. But I feel like I did talk to Avery for a minute and she really is looking for me too.

CHAPTER FOUR

Walls keep coming down. The whole south side of the living room is stripped to the studs and the wall between living room and kitchen is gone. What used to be the family room is now a pile of building supplies. The wall between that and the master bedroom is open. And over the last two days the old kitchen has been disappearing, carried to the Dumpster in chunks of cabinetry, tile, and drywall.

Our official Culinary Club at school has about twenty members, but only the core group—me, Kinz, and Duke—cook together regularly over the summer. We make dinner at least once a week, but for the fifth of July we've planned a big dinner party for everyone who didn't party enough on the fourth. We've invited more of the regular Culinary Club and Mac's bringing two friends he stayed in touch with.

Kinz and Camden arrive early to help me tidy the construction mess. We'll cook in the outdoor kitchen and eat on the patio, but when the bugs come out, we'll want to settle in the living room. I sweep the living room while Kinz wipes down the kitchen counters. Camden pauses sweeping the patio to talk to her mom. Camden voluntarily *talks* on her phone, in addition to texting, usually to her mom (also voluntarily).

I ignore Mac hauling trash bags out of the basement, but focus when he starts carrying boxes toward the stairs. "Where are those from? Mom said to leave the art upstairs under the drop cloths."

He half turns on the top step with two boxes in his arms. The bottom one says "Busts," which would make me laugh—except that top box is my super private box. I put it on my bed today because he told me to empty out my closet.

I stride across the living room to him. "Where'd you get that?"

"Your bed," he admits.

"Don't go in my room!" I grab the box and pull it against my chest. "This is not for the basement."

"You've got to keep your closet clear in case the contractors need to go through for the plumbing."

"Fine. Stay out of my room."

He snorts and carries the busts downstairs.

"Put those somewhere safe!" I yell after him.

I lug my box across the living room. This is a box meant to be in a closet stack, not carried around the house; it is not well taped. I try to shimmy my arms under it, stagger sideways and bump my shoulder on the wall. The box bottom opens. Four years of secret treasures dump onto the living room floor with a sound like a stone waterfall.

I drop to my knees and fold the bottom of the box together. I shove half the pile in but it won't hold. I need another box fast, but Mac is already back in the living room, drawn by the sound of disaster. He reaches the colorful pile.

"Jesus!" he shouts. "Holy sweet literal Jesus Christ!"

He waves my mint-in-box Jesus Christ action figure. His other hand mashes together two of my *Prince of Egypt* dolls. I'm so on fire, wanting to grab those out of his meaty hand, wanting to kick him, wanting to cry but less than I really really want to not cry right now.

"How long have you had Jesus?" he asks me. "'With poseable arms and gliding action,' that's rich! Do Mom and Dad know? God, they'd freak out. I'm sending them a photo. Who's this?" He waves the *Prince of Egypt* figures, then tucks the Jesus action figure into that same hand and crouches down. "Whoa, is this a rosary? How the shit do you have that?"

I look up when I hear Kinz stomping toward us. She plants her feet, hands on her hips, and glares at him.

"Blasphemer!" she bellows in a fair imitation of her dad's most dramatic preaching. Kinz's dad can be terrifying when he's preaching. And when he isn't.

Kinz follows up, "Those are mine and if you're going to mock my faith, you'd better put them down and step on out of here."

He stares up at her, across at me and over the rest of the open box. "Why was your stuff in Synclair's closet? Your folks are all over this."

"It's not all Christian," she points out.

"Oh, like they're going to lose it if they find you with..." He stares at the dolls. "Indian religious action figures? That's a thing?"

I don't know if that's a thing and I'm not going to tell him they're not Indian.

"Put them down," Kinz tells him. "You're being a flooding donkey."

He drops Jesus and the *Prince of Egypt* figures on the pile and heads for the basement steps. Kinz sits next to me and puts her arms around me. I'm sideways to her so my shoulder's pressing into her boobs. I turn and hug her but let go before it's long enough to be weird, especially with Camden here. She's been standing inside the patio doorway this whole time and must've witnessed all of it.

Half the time Camden and Kinz go to church together. It's not like they'd get why my atheist parents would be more okay finding porn or half a joint than my stash of religious stuff.

Kinz retrieves a packing tape dispenser from the kitchen counter and tapes my badly battered box. Camden sits by the side of the pile nearest the door, not across from me but not next to me either. She picks up the two dolls—Tzipporah and the Queen of Egypt (because they didn't make a doll for Miriam)— adjusts their clothes and sets the queen's hair back into its dark cascade. Then she picks up the Jesus action figure and reads the back of the box. Her lips part; her eyes soften.

"This is beautiful," she says. "I wouldn't have expected."

"Yeah, that's why he's still in the box."

"Why the closet?" she asks.

In the four months she and Kinz have been dating, she's been over a few times and never spent more than a few minutes with my parents. I guess she and Kinz don't talk about me that much.

"My folks are old-school atheists, the 'God Delusion' kind. If my mom saw this…I don't even know what kind of talk we'd have to have."

"You can't be serious," Camden says. "This? It's emphasizing Christ's work as a healer and a remarkable person. It doesn't go far enough in terms of his inclusion of the oppressed and fight for justice—and he's *really* white—but it also doesn't even call him the Son of God."

"Still Jesus," I tell her.

"You can't have prophets?" she asks, as if this is the most confusing thing she's heard this year.

"I could. I'd just never hear the end of it. They think only weak-minded people need religion."

"Better off without prophets or religion," Kinz says. She's finished taping the box and sets it down with a thump on the bare wood floor. "I wish I could get rid of mine."

She lifts my books, gently, into the box, followed by the rosary, a few small statues, the action figures. Kinz won't fuss about anything she sees in this pile. She's the one person I know who can disagree with me and not make it a big deal. And she knows not to tease me about this.

Camden tells Kinz, "If you would come with me to one of the Saturday sessions—"

"I said no," Kinz's voice is halfway to yelling. "You keep telling me God is noncoercive, so get off this."

Camden shuts her mouth tightly and hands Jesus back to me. She returns to the patio and sweeping.

Kinz asks me, "You okay?"

"Mac is going to tell my parents and they're going to be exponentially extra."

"You want me to put that box in my car?"

"I'll hide it under my bed with the porn," I tell her.

"You're hiding old school printed porn under your bed? Is it lesbian? Is it good?"

"Hah, no, no and no. But I should get some for the top of this box." I fold it closed. "Who do you think would have some?"

"Duke'll buy you some if you ask," she says. "Also, I think we got the wrong parents."

"Yeah, but your dad scares me."

"Me too," she says. Her hand rests on my shoulder and squeezes. "Still love you. Me and Cam will set up for dinner, come out when you're ready. I mean…you know what I mean."

I carry the box into my bedroom and put it on my bed. I flop back next to it. Why can't I be some other kind of abnormal? I don't like porn, not even the artsy stuff, and have zero interest in weed.

Since halfway into freshman year of high school—two and a half years ago—I've been avoiding churches, temples, mosques, meditation centers, as if not going into them would make it so I didn't want to. I still want to. I want a religion or a spiritual practice, but as soon as I tell my folks, there are going to be so many conversations. I need to get my answers sorted first. This summer is my chance.

* * *

I leave my room when I hear Duke's upbeat tenor yelling, "Seafood cooking *adventure!*"

The heart and soul of Culinary Club, Duke is our best chef and fearless leader. Meeting him turned around the worst part of my life. I'd spent sixth grade alone and thought seventh would be the same until this pixie-haired boy offered me a garbanzo-bean-flour cupcake. The texture mixed sand with gravel, but it tasted like strawberry sugar, so I ate the whole thing. Duke decreed that I was a keeper.

Now he's moving through the living room with a crutch under his right hand and a grocery bag in his left. He's in tan shorts and a button-front, patterned short sleeve shirt that screams "gay!" It's dark blue with tiny seagulls. There's a thickness under his sock and he's wearing the half-size-larger gray loafers that fit around ACE bandages or a brace.

"Ankle?" I ask.

"Again," he says heavily. "The sidewalk's an asshole."

He has hypermobile Ehlers-Danlos Syndrome, which means his ligaments are too loose. He gets sprains and dislocations way more often than the rest of us. His disorder affects the connective tissue of his body, including his gut, and can be triggered by gluten.

"What are we eating?" I ask.

"They had some great fresh scallops. Those with a summer salad, lots of fruit, and if I can get that oven to behave and the gods of gluten-free baking don't hate me, I'm working on my profiteroles: chocolate dough with salted caramel filling."

"Can we start with those?" I ask as I follow him onto the back patio.

"Maybe. For you."

On the patio, Camden and Kinz sit at the long table, chopping veggies for salad. Camden's best friend, Jay, has joined them. She's tall and also Black, but with a sporty, outdoorsy style instead of Camden's femme layers. She keeps her hair in loose, frizzy curls (Camden calls that "natural," which I had to look up): today they make a soft halo behind her head. Jay always looks like she's gazing into the sun—currently midday bright sun because her perpetual squint is gathering smile crinkles at its edges.

She must've gotten a ride here with Duke, which is weird because they hardly know each other. Jay started hanging out with us culinary nerds about a month ago, since Camden now spends most of her free time with us.

I know even less about Jay than I do about Camden. She complained at last week's dinner that it sucks being a straight girl who's taller and better at sports than the guys she likes. We informed her that hanging out with us would not help her cause—and that dressing like a lumberjack signals lesbiatronics to the Nth degree. She said she's not changing her style for anyone. Plus, with her pristine sneakers and mass of natural hair, she insists that her style is lumber-Black. She and Camden do Black girl fashion videos. Maybe "lumber-Black" will catch on.

Duke puts his grocery bag next to the vast counter beside the grille and drags over one of the stools that have been exiled from the kitchen. Our outdoor kitchen is bigger than the indoor one—at least until this remodel is done. He gets his cooking implements set out and I wash the fruit: nectarines, blueberries, and one Honeycrisp apple.

"You want to do the scallops?" Duke asks Kinz.

"Yeah!" She grins. "Let me go wash up!"

When Kinz hops up, Jay pulls her cutting board over and continues carving thin slivers from a green pepper. Duke chops garlic and basil. Muscles move in his arms. He's about as bulked up as Mac, but you wouldn't know it because he's shorter and not as lean. I've teased him that he's got the face of a generic white boy on a CW show, but he's objectively cuter than I am. Maybe cuter than Kinz.

Fruit washed, I settle at the table, across from Jay. Camden's at the head of the table measuring herbs into a bowl for dressing. We make our own; Duke wrote up instructions that we keep behind splash-proof sheet protectors in a small notebook.

Through the open back door I hear the shower near my bedroom turn on. I am trying so hard not to picture Kinz getting into it. The only rooms on the first floor that aren't being remodeled are my bedroom and the small bathroom next to it. Does this mean Kinz is going to get dressed in the little bathroom? Or in my bedroom?

I glance at Camden to remind myself that she, not me, is Kinz's girlfriend. She and Jay are the newest in Culinary Club—very much the newest of the club's summer group. The school's official club has about twenty members, but Duke, Kinz and I used to be the only ones who'd cook together over the summers.

Now the summer crew includes Camden and Jay, but I don't know enough about them. Awkward whiteness descends over me, as if no matter what I say next it's going to be wrong because I haven't had any Black friends before now.

So I open with, "Thanks for being cool about Jesus."

"Of course," Camden says. "Did you put him back safe and sound?"

From across the patio, Duke's head turns. "Where *did* you put Jesus, Synclair? And did he like it?"

"He's going under my bed. And I need some porn to hide him with, but nothing gross," I tell him. "Maybe teen gay boy stuff so my parents are confused and stop looking."

Duke snorts and turns back to measuring out flour.

"Your parents are going to stop if they find porn?" Jay asks. "My mom would have so many inappropriate questions. What does 'Jesus' stand for?"

Camden explains, "Sync has a great Jesus action figure in her collection of religious items."

"That you're going to keep under your bed with porn?" Jay asks, her cheerful squint deepening.

I pause my apple chopping so I won't nick a finger while I try to explain. "My folks are atheists and my mom's really serious about it and…she won't respect me because she thinks religion is for fools, as if the only people into it are right-wing nutjobs who voted the moldy tangerine into office. They sent me to church when I was little—and to temple with Duke—so I'd have a well-rounded cultural education. They never figured it would stick."

"Wait, where are your folks?" Jay asks.

"Greece for the summer. They didn't want to be in the mess and noise of the remodel. Plus their bedroom is getting torn up and they could move to an upstairs bedroom but those are getting repainted and it's all going to stink. My mom hates the smell of paint. They said I could come but I wanted a quiet summer."

"Hah, sure you did," Duke says. "That's why you had us all come over."

"Kinz invited you over," I point out.

Camden takes off her glasses and cleans them with a tiny square of blue cloth from her purse. When she puts them back on, she peers at the recipe page, but asks, "So religion stuck with you after all?"

I shrug but I also nod. "Kind of like being queer. I could avoid girls but I'd still know I like them. I guess I figured if I didn't go to church or temple or wherever, maybe I wouldn't want to learn to pray or meditate or have a spiritual practice in my life."

"Not working?" Jay asks.

"I feel like I'm missing something huge."

"Huh, I have never felt that way about religion," Jay muses. She pours her cutting board of pepper bits into the giant orange salad bowl.

"Or girls," Camden adds with a smirk as she stirs the carrots into the pool of dressing in the bottom.

"Truth," Jay affirms. "Your folks are that strict about *not* doing religion, Synclair?"

I pop a cherry tomato in my mouth. "They wouldn't tell me not to do it, but they'd ask questions. My mom would be all 'how can you believe this?' and 'what are you getting out of this?' with a sense that I'm into something gross. I don't want to have to field those questions until I have rockstar answers. I figure this summer I can study meditation and spirituality and know where I stand before I have to talk to my parents."

Camden half laughs. "Like going to the library and reading all the queer books before you come out?" She might be in the process of doing just that.

"You know, telling your mom to back off is also an answer," Jay points out.

"You tell your mom 'back off'?" Camden asks her.

Jay snorts. "Not in those words. Try, 'you're impeding my self-actualization.'"

"No!" Camden tosses a sprig of parsley at her. Jay retaliates with a stray carrot piece that drops perfectly down the front of Camden's shirt.

"It made her laugh," Jay says while trying not to snicker at Camden fishing up under the bottom of her shirt to get the carrot piece stuck in her bra.

"Self-actualization might work on my mom," I say as I type a note into my phone. "I'll try it." Note saved, I look from Camden's carrot-fishing expedition back to Jay. "You don't go to church?"

She shakes her head. "Atheist. Church was fun when I was a kid because of the singing and getting dressed up, but the religious part doesn't make sense to me."

From across the kitchen, Duke asks, "How long have you two known each other?" This is a very legit question about Jay and Camden, since we all know that Camden goes to church every Sunday.

"Three years," Camden tells him as she pops the freed carrot piece into her mouth. "How do you know Kinz? She hasn't said."

Duke chops a pile of chocolate pieces with a speed that blurs his knife, then says, "I found a young squirrel that had been attacked by a cat. Dad and I took it to that wildlife place where she volunteers. We got into this super intense conversation about shapeshifters who turn into squirrels. From that moment on I knew that with me and Synclair, we'd be a trio of inseparable queers. That was mid-eighth grade. Also for the record, she thought Culinary Club was a stupid idea and is still making that up to me."

I've heard the stories about that too many times, so I ask Camden and Jay, "How does it work that one of you is super into religion and the other isn't?"

Jay says, "In her paradigm, Camden assumes I'm in a relationship with God whether or not I'm aware of it, and she knows I'm doing okay, so she doesn't worry. In mine, I figure religion takes care of many psychosocial needs for her, and everybody needs awe or wonder, so she's good. We've never tried to tell each other how to be."

Kinz comes back onto the patio during Jay's explanation. She stops adjusting her light green T-shirt to blink hard at

Jay. "Wait, if you're an atheist," Kinz says, nodding toward Jay. "Cam, how come you want to explain all that theology to me and not Jay?"

"She already explained it to me," Jay says. "It's cool, it's just not my thing."

"It's not my thing either," Kinz points out.

Camden shakes her head. "You don't know that because the only way you've been exposed to Christianity is toxic. What if I hated nature? You'd want me to give it a try."

"Synclair hates nature." Kinz winks at me.

"It hates me," I remind her. "I tried to make that relationship work. It dissed me hard. I still itch when I think about it."

Camden doesn't have to say that Kinz could try to make it work with God, we all hear the implication hanging in the air.

"What do you believe?" Jay calls across the patio to Duke.

He turns on his stool, head tilted. "I'm Jewish and my family's into Kabbalah, so I'm for full-on mysticism. But that's not about belief, it's about practice. Who cares what you believe? It's what you *do* that matters. I study God. I do good things and I feel like God and I are on the same team about that. God helps me out and I help Them."

"God is nonbinary?" Kinz asks.

"Of course. You can't define God—that'd be idolatry. There's rules about that," he says with a smirk.

I love Duke's concepts of God, but sometimes they leave me feeling lonely. I want a personal God. What I like about Jesus is the feeling that I could talk to him, maybe hang out, have him tell me I'm doing okay. And I could use a God with advice about me and Kinz.

CHAPTER FIVE

Two of Mac's old friends show up for dinner and afterward take over the stretch of lawn between the patio and the woods so they can toss a Frisbee around. He introduced them when they arrived, but I've already forgotten their names so I ask Duke.

"Matt and Mark? Mike and Marty?" he suggests. "I don't remember. They need nicknames. Something foodie and funny so I don't try to flirt too much."

"Mac and Cheese," Kinz suggests.

"We already have a Mac and that seems unfair to whichever one we call 'Cheese,'" I point out. "Same problem with Sweet and Sour."

"Ham and Eggs?" Jay offers.

"Should be fancier," Camden tells her. "We have a Culinary Club rep to maintain."

Duke snorts. "How about Gnocchi and Risotto? The thick one's Gnocchi and the tall one's Risotto."

"Dibs on Risotto," Jay says with a grin.

There's a huge, tarp-covered hole by the edge of the patio and top part of the lawn, where the construction people are digging to put in a hot tub. Mac almost tumbles into it and switches them to a lawn bowling game. Jay joins in and dominates with her amazing aim.

As if reading my mind, which isn't hard because I'm thinking of Avery one out of every two minutes, Kinz calls across the patio, "Too bad Avery isn't here."

"She made her up," Mac hollers from the lawn bowling arena. "Synclair's always had a ton of imaginary friends. She probably saw a pic of Avery from back in the day and got thinking what if she grew up hot."

"I didn't," I tell him. But he's not saying anything I haven't wondered myself the last two weeks. If all that happened, where is she? I can't be *that* hard to find.

"Leave Synclair alone," Jay insists. "Can't you see she's heartbroken that she might've run into the love of her life and lost her again? If we weren't so self-absorbed, we'd be helping her look."

"Ten bucks says she's made up," Mac replies. His taller friend, the one we nicknamed "Risotto," starts putting together a betting pool about whether or not Avery exists and when we'll figure this out.

"Flood you all," I say and go into the house pretending I need a drink but really to get away from them.

I wash my face in the bathroom then swing through my bedroom to see if there's anything I'd rather be doing. There isn't. I stand in the middle of the room wishing for Avery.

The doorbell rings so I head for the front door. More kids from Culinary Club, probably—there are three lacrosse guys Jay is hoping will show up. I really hope they brought ice cream. I swing the door wide.

Avery grins at me.

It's like someone stepped on my lungs and mashed them down into my pelvis. I know my mouth is open and I'm blinking at her, but I can't move.

Her clothes still resemble pajamas: a cream-colored shirt with two-inch blue stars on it, plus flowing navy pants with little flowers. There's a silver pendant around her neck, a tree in a circle, hanging below the dip between her collarbones. Hair blacker than I remember, eyes exactly the same: one deep brown, one keen blue.

"Hey," she says. "I'm here for the party."

I push air through the words, not sure my lips are forming them right: "How did you know?"

"You invited me."

"In that dream?" I ask.

"On my phone," she says, looking as puzzled as I am. I am definitely getting good at meditation if I could project an invite onto her phone!

Avery breaks our confused silence by saying, "I hope it's okay that I invited Nadiya. We brought pop and ice cream."

"She needed my car," Nadiya says with a smirk.

I should really say hi to the shorter, rounder, dark-haired girl standing next to Avery, but instead I ask Avery, "You're not a telepath?"

"Not yet."

I step back from the doorway, feeling loose and floaty, as if we're back in the dream. In no way do I understand what's happening here. I'm worried that when we get to the backyard, she'll vanish. Brain tumor? Hallucinogenic mushrooms in the burgers?

"Come on in. Both of you. Nadiya, welcome." I lead the way through the living room. I should treat this as real until proven otherwise. "It's great you both came. My folks are redoing the house. Also, my brother thinks I made you up. And I'm not sure I haven't."

"I can poke you later if that'll help," Avery says and her cousin laughs, a higher bell sound than Avery's.

I step onto the back patio. Since there isn't a door to slam open or a pot to bang, I yell, "Hey everyone!" When they've all turned toward me, I step aside. "This is Avery."

Kinz falls over herself coming to say hello and then everyone is crowding around, introductions being made, Mac helping Nadiya stow the ice cream and pop, Duke proudly talking up the food options.

I lean against the back wall of the house, enjoying being right and watching Avery—how real she is and, especially in the golden light of the afternoon, beautiful. She's almost as tall as Kinz and Jay; as kids, she was always smaller than me. She's still thinner, not stick-skinny, but slender, except for her chest, which I'm not checking out except to the degree that I completely am.

She seems older than me too. She is, by three months, but her gracefulness and fancy pajamas style give her a sophistication that seems older. Maybe that's from living on a coast. Duke, Camden, and Jay are as intentionally dressed as Avery, but the rest of us look like we just grabbed some things at Target, which is provably true in my case.

Avery gets a veggie burger from the grill with salad and sits at the smaller patio table, patting the seat next to her. As I'm on my way over, Kinz catches my eye and waggles her eyebrows at me.

"Is it really okay that I brought Nadiya?" Avery asks. "You didn't say."

As if I'd said anything? "I didn't text you. I don't have your number. I can't figure out how you're here. How do you know where I live?"

"You gave me your address," Avery insists. "I've been texting you for days."

"No." I open the messaging app on my phone and show her the names next to my most recent conversations: Kinz, Duke, Mac, my parents.

She shows me her messaging app. At the top is a contact named "Em" and a photo of someone in ski goggles. I can't tell if the goggles are ironic, because it's summer, or if this person is that hardcore about skiing. Wait! There is a bratty kid at my school who loves to ski and hates that she keeps getting mistaken for me because our names are so similar.

I lift the phone out of Avery's hand and tap the conversation to confirm my guess. Yep, that's not my phone number. And I don't talk like that.

"You texted *Emily* Sinclair, not Emma," I tell Avery. "She's a sophomore at my school and kind of obnoxious, at least about me. She gets lots of emails from teachers that are meant for me. She must've figured out you were looking for me and gave you my address thinking it'd be awkward for you to show up here expecting a party. Joke's on her. She should've picked a day that isn't one everybody's going to have a party on."

"Maybe she couldn't help it," Avery says. "Greater forces at work."

I cannot in the least argue with this. In fact if Jesus or God or Goddesses want to prove to me that they're real, I can think of no better way.

Avery is chuckling, shaking her head. "I thought you were being weird, stalling about having longer conversations. Figured it might be the crush thing. I searched and found an Em Sinclair at the local school and couldn't really see her face but what are the chances there'd be two?"

"One hundred percent, apparently. I'm just Synclair on my accounts now, with a y," I tell her. "I looked for you—online and stuff. But I don't even know your last name anymore."

"Hamidi. I changed it with Mom when she went back to her family name. I wasn't going to keep that asshole's last name," she says, face clouding for a moment. "You're just Synclair? One name, like Beyoncé?"

"I wish. But yeah, as much as I can."

She taps the back of her phone, still in my hand. "Put your number in my phone."

I do.

She takes her phone back and texts me: *Hi, real Synclair.*

I reply: *Hi real Avery Hamidi. I'm glad you could come to my party.*

Kinz and Camden drop into the chairs across from us and Kinz asks, "What are we doing?"

"Texting each other to make sure we have the right numbers." I explain about Emily Sinclair sending Avery over here as a joke.

"Coincidence or divine intervention?" Avery asks, eyes shining.

"Are you sure there's a difference?" Camden asks.

"It's not as if God answers everyone's prayers or we'd live in really different world," Kinz grumbles.

"Prayers aren't wishes," Camden tells her. Her eyes have a burning brightness that suggests she has a whole lot more to say on the topic and is trying not to.

"But you think God sent Avery over here by using some girl?" Kinz asks.

"Maybe that girl is good at hearing God's calling." Camden puts a hand on Kinz's arm and turns to Avery. "I promise you we're not always this way."

"I don't mind," Avery says. "How does God's calling work?"

Camden explains, "God calls to us with the best possibilities given any individual situation and we can choose to follow that or not, because of free will and all."

Kinz snorts. "Then why doesn't God call people to be less hateful and evil? Who's pulling them toward evil? The devil?"

"Evil is a possibility in the system," Camden tells her.

"But God made the system, so God made evil. If God's all love and great possibilities why is the world a Dumpster fire?"

"You don't even listen," Camden says. "I'll explain it again if you'll listen."

"I don't need it. But go ahead and tell them."

"As if I need your permission?"

"Synclair was my friend first," Kinz points out.

Camden closes her eyes and I'm pretty sure she's praying. Slowly, she says, "God calls us to follow the best possible paths to good futures and we still have free will. We can choose differently. Because we're all connected in this world, those choices have consequences—some of them create evil in the world." Camden takes a breath and opens her mouth to continue, but doesn't get a chance to.

"So stuff that happens to me is my fault," Kinz says.

"Why did you tell me to explain it if you were going to come at me about it again?" Camden asks her.

"She's not," I say and now everyone is looking at me intensely. No way am I explaining all Kinz's religious baggage to Camden.

Camden opens her mouth, pauses, peeks sideways at Kinz. Into that silence, Duke yells, "Éclairs!"

"God's calling?" I ask.

Camden grins. "Kind of like that. But different. Come on, you have to taste these."

Camden and Avery get up from the table. Kinz says, "Be right there." She and I watch two beautiful girls walk across my patio and everything is right with my summer.

When I do get up, I clear a round of paper plates and cups, biodegradable of course. I would use our regular dishes, but they're all packed up since the contractors have been tearing out the kitchen cabinets.

Avery stands by the eclairs talking with Duke. I want to watch them more even than listen to them. She's here. *She is here*. And real. And came to my party even though I'm certain that Emily Sinclair's phone game is terrible, especially with girls, since she's straight.

I go into the kitchen for another trash bag and more napkins but the storage cabinet has been torn out. Basement? There's a crowded jumble at the foot of the stairs. I spot a box of construction-grade paper towels and grab that.

In the kitchen, Avery is pulling ice cream out of the freezer. I step next to her and she sets pints on top of the paper towel box. We carry all that out together.

"We're one pint short," she says, so we go back inside.

That pint is the very aptly named Karamel Sutra Core—caramel ice cream on one side and chocolate fudge chip on the other with a solid caramel core.

"I have strong feelings about caramel," I say.

"Pro or con."

"Extremely pro."

"Maybe we shouldn't let anyone else know we have this," Avery suggests.

We fill bowls and sneak the rest back into the freezer.

"Come on." I lead her into my bedroom. I sit at the head of my bed so she can take the desk chair or the foot.

She puts her ice cream on my desk and turns slowly, examining my books and photos, my posters and art, all the silly things on my desk. Then she grabs her bowl and sits at the foot of the bed.

"How's your meditation going?" she asks.

I want to tell her about trying the awake-dreaming state in the middle of the day and flying on a winged horse to meet her amid the ancient trees, but I don't know how to do that. I settle on saying, "I dreamed that a winged horse took me to find you, so that seems like progress."

"Winged horse? That sounds symbolic."

"Really? I'll look it up." I type into my phone: "dream interpretation winged horse."

A common theme in mythology, the winged horse is a symbol of unrepressed sexual desires.

"What does it say?" Avery asks.

It says I should've taken the teleportation, but I can't say that out loud. I scan down the entry to find something I can say.

Sexual drives are rising to join with your consciousness desires. Having sex will cause the fulfillment of this energy and it will fall. However, if this energy is maintained without full sexual release, it will continue to build and rise, carrying your awareness upward and outward to greater knowledge of life itself.

While I skim, she crawls up the bed, bowl in hand, to sit between me and the wall. Her fingers curl around mine and tilt the phone so she can see it. Her fingers are so warm, stronger than when we were kids, and I imagine them on my waist, pulling me closer. Realizing what she's reading, I jerk my phone away and put it facedown on my bedside table.

"Aww," she says. "What was the part after they tell you not to have sex with your rising energy? That's as far as I got."

"It keeps building and, you know, more stuff. I'm sure that's not what it meant in my dream."

"What were you doing with the horse? Riding it?"

If it's possible to die of blushing, I'm going to find out.

"That's kind of what people do with horses," I say.

"Some people use them to pull carriages, carry heavy burdens, plow things. Not everyone wants to ride their desires to higher consciousness."

"That's not..." But actually I do want that. It sounds amazing. "Is that a thing?"

"Yes. You draw the energy in your lower belly up the inside of your spine. Except it's not that simple. You have to be careful with it—with the kundalini energy. It's the energy of Shakti in your body. Oh and stop at the heart for a while. If your heart isn't open, you're not ready to go higher."

"Is yours?" I ask.

"It's getting there," she says and takes my fingers in hers.

She tugs at me and I'm not sure if we're going for a kiss or not. I lean in but she's going the other way. We hug awkwardly, pelvises side by side, upper bodies together. Her hair falls in a silken wave over my face, smelling of mandarin and rose, coriander and juniper, and burning sweet sage. I want to kiss her but I can only reach her neck or the edge of her cheek and that seems presumptuous before her lips, so I press my cheek to hers and she returns the pressure.

I'm hot all over, except my lap, which is strangely cool.

As I'm working out how to turn this hug into a kiss, my bedroom door bangs open against the wall. I jerk out of the hug to see Camden pressed against my door, being kissed hard by Kinz.

"Hey!" I yelp.

"Whoa, kids," Kinz says, pulling back a fraction. Camden's glasses are askew and two braids have come out of their thick ponytail.

"You two are busy." Camden points somewhat lower than our faces.

I look down. My lap is full of melting caramel ice cream from where Avery's bowl tipped over when we hugged.

Avery crawls to the foot of my bed, lithe as a cat, and pads out of the room.

"Having a good time?" Kinz asks.

Rivulets of ice cream are soaking through my shorts and I'm afraid if I stand up, it's going to glop all over my comforter and soak through to my sheets. My lap makes a bowl, containing the mess. I scoop up with my fingers the parts that aren't completely liquefied and put them in Avery's bowl, setting it on the bedside table.

Avery pushes by Kinz again and climbs back into my bed, towel in hand. She presses it into my crotch to soak up the freezing ice cream, then realizes what she's doing—but not before I feel energy shoot up the inside of my spine and think that this kundalini thing is going to be a breeze after all—and pulls her hand away.

I endeavor to get more ice cream into the towel than in my pants.

"Is Synclair in there?" Mac asks. "Did she take the—" He's come up behind Kinz and can see me sitting in bed with a towel pressed to my crotch and Avery next to me.

Once he starts laughing, he can't stop. Or doesn't want to. I hear his laughter echoing in the living room. He is definitely going into the backyard to tell his friends whatever he thinks he saw, and not caring if the rest of my friends hear.

I change into clean shorts and go rinse off the ice cream in the bathroom sink. I take my time wringing out the shorts and hang them over the towel bar to dry. Am I ready to go face my friends after this? With Avery out there I sure am.

When I open the bathroom door, she's standing against the wall beside it, waiting. Her posture is loose, her pajama-like clothes hanging gracefully, but worry wrinkles her forehead. She's worried about things being okay with me. I grin.

She grins back. "You okay? Are your shorts going to make it?"

"That's the most exciting thing that's ever happened to them," I tell her.

She holds out her hand and I take it, expecting that she's going to pull me closer, but we stand there, grinning. I should pull her toward me and my bedroom, assuming Kinz and Camden didn't claim my bed.

"Do you want another bowl of ice cream?" I ask. "You didn't get to eat most of it."

"Can I come back for it? Nadiya wants to leave. She's got some party she wants to go to tomorrow and can't be out late on sequential nights or our grandparents think we're misbehaving. But you have my number now for real, text me, okay?"

"Can you come over again?" I ask.

"Of course." She squeezes my hand and I slide a half step closer. I want to kiss her but we're in the hall outside my bedroom with an open archway between us and the living room.

Avery releases my hand and goes to find Nadiya. I walk them to the front door and when I've shut it behind them, I'm left with that feeling that she's not quite real.

CHAPTER SIX

My brother's nickname for me is now "messy shorts." I suspect he means it in a sex way and not a scatological way, but knowing him, he's trying for both. When he still lived here, when I was ten and eleven, he and one of his friends were super into jokes that involved celebrities who'd farted during sex. That was half my sex education before I came out. To this day I'm terrified that when I do have sex, the subconscious ideas Mac planted in my brain will cause an unholy amount of flatulence.

That wasn't a huge consideration this summer until two weeks ago, finding Avery again, almost kissing her last night. I really want to kiss her, but I also want to talk to her about everything. How do I describe to her the dream that wasn't a dream—without ending up back at the winged-horse-is-about-sex interpretation?

I chicken out about that, but we start texting as soon as we're both awake and cover so many details of the past six years that it doesn't matter. I learn that she and her mom moved to the DC area first, because her mom's sister lives there, and then

New York when her mom got a new job. Avery's at an artsy high school, taking some dance and a lot of acting. She thinks our Culinary Club is great, even if I'm still bad at cooking. I try to come up with what I am good at, but most of my hobbies are borrowed from Kinz. I can ride horses, but not well, and feed baby wildlife from tiny bottles.

Mid-afternoon, Avery texts: *Nadiya wants to go to a party and bring me, do you want to come?*

I type: *Can Kinz come? And maybe Camden?*

Minutes later, she replies: *YES! It's out in the sticks. They're going to fire off all the rest of the fireworks everyone has. I'll send you the address in a few. Bring anyone you want. There's drinking, though, so don't bring anyone who'll freak out or get in trouble.*

I text all of that to Kinz who says: *If we bring Jay, then Cam and I can tell our parents we're staying over at her house and we're all in the clear. You think Duke wants to come?*

I text Avery: *What % of the guests are queer?*

She replies: *Probably 10%. It's my cousin's mostly straight friends.*

That means I can invite Duke but he won't show up. On the other hand, Jay is going to be thrilled.

We meet up at a pizza place and I feel medium shitty because it doesn't serve gluten-free so this only works because Duke isn't here and I miss him. I don't spend as much time with him as Kinz, but I've known him longer and he's always around for the big moments in my life.

Avery is the same amount of amazing as the last two times I saw her. I can see the echo of her kid self in her face, but who knew she'd grow up like this. I look like a bigger version of my same dorky self. Avery lost all of the baby fat on her face, turning it into an elegant oval that her ebony hair frames, showing off her cheekbones and lips.

She chats with Kinz and Camden like they've been friends all school year. Nadiya and Jay get into a long thing about which pop star boys are cutest, but I tune them out and focus on Avery, Kinz, and Camden.

"I couldn't tell from what you were saying last night, did you two both grow up Christian?" Avery asks.

"Boy did we," Kinz says.

"Her dad's a preacher at a fundamentalist church," Camden says. "My family's African Methodist Episcopal."

Avery shakes her head. "I understand almost none of what you said. Translate for a Wiccan Buddhist, please. There's Catholics and Protestants, right?"

"Protestant is a very big umbrella," Camden tells her. "And my denomination falls under that umbrella but Kinz's doesn't; they're nondenominational, which often means fundamentalist."

"It's not *mine*," Kinz says. "It's what my parents make me do. In addition to never listening to me when I tell them I'm lesbian but then giving sermons about the evils of homosexuality. Oh, and my dad doesn't only give those sermons, he asks me about them after and wants me to tell him what a theological genius he is."

"That's horrible," Avery says.

"She comes with me as often as her folks will okay it," Camden tells her.

"And your church is better about being queer?"

"The denomination has some struggles, but nothing like… that." Camden stopped herself from saying "Kinz's church."

"Are you out there?"

"No," Camden says, but she's chuckling. "At least I don't think so." She turns to Kinz. "I think my mom's been trying to ask me about you but doesn't want me to feel like I have to say anything I'm not ready for."

"For real?" Kinz asks.

"She's been doing that thing where she'll ask a question and then drop it and then ask another a few hours later, like I won't realize the questions are related. So she asked how I like the new younger minister, the one who's been giving the really inclusive sermons, and I said that I think she's great. And then she waited and asked if any of my friends are gay. There were a few questions about that, over about two days, and yesterday she asked, 'Does your friend Kinzey want to come to church with us every week?'"

Jay leans in from her conversation to say, "Oh yeah she knows."

Kinz shakes her head, which makes her braids jingle together, but she's smiling. "Yeah, I totally want to come to your church if I have to go to one, but my dad will…pass a bowling ball out his colon, or something else I don't have the words for."

"Shit a brick?" I offer.

"Multiple bricks."

"What if we needed you for Sunday school?" Camden asks. "Mom and I were brainstorming ideas."

"To make sure that me—your girlfriend—comes to church with you?" Kinz sputters. "That isn't. That doesn't. How?"

"She wants me to be happy," Camden says. "And she gets that my life is between me and God. The new minister is really great. She's touched on queer and trans inclusiveness a few times in the last months—explained how not being inclusive is a sin. Mom's sharp, she sees me sit up and grin during those. And I guess she was pretty boy-crazy at my age so the fact that I'm not has been sticking out more and more. Are you cool with me telling her you're my girlfriend?"

"A thousand percent," Kinz says.

* * *

After dinner, we follow Nadiya and Avery on the highway to a smaller road that leads to an even smaller road that leads to a dirt road and then a dirt driveway. Cars are parked all-around a big open space in front of a three-story house. Huge old house in the middle of the woods? This is obviously the setting of a horror movie.

My skin prickles and I brace for a jump-scare as Avery takes us through the first floor, showing us the kitchen and bathroom. But when we get to the back, I see a boat launch. The only valid reason to have a big house in the middle of nowhere is to be on a lake. Maybe we're not in a horror movie. Dim golden lights around the lake hint at other houses hidden in the trees. This could be a romance setting. Or romantic comedy, knowing my life.

The backyard is like mine but bigger, with more lawn before the trees start. In this open space, people stand around boxes on the grass, arguing about the order in which fireworks should be lit. Younger kids dash around with sparklers while their parents watch. The parents are younger than mine, but old enough that this party isn't going to get too out of hand.

How did I start out determined to learn to meditate, two weeks ago, but keep ending up at parties? Is God trying to tell me something? I guess I'll roll with it and see what happens.

We join the awkward dancing in the living room. Scratch that: Kinz and I are awkwardly dancing with each other. Camden and Jay dance together because they're intimidatingly great, but open ranks for Avery whose style is belly dance with hints of Bollywood.

Kinz and I duck out to get water and then I head into the backyard while she goes back to dance with Camden. Evening is becoming night, the air cooling, a breeze off the lake almost chill. People start setting off the fireworks while continuing the argument about the right order for them.

I like being at a party where most of the people don't know me and don't expect anything but are still keeping an eye on me. One of the young parents makes sure I know when fresh brownies have hit the food table. Another one thanks me for making sure her kid doesn't run out toward the fireworks. Avery comes to stand beside me, but Nadiya calls her away.

I turn from the sparkling colors of the fireworks, their bright trajectories reflected in the lake water, so I can watch Avery walk back into the house. She's here and real and back in my life. I want to chase after her and hug her again. I want to keep touching her to reassure myself, and maybe for a few other reasons.

Was she my first crush too? At eleven we'd been inseparable. Or that's what I'd thought.

EMANATION THREE:

Understanding

Toward the end of fifth grade, Avery gave me a goddess statue, my first sacred action figure. She'd brought it over in her backpack, wrapped in one of her pajama tops because she didn't know how to wrap a gift that unevenly shaped. I hadn't cared if it was wrapped or not. We gave each other stuff all the time, loaned toys for however long, and books and clothes. But this was a weighty gift, literally, and thick with meaning.

I unbundled it and turned it in my hands. Three women faced outward, one carrying a key and holding a snake, another carrying torches, the third holding a knife.

Avery explained, "She's the triple goddess, Hecate from Greece. She'll protect you."

"From what?" I asked.

Avery shrugged. "Whatever. See, her aspects are the maiden, mother, and crone. I think the one with the key is the crone because she's wise. The knife is about intellect and the torches are creativity."

"I love this," I told her and put the statue in the middle of my stuffed animals. Eleven wasn't too old for stuffed animals as long as they stayed on the low bookcase beside my bed and not in my bed.

Hecate lived amid my plushies for about a month, as the school year ended and the lazy, humid days of summer started. That's when my mom saw her hanging out with the fuzzy bears and dogs. She picked her up, puzzled by the heft of it as well as the subject matter.

"Where did you get this?" she asked.

"Avery gave it to me."

"Should she have done that? Is it valuable?"

"I don't know."

"What did she give it to you for?" she asked.

"Protection."

"You know that's not real, right? Emma, we are going over there tomorrow and you're going to give this back."

"I don't want to. It's mine!"

Which sparked an evening-long fight with yelling and a lot of crying. Would I even have wanted the statue that much if Mom hadn't told me to give it back? Who knows? Goddesses work in mysterious ways.

But probably, because Avery gave it to me.

I slept with the statue in my bed that night, despite its sharp points and heavy bronze. In the morning I hid it, but Mom asked me to go get it. If I refused, there'd be another fight and I'd get grounded—and I figured if Avery had the statue, I could see it at her house, so I might as well give it back to her and tell her all about this later. Maybe we could wait a few months and smuggle it back over to my house, hide it in my closet.

We drove because Mom wanted to run errands after, even though Avery's house was close. On the way over, Mom said, "You need to tell her you don't believe in this and she shouldn't give you religious items."

"I don't know what I believe," I said.

She laughed—not a nice laugh, a scoff. "You can't possibly believe that's real. Gods and goddesses standing over us, puppeting our actions."

I couldn't figure out how to put into words, or if I wanted to, my sense that something was real, something huge and important, something beyond everyday life: beyond my school, the house, even my parents.

"A lot of people are religious," I said. "Most of them."

"Honey, you're too young to understand that most of them are pretending and the rest are deluded."

She sounded so sure, but there were billions of people in the world. Could they all be wrong or faking? It seemed more likely that Mom was wrong.

When we pulled into Avery's driveway, I said, "I don't want to do this. Avery gave me this; it's mine."

"It's important that Avery and her family respect our beliefs," Mom said.

"But I don't believe there are no gods," I told her, the first time I'd said that out loud.

"Oh? What gods do you believe in?"

"Maybe these," I said, lifting the statue.

"You're only saying that because Avery is your friend. Let's take this back and next week you'll be into something else."

I absolutely did not want to walk up to Avery's door, but I got out of the car. Mom wasn't going to take us home until I'd given back the statue. I could get stubborn and stay in the car, but then she'd take the statue in by herself and I'd be grounded.

My parents weren't strict and I'd only been grounded twice in my whole life. But sometimes one of them got stuck on something—like the time I'd forgotten a sandwich in my book bag and it got disgusting and stank up my room. It had been a mistake, but Dad made me clean everything and forbade me having food in my room for months afterward. Plus he kept doing random checks of my backpack and drawers.

This wasn't the same, but I couldn't fight and get what I wanted. As I walked up to Avery's door, I felt part of me hang back, stay by the car—like my body couldn't refuse but part of my soul adamantly would not do this.

The rest of me in my body felt hazy and unreal without that larger part of me. That made it easier to climb the porch steps and ring the bell. Avery's dad answered: a bigger man than my dad, with lots of thick, black hair on his head and arms. He scared me, not because of his size or all the hair, but because when I was playing with Avery, he'd sneak up on us. Whatever made a guy his size adept at sneaking, it couldn't be good. He'd be standing silently in the doorway watching us for a minute or two before we noticed, but Avery never closed her door. She wasn't allowed to.

"We came to return this to Avery," my mom said, pointing to the statue. "It's too nice and not appropriate for Emma."

"Ave!" her dad yelled up the stairs and she came running down. "Why'd you give this away? It's not yours."

Her cheeks turned dark red while she stared at her feet. Her dad held out a hand for the statue. A cold feeling dripped down inside me. He shouldn't touch it.

"I want to keep it," I said. I turned to run, but Mom caught my arm and took the statue away from me. She put it in his dense hand.

"What else do you have to say?" Mom asked me.

"Thanks," I told Avery. "It was really cool. I like it a lot."

Mom sighed and shook her head. "We don't believe in all that nonsense. Please don't give my daughter any religious gifts."

Avery's dad grumbled, harrumphed and shut the door.

"I don't recall him being that rude," Mom said on our way back to the car. "But do you see we did the right thing? It wasn't even Avery's statue to give."

I didn't respond. The part of me that had stepped outside myself was back at Avery's house, gliding up the wall and into her room, putting my ghostly arms around her, shutting the door between her and her dad.

In my memory, that was when Avery left. In truth, she went away weeks later. We must've hung out a bunch more times. I don't think we talked about the statue. She did bring me a classic Wonder Woman action figure and I gave her my favorite plush dog. I didn't realize these were parting gifts. I'm not sure she knew that either. She never said goodbye in a final way.

She and her mom went to see family for the weekend of July 4th and never came back. I was afraid to ask her dad where they'd gone and then later, months later, when I asked Mom about it for the hundredth time, she said they hadn't left any forwarding information.

"Avery's mom left her dad and she doesn't want him to contact her," she said. "It's a grownup thing. Someday you'll understand."

I knew what she meant. I never did understand.

CHAPTER SEVEN

I'm watching the fireworks arc above the lake and trail sparks down to the water where they're absorbed into their reflections. Avery walks up behind me. I smell woodsy jasmine and the skin on my back tingles. "Pretty," she says in my ear.

"Very," I tell her.

We're alone in the vastness, like at the lake in my neighborhood. None of the people here notice us. A perfect place to kiss her under stars and sparks, except that my phone is buzzing like a trapped hornet. I dig it out of my pocket to see Mac texting an excessive number of times, asking where I am.

I text him: *Still at the party, not drinking, it's cool, there's adults, might sleep over at Kinz's.*

If you're lying and get arrested, I'll kill you, he writes back.

I promise not to get arrested. You'd better not either!

Text me when you've gotten to the place you're staying tonight, messy shorts.

I don't grace that with a reply because as I'm texting, Avery leans softly against my back and puts her hands in my front pockets. I pull her right hand out, stick my phone in that pocket, and lace my fingers with hers.

The last booms of the fireworks fade. People walk toward the grill and coolers. Can I turn around and kiss her? I mean, of course I *can*—but can I do it without missing her mouth or kissing wrong.

"Hey, there you are!" Nadiya calls from the edge of the patio, waving. It's like it's her job to interrupt the two of us. Is she doing this on purpose, not wanting us to be together? Is that paranoid? She isn't even two years older than Avery, so I assumed she was cool, but maybe she's stealth homophobic and doesn't want her cousin kissing a girl.

Avery slides away from my back, shifts my hand to her left and tugs me in that direction.

"What?" she asks her cousin.

"They're playing a game upstairs and we're running out of people. Come join."

"What game is it?" Avery asks.

"I don't know the name and I can't tell you how to play 'cause that's the point."

Avery raises her eyebrows at me, so I say, "I should check in with Kinz."

"She's up there," Nadiya says. "She played already."

"Did she win?" I ask.

"That's hard to say, more like she survived and so did Camden. Jay won."

"I guess if they're all there, we might as well." I shrug at Avery and she shrugs back, the motion rippling through our joined hands.

We go through the kitchen and up the stairs to the end of a hall, where we enter a bedroom that's probably a teen guy's. He's got a ton of sports stuff, posters, trophies of dudes with hockey sticks, actual hockey sticks. He's not here; as far as I can tell, we're all girls. They're crammed in around the walls with nobody sitting on the bed. The horror movie feeling starts up again, except I'm with Avery and two of the people leaning against the wall to the left of the door are Kinz and Camden, Kinz's arm easy across Camden's shoulders.

Jay is talking with three girls I don't know. I catch snippets about college basketball and guess they're close to Nadiya's age, all of us in late high school or early college. So this is less like a horror movie and more of an initiation into a secret coven of witches? Okay then. Clever to disguise it as a game.

I've wanted an initiation ever since Duke's bar mitzvah. He went to Hebrew school for years and had to learn a Torah portion and get up in front of everyone to read it. I felt his religion wrapping him and me—like his joint supports, not the ones he uses when he's hurt, but the ones for working out, the ones that help his body to be stronger. I wanted that, but of course when I asked my parents if I could have a bat mitzvah, they told me to stop going to temple with him. At least I got to attend his bar mitzvah, but afterward Mom didn't want my head filled with "all that religion nonsense." Way too late. Some days there's more of that in my head than anything else: the trees and the lake and the fireworks all talking to me only I don't know how to understand them—but I really want to.

So let's get on with this mystic initiation. Or is this just a weird game in a stranger's bedroom? Unless this is when the escaped serial killer with the power drill leaps out of the closet and terrifies us all.

"Avery and Synclair will play," Nadiya announces and the room gets quiet. I wait for horror music to start. She asks, "Who's first?"

"I'll go," I say. That way Avery has a better shot at winning, or whatever.

"Gonna be a short round," Kinz says.

I almost don't worry obsessively as Nadiya tells me, "Sit on the bed."

When I'm sitting, she picks up a black cloth and brings it toward my face. I put up a hand to intercept. "Whoa, you're going to blindfold me for a game to which I don't know the rules in a room half full of strangers?"

"Nobody's going to touch you," she insists. "It's psychological."

"That is *so* comforting," Avery says. She's leaning against the wall next to Camden, facing the bed where I'm sitting.

I shrug and take off my glasses, setting them on the bedside table. She was probably going to tie the blindfold over them and I should've let her, but that could get uncomfortable fast. I don't want to have to deal with eyeball sweat while I'm trying to be smooth.

Nadiya ties the blindfold behind my head and sits back, away from me. I relax enough that my nervousness floats inside of me on the surface of—not quite calm—but at least a mental pause, curiosity, maybe wonder.

Nadiya says, "Think of someone you really want to have sex with, real or imagined or movie star, anyone you want."

Wow, so not what I expected. Not even when she said "psychological." How did Jay win at this? Do you have to pick a specific person? And if so, how did Kinz not win?

"Am I going to have to say who it is?" I ask.

"No."

I think of Avery, of course. But sex? That's so far off. I'd tentatively scheduled it for sophomore year of college. And even though Nadiya says I don't have to say who it is, how can I be sure? I don't want to have to admit how into Avery I am in front of all these people.

Have to think of someone else.

Kinzey.

No.

Yes.

Okay, yes, but also not someone I'm going to pick for this game. Especially since she's in the room—with her girlfriend!

Who, come to think of it, I also would not turn down a kiss from.

Jeez—er, I mean, Geppettto—is there enough meditation in the world to get me to stop thinking about every queer girl within a hundred yards of me?

"I'm thinking," I say, because the silence is getting longer and weirder.

"Want help?" Kinz teases.

"Shut up," I tell her.

Could be a movie star, TV star, pop star. I can't think of a single one right now because I can smell the jasmine scent of Avery and she's such an obvious answer.

Maybe I should pick Gaia. Would picking a goddess get me points from Avery if I do have to say this out loud in the end? Except Gaia is Greek and is that me objectifying Greek religion and therefore Avery, since she's part Greek? What other goddesses do I know?

The other goddess Avery named is Inanna. I did Google her days ago while still searching for Avery. There was a great painting of her as a badass Middle Eastern queen with long, very black hair and—you know, she actually looked a lot like a grownup version of Avery but without the blue eye. Okay great, I'm picking Inanna and if she happens to look like Avery, we're good.

"Got it," I say. "Er, her, I've got her."

"All right, now imagine she's here in the room with you," Nadiya says. My heart lurches sideways and threatens to flop out of my body like a beached whale. Fortunately, she keeps talking. "Imagine she's here, in this room, and she wants to have sex with you too."

Does Avery? I mean, kissing at least. I'm so not ready for sex. Could I get ready for sex? Is she? Would she want that? The entire skin of my body is sparking with the remnants of the fireworks.

I spin the image of Avery in my mind back into Inanna.

"Uh, sure, okay. So you know, I am not air kissing anyone," I say.

That gets laughs from around the room. I can pick out Avery's chuckle and Kinz's snort.

Nadiya says, "Don't worry. Imagine she's here and wants to have sex with you and you're dressed exactly as you are now. What would you take off first?"

I shrug because that's easy. "My shoes."

"Take them off," she says.

I reach down until I feel the laces of my sneakers and untie them, then slip them off and let them fall next to the bed.

"Dressed just exactly like you are now, what would you take off next?" Nadiya asks.

I can guess where this is going. There has to be a trick to it, but my mind isn't functioning beyond turning Inanna back into Avery every time I stop concentrating.

I say, "My socks," and pull them off to demonstrate that I've caught on at least this far.

"Good," Nadiya says. "What would you take off next?"

"Dressed exactly as I am now?" I offer, thinking about my shorts and T-shirt and how after those come off I'll be in my bra and panties. I should've done this in winter. Is this like strip poker? I haven't played that either.

What am I missing? If Kinz thought my playing would lead to a short round, there has to be a trick. There's no way that she or Jay or Camden stripped down to bras and panties in front of strangers. How did people get out of this? I wish the blood thrumming in my ears would make it to my brain instead of all the lower parts of my body. Maybe if I'd meditated on the breath at the tip of my nose for, like, twenty years.

"I think I'd take off my necklace, you know, so it doesn't get in the way," I stall.

Someone laughs quietly. How many times has she been smacked in the mouth by a date's necklace?

"Take it off," Nadiya says. The air is so thick with energy that it surprises me how quickly my hands move to unclasp the silver chain with its two stamped aluminum disks that say: *not my circus, not my monkeys.*

I hold it out in front of me. The floor creaks as someone steps toward the bed. Avery's hands cup mine and take my necklace, skin sliding over skin.

"What would you take off next?" Nadiya asks.

"My shirt."

"Synclair," Avery only says my name but I understand she's asking if I'm okay, if I want to stop.

And I don't. I want to know the point of this. I want to figure it out. I want to figure everything out: what am I supposed to be doing? What does God want from me? Which God? Can I simply pick from any long-ago religion and have that work?

In the near silence of the room, my thoughts are thunderous. Distantly, I hear women shifting, feel them watching me, but there's a way in which I'm alone with Inanna—as if she's in this room and beyond it. She's both the image of Inanna, which helps me focus, and a greater reality watching through that image, waiting to see if I can do this, if I can pass this challenge. Will I like what I find on the other side?

I slip my arms inside my shirt, use my hands to hold the neck open so it won't snag on the blindfold, and pull it off over my head. At least I'm wearing a good bra: plain black and simple.

Avery didn't step back after taking my necklace. I know she's as close to me as Nadiya, maybe closer. Is she breathing as fast and shallow as I am? Can she feel the energy surging between us like the ocean crashing up between two stones? Is that between me and Avery or between me and Inanna and all She represents? A person by the wall blows out her breath quickly, but the sound slides off my ears into oblivion.

I stand beside the bed and tug my shorts down over my hips, step out of them. Because this is next, right? Nadiya is going to keep on asking until I'm naked. A bat mitzvah would've been so much easier. Well, unless I had to read Hebrew.

I ask, "Are you going to tell me what the trick is?"

"It's not a trick," Nadiya says.

So this isn't a game. It's a gateway, an initiation.

The darkness behind the blindfold is shot through with flickers of color that fade into infinite distance. I ask into that infinity: *Are You there, looking for me? Why haven't You found me yet? Why haven't You come into my life with more than hints? If I have a spiritual calling, why is it hidden from me? Am I not dedicated enough? Can't You see me?*

I shrug off my bra and drop it onto the bed. Then I pull my underpants down and step one foot free of them, legs open only enough to give me balance. I fold my arms over my breasts and try to glare through the blindfold in Nadiya's direction. I know what I look like naked: very average, five-foot-four, boobs that need a bra for working out or dancing but otherwise can go without, nerdly amounts of muscle. Is Avery disappointed?

"Is this what you want?" I ask. But I'm really asking: *Do You see me now? What more do You need from me?*

Nadiya stands up, the bed giving a querulous creak, the rest of the room in held-breath silence. Her fingers brush the middle of my cheeks where the blindfold starts.

"Apparently you're going to have sex with whomever you chose while still wearing this blindfold," Nadiya says as she pulls it away from my eyes.

I'm released back into sight. I *have* passed an initiation because I'm standing naked in a room full of women and nobody can meet my eyes except Kinz. She gives me a giant grin and a thumbs-up. Also I want to kiss Avery so badly I feel punched in the chest.

I turn away and get my glasses. As I pull on my underpants and bra, the room erupts into sound. I get a lot of congrats, as if I *have* won a game. Half the women leave, to get drinks or take a break, or maybe this is over and Avery won't have to do it because now she knows the secret.

"You're my hero!" Kinz says.

I grab my shirt off the bed, jerking it on. The presence I felt while imagining Inanna is close now. How can I be feeling this much power and blessing and anger at the same time? How do I put all this together? Are all initiations like this?

Avery hands me my shorts, asking, "You okay? If I'd known… I'm sorry."

"I am actually okay," I tell her. "I'm weirdly very okay. And I'm mad." I wave at Kinz, Camden, and Jay. "You guys could've told me. They said you won, Jay, what's winning?"

"Took off the blindfold first, tossed it at Nadiya," Jay says. "And made a joke about not wearing one unless we're clear about a safe word."

"We'd have stopped you but who knew you were going full monty?" Kinz says. "My absolute hero."

Camden puts a hand on Kinz's arm and the gesture is not cuddly at all. "That was dubious *and* shady."

I ask Camden. "What did you do?"

"I started with my shoes too but about the third time she said 'dressed exactly as you are now,' I caught on and took off the blindfold. Kinz got down to her shirt and that caught on the blindfold and she pulled both off."

I ask, "And everyone else?"

Kinz and Camden share a glance that I can't translate. Jay answers, "Another one took off the blindfold first and the rest got to their underwear, chickened out and quit."

"Quitting was an option? Crap. I'm the only one who got totally naked?"

"You're the only one who didn't quit," Kinz says, like this is a demonstration of great fortitude. Which it is.

"And my prize is being naked in front of a bunch of strangers and you guys?" I'm about to say this is a pretty shit game, but the feeling of initiation presses me from behind, heavy and new, like I have won a prize; I just haven't figured out how to unwrap it.

"You've seen me naked a bazillion times," Kinz points out, because she does change in front of me without hesitation.

"She has?" Camden asks.

"We're BFFs, of course she has. Plus we've had the same gym period for two years, we're naked together in the locker room plenty."

I catch Kinz's eye and say, "Can we go home." It's not a question.

She nods and gets her bag. Avery follows us down the stairs. "I didn't know it would go like that."

"I know," I tell her. "It's okay. But I'm not partying in a group of people who've seen me naked."

What I mean is: I'm not partying with Avery right now when she saw—I can't think about it without starting to blush. How did I look to her? We'd seen each other naked when we were eight or nine or ten, which is so different from now. And I can't stop thinking about what would've happened if she'd gone first. Even if she didn't get all the way through, could I have seen her with her shirt off? Seen her bra and her dancer's stomach, the long, slenderness of her, the fineness of her collarbones.

We haven't even kissed and she's seen me naked. I want to be home, alone in my room and work apart the snarled cords of these feelings.

"Text me," Avery says.

"Sure." I head down the stairs. Kinz and Jay are in the entryway. I crawl into the back of Kinz's car, my feet propped up by the horse blanket, and stare out the window.

I'm shrouded in layers of past and present: my feelings for Avery then and now, the losses, the confusion, the possibilities. How do I unwrap all this?

CHAPTER EIGHT

Avery sends me apologies during the drive home and a bunch of thanks because she's realized she could've been the one naked. That's still nice to think about but absolutely not how I'd want to see her like that. I tell her it's okay and I'm going to sleep.

We drop Jay off at her house. On the next stretch of freeway, Camden says, "I should've stopped it. I was going to and then you stood up and took off everything else and…if you need anything, support or something, I'll help you figure it out."

"I'm really okay," I tell her. But I might be blurred with exhaustion from so many hours with people around while I wished for time with Avery. "Ask me again in the morning."

"I will," she says. I believe her.

I don't feel dubious, like Camden said. I feel bright inside and split into two people. There's everyday me who is too flooding embarrassed to leave her house for the rest of the summer and praying that nobody in the room took a phone pic of me. But under my surface, there's another me, called forward by the strangeness, the pureness of the moment of being alone and surrounded, naked and strong, revealed to myself in a new way. And that version of me knows no one took a pic because we were all wrapped up in that thick magic.

There've been two of me for a long time—since that day at Avery's house with the statue, if not before. One of me has been living in the world of my dreams and dolls, the world of God and gods—while the other walks around the everyday world of physical things. Tonight the two of them swapped places. The spiritual me stepped forward and I am not ready for how fearless she is...I am.

Kinz pulls into my driveway, next to the huge Dumpster piled with demolished cabinetry, broken marble and tile, chunks of drywall and wood. "You want us to come in?" she asks.

The basement lights are shining up through the windows on the north side of the house, so Mac is home and awake. What I really want is some ice cream and about ten hours of sleep.

"I'm tired," I say. "You guys go home. Thanks for the ride."

Kinz rises out of the car and opens her arms. I lean into her and get hugged hard.

"I'm weirdly okay," I tell her.

"Hero," she says.

"Jerk," I reply.

"BFF," she says and kisses my cheek.

In the house, I go to the top of the basement stairs and yell down to Mac that I'm home and going to bed. He yells back an inarticulate blend of syllables, "Heyyaaargh!" half meant for me and half for his game. Good enough.

There's nearly a half pint of Karamel Sutra in the freezer that I take into my room. I sit in my bed eating it, gazing at the action figure sitting at the top of the box in my closet. She looks a lot like Inanna.

* * *

The next two days are a storm of texting, everyone making sure I'm okay—and I am, except I want them to leave me alone so I can feel everything that's opening up around me. But also I want Avery to come over again so I can kiss her. We settle on Tuesday night for a late dinner and hanging out. I'm hoping we end up sitting on my bed, eating ice cream, watching a movie on my laptop. I do my best at meditating, breathing through my nose, and praying some, and trying everything I can think of to make this go right. Can it work that way? Can my meditation sessions be cosmic bank deposits and at a certain point the universe owes me a favor?

Not this time, because everyone comes over again. Kinz invites herself—because she must know how my situation with Avery is going—and of course she's going to bring Camden, and then we have to include Duke and Jay. At least the weather turns out perfect: the air warm and close, the sun setting a little earlier than a few weeks ago, so by eight thirty when we're finishing up a late dinner, it's not too hot and the right amount of dark to see a few fireflies winking at the edge of the trees.

"Let's go for a walk," Avery suggests when we've carried our plates into the kitchen.

"To that beach?" I ask.

"What's in the trees at the back of your yard?"

"There's a cute creek that goes down to the river. But you can't walk along it very far."

"So nobody else is going to be walking it. We don't have to go very far to be alone," she points out, like the genius she is.

"Yes!"

I head into the backyard and tell everyone we're going for a walk, which causes a super knowing look to pass between Kinz and Camden. Kinz opens her mouth and I know she's going to say something stupid like, "Don't come home until you've kissed her," but Camden puts a hand on her wrist. Kinz closes her lips and smirks.

"There's pie in forty-five," Duke says.

"We'll be back," I promise.

We walk into the trees without me stumbling over a million roots, only three or four. Avery is light on her feet.

"Dance lessons?" I ask.

"Yep," she says and pauses to wiggle her hips. "Including some belly dance."

"Do I get to see that?"

"Hmm, seems unbalanced, what do I get to see?" she asks.

"Other than me naked?"

She stumbles over a root and catches herself against the next trunk.

"Sorry," I say.

"Don't, I should've gone first or stopped Nadiya, it's...just, sit down."

The trees block out most of the distant backyard lights from the houses around us, but the moon is already up and nearly full. I sit on a fallen tree and she moves so the moonlight is behind her.

Avery dances, hips swaying and circling, arms making impossibly fluid sweeps in the air. When we were little, she was only ever graceful when she danced. Now I can see how that grace has permeated her whole body.

"What song are you dancing to?" I ask, because the only sound in the night is crickets and one complaining frog.

"Sosin," she says, twirling and swaying. She sings a line in a language I don't know and couldn't name, the only part I recognize is the word "sosin" repeated four times.

"Which is?"

"Sosin means 'lily' and what I remember of the translation, and I'm probably messing it up, I don't know Kurdish, is that the women are dancing with their scarves and the fever of their kisses makes wisdom abandon passion. I think traditionally it's implying that men are kissing the women, but I prefer to think of it as the women going out together, dancing and kissing each other."

"I like that," I say. "A lot."

She stops and holds out a hand to me. Inviting me to dance? I stand up, but shake my head.

"Remember how I was also a clumsy kid," I start.

"Most kids are," she says.

"Well I'm about twice that clumsy now."

"You don't have to dance."

I put my fingers in hers and let her tug me a step closer.

"I don't know how to kiss you," she tells me. "I've wanted to for so long. I wanted to when we were eleven, but in a different way. And I had this idea that maybe we'd go to college near each other and I'd see you again and it would be…like this. Except." She stops and shakes her head. "Almost like this. Not quite exactly. Emma… Synclair."

"Avery," I say. I touch her cheek and her lower lip that is so much more kissable than at eleven, but then, to be fair, I wasn't thinking about kissing anyone back then.

She's shaking, which makes it easier for me to feel confident, to slide my fingers up her cheek and align myself so that I lean in and kiss her softly, solidly on her lips. She pulls back and ducks her head, dark hair falling across her face. I drop my hand but she catches it, puts it back on her cheek and kisses me.

We stand by the creek and kiss each other, despite the water edging into one of my shoes from the damp ground, until in the distance Kinz bellows, "Pie!"

We walk out of the woods holding hands and Duke yells, "Huzzah!"

Mac says, "Jesus, finally," and then with a glance at Kinz adds, "Sorry."

She shrugs. "If He has a problem with it, I trust He'll take it up with you." She still says Jesus's pronouns with capital letters, you can hear it. "But if you wind up in hell, don't say I didn't tell you so." She's trying to joke, but it comes out with the edge of having grown up with her parents, like sometimes she needs to slap us around with religion because our coping with it becomes hers.

"Atheists go to heaven if they follow their conscience or their ideals," Jay says, matter-of-factly. "According to some traditions."

"What, really?" Mac asks. "Why do you bother with all that other stuff?"

"It's not a bother," Camden tells him. She asks Duke, "Is there a Jewish hell?"

"Heartburn, if you listen to my dad. But not really, at least how I was taught. There's a kind of purgatory-like space that a person can spend just short of a year in, but not longer."

"That's cool," Camden says. "Some Christian theologies don't have a hell outside of this world, only heaven."

I want to hear more about that, but I'm afraid of how much I enjoy hearing Camden talk theology, so I ask Avery, "Is there a heaven in Wicca?"

"Depends on whatever their personal beliefs are."

"What are yours?" Kinz asks.

She looks at me. Kinz groans the "ugh, this is so sappy" groan, which is profoundly unfair considering what I've had to put up with involving her and Camden.

"I think we reincarnate," Avery says. "But it's hard to remember past lives so it's best to live this life as if it's our only one."

"You two weren't star-crossed lovers in some past life?" Duke asks us, smirking.

Avery plays along. "Oh it was a terrible tragedy. Synclair was but a lowly groom in the stable and, sadly, I was one of the camels."

Jay snorts, inhales the juice she was drinking, and sputters as we scramble to hand her napkins. I'm grinning so hard half my face might fall off. And I'm counting the seconds until I'm alone with Avery again.

CHAPTER NINE

Clearing the dishes from the pie course gets everyone inside. Mac fires up a movie on the Xbox-connected-TV and we sprawl on the living room blanket watching it. We can only furnish the living room with blankets and cushions that we can carry down to the basement at the end of the night, so the space is open when the contractors arrive in the morning. We've got a bunch of couch cushions up from the basement so it's nice, like camping out in my own house.

But I'd rather be camping only with Avery. I want to kiss her again, kiss her so many times that at the end of the summer when she has to go back to New York, I can never forget how it feels. Maybe I could go visit her there. Could we keep dating? Are we dating? We definitely need to talk about this instead of watching the visually stunning but plot-wise boring *Godzilla: King of the Monsters*.

"I have questions about Mothra," I say. "I'll be back."

Instead of going into my bedroom, where I could theoretically be looking up answers about Mothra, but also would be still way too close to the living room, I walk into the backyard as if I'm going to examine actual moths.

No one is fooled by this, least of all Avery who follows me out a minute later.

"Mothra usually generates offspring when near death, which is symbolic of reincarnation," Avery says as she joins me on the far side of the patio.

"You're a Mothra fan?"

"No, I looked that up on my phone a minute ago to impress you."

"You don't need monster lore for that," I say. "You could always dance again."

"There's a limit to how much I can dance without music. We could look at the stars and I could pretend I know the constellations."

"Great," I tell her and lead us over to the part of the lawn beyond the outdoor kitchen.

There's an open space of grass where Mac and his friends play lawn games. It's a half-crescent with trees all along the curved side. Random lawn sports gear is scattered over the lower half, plus that part's really visible from the house. If I want us hidden by the half wall that borders the patio—and of course I do—we need to be in the space between the hole being dug for the hot tub and the trees. There's plenty of room for two people. I sit on the grass a few feet from where the tarp is marked off with stakes and string.

Avery sits next to me, then lies down, so I do the same. I roll onto my side, scoot closer to her. She turns to face me and I kiss her. Lying down it's easier. I fold one arm under my head and she does the same, putting our faces level. We kiss studiously, then breathlessly.

I need a pause so I pull back a fraction and turn to stare up at the few stars visible despite the brightness of the moon. "That constellation is probably Mothra," I say.

"Orion's going to have feelings about that," she says. Her hand moves from my hip to find my hand and lace our fingers together between us.

"He should take them up with Godzilla. Actually, I'd watch that. Orion vs. Godzilla. But only if Godzilla wins."

"He always does," she says, but her voice sounds far away and low.

When I peek over, a tear is streaking down the side of her face.

"What's wrong?"

She lets go of my hand and rolls into me, tucks her face against my shoulder. I wrap my arms around her, the beat of my heart strong in my ears, repeating: *Avery, Avery*. Will I ever get used to her being here? To holding her without feeling like the dreaming and waking parts of my life switched places?

"I go back," she whispers. "In a few weeks."

I hate that too. My throat burns, but I say, "Yeah. We can figure something out."

"Oh, Synclair."

"That doesn't sound good. That was like 'oh Synclair, I forgot to tell you I'm an alien and when I said New York I really meant Jupiter.'"

"Not as far as I know," she says, still not upbeat. She's pulled back a few inches, watching her fingers play with my necklace. "I should've said this days ago and you're going to think I'm terrible."

I wait, wondering if I should stop her from telling me because I don't want anything other than this, than right now with her elegant fingers turning the discs of my necklace back and forth.

"When I go back," she says. "I have a girlfriend."

"What?" I scoot back, far enough to stare at her.

"We decided to take a break for the summer. I'm not doing anything out of bounds. But I couldn't have imagined that I'd run into you and you'd be so amazing and also queer and single—so much has to line up for that. I thought maybe I'd fool around with some stranger at a party, not that I'd be falling...I don't know what to do."

Of course she'd have a girlfriend, she's freakin' beautiful. What kind of bizarro woman lets her beautiful girlfriend take a break for the summer? What is that?

I want to be so mad. I want to be furious and fuming and steamed and slightly-to-moderately rageful. Mainly I feel grateful that I still get to kiss her because of this break dynamic. And I've only known her for a week, but also for years. I get why she doesn't know what to do because I sure don't either.

"We have some time," I say and it sounds flat, so I tug at her.

She slips into my arms and we're kissing again but hard this time, desperate, her half underneath me and still crying. Fresh tears slip between our cheeks. I've never had a girl cry over me before. I feel huge—way beyond my skinny arms and doll face—and important.

She pushes me sideways so I slide off, drags her wrist across her face, then tugs me back on top of her. I kiss her cheeks, but this doesn't make them any less wet.

"I'll get tissues," I tell her and roll to my right so I can stand up without accidentally kneeing her. Her fingers trace the side of my face and I'm trying to memorize her face.

I pull myself away—and fall.

Plastic crackles around me, there's too much air. I slam into dirt.

There is dirt in my mouth. And in my eyes. Which is for sure not the only reason they're watering. I fell too fast to get my hands out and landed on my boobs and my face and my knees. I figure all this out while I'm still wrapping my brain around the fact that I'm facedown in the future hot tub pit.

There's pain radiating up my legs, but I can flex my ankles and, carefully, my knees. I don't think I broke anything. I turn my head enough to lay my cheek against the cold dirt.

"Synclair, gods, Synclair are you okay? Can you hear me? I'll get help, stay there."

"M'okay," I grumble, but it comes out as a wheeze because most of the breath got knocked out of me.

I hear Avery's feet slapping on the patio and then yelling in the house. More running, followed by the sound of a person scrabbling down the dirt wall on the far side of this pit. I'm starting to relax even before Kinz puts a solid hand on my shoulder because I knew that would be her.

"Take it slow," she tells me.

From above, Mac yells, "Jesus!" Nobody corrects him.

I want to crawl into Kinz. Because I only do active things when she's around, she's been at the scene of every injury I've had in the last three years. Not that many. Falling off a horse a few times, sliding elbows-first down a rocky slope, and grabbing a pot that was fresh from the stove, though usually Duke saves me from that.

I reach across the dirt and put my hand on her leg, manage a few breaths and wheeze, "I'm okay."

"Nothing looks bad," Kinz says. "What hurts?"

"Need a sec." The words come out sounding like: *need sex.* And that gets me laughing and then choking and I'm probably crying too but I don't give a crap. I push my hands against the ground and that feels good, so I roll over and push up to sitting. Kinz's hands stay on my shoulders, guiding me, which I'm super grateful for because my head is spinning from dropping into an actual pit where I'd forgotten there was one.

"Stop moving," Kinz tells me. She presses my glasses into my hands. They must've slipped off my face when I fell. They're bent but I bend the side piece back to about where it should be and put them on. She sits next to me and wraps her arms around me. I can lean into her.

"Do you remember what happened?" she asks.

"I fell in a pit."

"Before that?"

This must be a concussion test so I give her some details: "Godzilla. Went outside with Avery. We were lying in the grass. Rolled over and fell. My head's okay. My knees hurt like blazes. How am I going to get out?"

Avery, Duke, and Camden lean over the edge of the pit. Mac must've gone for a ladder, not that we really need one, the hole isn't even five feet deep. If I can stand up, they could pull me out, especially if Kinz will give me a leg up. But my knees are throbbing so maybe I could use steps or something. The contractors use a ladder but they took it with them.

To get into this pit, Kinz scrambled down the far the wall, the one nearest the patio. Maybe she knocked enough dirt loose to make footholds. In the bright moonlight I squint at the crumbling dirt she knocked loose.

Tree roots are sticking out of the wall Kinz scrambled down, but there's no tree. I squint and lean forward. The fragments of white come together and make sense: a skeletal hand is reaching out of the dirt next to the top half of a skull, eye sockets filled with dirt.

I am wrong about everything. Hell is real; I'm in one of the antechambers. This is all a warning. I should not be making out with girls who have girlfriends back on Jupiter. I should at the very least master meditation so I can go to nirvana and not this place. My mind seems half-calm thinking those things, but I'm screaming and pointing, which is horrible because the skeleton is also pointing back at me, so it's like I'm looking at a mirror dead image of myself, which makes me scream more.

I know Kinz has seen the bones because her breath stops. Then she scoots between me and the skull. Her jaw is clenched hard, she's at least as scared as I am, but as long as I'm hurt and scared, she'll muscle through.

"We're getting out of here," she says.

Avery jumps down into the hole but then freezes, looking in the direction of the skull. I can guess what she's thinking: it looks way more real up close.

"Wow," Mac says. "Mom and Dad are not going to like this."

Two seconds later, he's on his phone to 911 giving them our address.

I'm shaking and Kinz is trying to calm me down, but she's also shaking. Camden paces the side of the pit like she wants to comfort both of us but can't get herself to come down here. Or maybe she and Jay are working on the best way to get the ladder down to us without disturbing the very actual skull.

Duke repeats instructions to Avery until she stops staring at the skull and hand, "See if Synclair is bleeding. Check her eyes. Are her legs connected to her body the right way? Should she lie down?"

"I'm no way lying down!" I yell up to him.

"Okay, cool." He nods at me. "Ambulance will be here soon."

"I don't need an ambulance," I say, but then add, "Well, honestly, I wouldn't mind being checked out. But can I get out of this death pit?"

"Don't call it that!" Mac insists, putting his phone back in his pocket. "You can't tell Mom and Dad there's a death pit under their hot tub. It's a…death feature."

He jumps down and has Camden lower the ladder to him, setting its feet into the dirt by my legs.

"Are you sure you don't want to wait?" he asks. "If you have a concussion this might suck."

"I'm in a death feature with a skeleton—I want out," I tell him.

He puts his shoulder under one of my arms and helps me stand up, with Kinz supporting me on the other side. I wrap my hands around the ladder and it's okay. I get situated with hands on rungs and a foot on another. Everything hurts and I'm not sure how my body is connected.

Mac moves behind me, hands on my waist, and guides me to the next step up. I am mightily dizzy, but I can't tell if that's from hitting my head or falling or how weird this whole night became. The two figures at the top of the ladder blur and condense into Camden and Duke, kneeling on either side. They take hold of my arms and help me up the next few rungs. Time skips ahead a minute or three because I'm leaned back against someone softish and warm with a cold, wet cloth on my forehead. I have a vague memory of them pulling me to a safe part of the yard, but I was too busy shaking and freaking out.

An EMT starts asking me questions. He's a youngish Black guy with close-cropped hair, slender with a nerdy overtone, friendly. I tell him that I don't want to talk about who's president and I'm fairly sure it's still Tuesday. A sharp light hurts my eyes but my pupils do the right thing because he says, "Good responsiveness. Not a concussion, but a really bad hit. You're going to have some amazing bruises. What else hurts?"

"Knees," I say. "And every muscle in my back." Oh and also my pride, so much, because Avery has a girlfriend and also I freaked out in front of her and I'm now covered in grave dirt.

Because there's a dead body in my backyard.

The EMT is saying I could go to the hospital and get scanned to be sure, but I so don't want to leave my friends right now. He ends up talking to Mac while Duke tells me, "You need a lot of painkillers and a lot of water and a lot of ice and lying down."

His voice is super close to my ear, so I reach back and pat his hip. "That's you?"

"Kinz went to get ice," he says. "Mac's talking to the cops. Avery isn't sure how you feel about her and Camden went to check on Kinz. Want to borrow my crutch?"

"Can I borrow your wheelchair?"

"Of course. But your house isn't very accessible right now. Maybe Mac and I can carry you to bed."

"You'd love that."

"He did look pretty heroic getting you out of that hole," Duke admits.

I groan and lay my head back against his shoulder. "Do I have to move now?" I ask.

"Nope."

We're still there, sitting on the lawn in the darkness, Duke behind me as the cops arrive and hop down into the hole that doesn't even look that deep from here with their spotlights illuminating it. Kinz brings me two towels full of ice for my knees and a pillow to go under them, and then sits next to us, staring in the direction of the cops, but without focusing her eyes. I take her hand and she grips mine back.

Camden joins us, sitting on Kinz's other side, holding her other hand. Avery settles next to Duke and he pats her on the back. Mac is crouched at the side of the pit, answering the cops' questions: where our parents are; how long we've owned the house; when the construction started; how many serial killers we've met in the neighborhood who might want to stash bodies in our yard.

How did the contractors not see this? They were so close, but the skull and hand must've still been covered in dirt until Kinz slid down that side of the pit. My luck is terrible.

Another day or two and they'd have found the body, not me. Plus Avery's girlfriend. Those facts have multiplied in my brain, like there wouldn't be this skeleton now if she didn't also have a girlfriend—or is it the other way around? Skeleton means girlfriend? I need tonight to be over.

More cops arrive. Avery goes into the house and comes back with water for everyone. We keep sitting. The moon moves an inch across the sky, maybe two. Kinz has taken the ice off my knees and put it back on at least once, then takes it off again. Duke says I need crackers and Kinz finds me a box of Saltines. I nibble a few and when those stay down I take all the painkillers Duke insists I should.

Then he tells Kinz, "Get over here," and swaps out so she's sitting behind me. "You serious about borrowing the chair? It's in the trunk."

"I need to get to bed," I say. I can't crawl because of my knees, but I'm not sure I can walk.

"I can get it," Mac offers.

"You don't know how to unfold it," Duke points out. "I'd better come help." He's in heaven for the next five minutes, I'm sure, getting to do a heroic side mission with Mac. They get the chair set up at the edge of the patio and then rejoin us. More cops have arrived and they're taping off the death feature with yellow crime scene tape.

"Come on, let's get you into bed," Mac tells me. "You're only going to get stiffer."

"It's not that bad," I say, until he and Kinz help me stand up and I say a whole lot of very unchristian words because it *is* that bad. They fireman's hold carry me to the wheelchair and then Mac wheels me into the house and to the bathroom next to my bedroom. This involves him having to lever the chair up over the lip of the patio, the lip of the door going into the house and yet another difference in floor levels leaving the living room. He's muttering to himself about how our parents have got to agree to make this accessible.

At the bathroom door, I insist, "I've got this." I'm not letting Mac help me to the toilet. Or Kinz or Avery or any of them.

Screw our nonwheelchair accessible bathroom. Mac needs to talk to Mom and Dad about remodeling this too. I stand and shuffle to the toilet, grateful that Mac has closed the door behind me. Tears are running down my cheeks, but half from self-pity because the painkillers are working. I make it to the toilet and sit, then work my shorts and underpants down. My legs are mostly straight out because it hurts to bend my knees, plus the swelling.

I pee and then snag the hand towel. I can reach the sink next to the toilet and clean up as best I can while sitting there. I leave my shorts around my ankles and get my panties on, then push up to standing so I can brush my teeth twice.

Then I turn to the door, leaning back against the vanity, and raise my voice. "Okay you can come rescue me now."

Kinz bursts in and puts my arm around her shoulders. We shuffle to the door where there's room for Mac to take my other arm and help me into my bedroom and bed.

"You want your bra off?" Kinz asks.

"Yes, you lovely person," I say.

She gets me a clean T-shirt and helps me change into it, sitting on the side of my bed. My upper body isn't the mass of pain that my knees are, it's only stiff and creaky.

"We're supposed to elevate your legs," she says. "Mac's getting more pillows."

"Where's Avery?"

"She was hovering outside your door for a bit. You want her in here?"

"I don't know. But I want her to be okay. Is everyone okay?"

"Well I'm still screaming in my mind, but otherwise I'm golden. I'll go ask, if you're good for a sec."

"Oh yeah," I say, letting my head sink more into the pillow. "Peachballs."

I doze for a bit and hear Kinz talking in my doorway. She says, "I think she's asleep… Yeah, there's a glass on her bedside table… You're staying? I could stay. We could both stay…I guess not."

I want her to stay, but the fuzzy painless haze of the pills drags me into sleep.

EMANATION FOUR:

Kindness

In the middle of the night, I flick on my bedside light. My left knee isn't as bad as I expected, heavily scraped and red in a few places, but I can bend it fine. My right is swollen and dark red. I make it to the bathroom by limping and keeping that leg straight when I sit. My neck and shoulders ache and there is a red, swollen lump down by my jaw on the left side.

"You should see the other guy," I tell my reflection.

Then I remember the other guy is a skull, and shudder.

Back in bed, I pull the blanket all the way up to my chin, even though it's not cold in the house. There's been a dead body in my backyard the last three years at least? Who is it?

Were they old when they died? Did they have a full life that they enjoyed? Or were they my age? What would happen if I died now with so much undone? I don't want to. I'm shivering in my bed, holding the blanket close.

I want to curl up next to someone. Did Kinz stay? I used to sleep over at her house a lot, before she started dating Camden, and of course we'd both sleep in her bed. Not in a super gay way, unfortunately, more like cats sleeping near each other.

As the kid of the family, I'm used to having people in the house and being able to go wake someone up or climb into bed with them if I'm scared. If my sister were here, I could maybe do that with her. But I don't want to be that baby. I'm seventeen now. I've only got a year until college, what would I do in the dorms if I can't sleep alone in the dark? Though, to be fair, I don't plan on seeing skeletons in the dorms—and a skull with dirt filling the eye sockets is terrifyingly worse in real life than on TV.

I take more of the painkillers next to my bed because enough time has passed and Duke would tell me to, and stare at the blurry blue-gray of my ceiling some more. I should get up and watch something, but that feels like defeat.

My folks found it funny that I enjoyed going to church with Kinz as a kid, until I hit thirteen and asked about confirmation or maybe a bat mitzvah. For half a year I obsessed about which one I should have. Mom and Dad finally shut down the obsessing by telling me I was no way getting either of those rites of passage. I guess the joke was on them since I'd ended up having a sort of lesbian magic initiation after all.

"I really don't want to die any time soon," I tell the space of my room and whatever's beyond it. "I don't want my skull filled with dirt. What happens when I die? Can you clue me in because I'm freaking out pretty hard right now."

A presence is in the room, warm and full, covering me more than the blanket can. I'm not alone and I'm not as scared. I close my eyes.

I'm not aware of falling asleep, but after a while someone picks me up and carries me through the back of my closet, so I must be. I'm standing by myself in the big, ancient forest and my body feels good. I don't hurt and it's easy to walk through the trees. I go until I see the treehouse in the distance and head for that. As I get closer, I spot construction workers tearing out one of the walls.

Avery stands among the roots of that tree.

"Is your house under construction too?" I ask her.

"That's yours," she says.

It's night here, but the space between the trunks is softly luminous, as if the bark glows too faintly to see the light of any one tree, but all of them together illuminate us. Avery holds out her hand and when I take it she pulls me close. She kisses me and then holds my face in her hands and looks at me.

Both of her eyes are brown and in the dimness of the trees, they look blacker than her hair. There's a presence in her that's far beyond what she is, what any of us are.

"Why?" I touch the side of her eye that should be blue.

"You ask good questions," she says. "But I can't tell you." The inside of her mouth is golden fire, like a sunrise over water.

She kisses me again and I wake up.

My room is still dark and filled with warm presence.

I get my phone and stare at it. She hasn't texted. Freaked out by the body? Or maybe I'm a terrible kisser and a dead body is the excuse she needs to run for it.

I turn off my phone and fall asleep again. This time I get a normal dream that Duke is baking religieuse pastries—the ones shaped little nuns—with bright pink frosting.

CHAPTER TEN

In the morning I fumble for my glasses on the bedside table and, staring carefully at the floor as I go, make it into the bathroom without having to bend either knee too much. The very red knee does not want to bend, but the other one is okay. I manage to pee and splash water on my face. I badly want coffee but don't want to have to limp across the whole living room to get it. Mac is way down in the basement, in one of the back guest rooms. I could text him, but that won't wake him up.

I take the few steps to the arch between the hall and the living room. A sleeping bag makes an army green lump against the near wall, black hair spilling out the top.

"Avery?"

She rolls over and blinks up at me. "Should you be up?"

"I am up. What are you doing?"

"I meant standing." She sits up. She's in one of Mac's white tank tops. It's too big for her and semi-transparent—and I've forgotten how to inhale. I'm following one exhale with another, especially when she says, "I'm here to take care of you."

I grab the arch's molding next to me and mutter, "I was, just coffee, then lying down."

She laughs. "Are you always like this without coffee?"

I can't answer that because she's climbing out of the sleeping bag and she's also wearing Mac's boxer briefs above her long, really smooth legs.

"Where's the coffee?" she asks. "I'll bring you some."

"Outdoor kitchen. French press. The cabinet by the other cabinet."

She snares the throw blanket by the Xbox console and wraps it around her body before opening the sliding glass door to the patio. I limp back into my bedroom, holding on to the wall. I shove pillows against my headboard and sit, wishing my bedroom had a window on the backyard, imagining Avery out there heating up water and bending down to look for the French press, with the blanket falling away and the dense curve of her butt in those boxers that I don't even care where they came from.

Avery comes into my bedroom, looking even better than in my imagination. She's got the blanket wrapped around her body and over one shoulder, two mugs in one hand and a plate in the other. I'm sure there's food on the plate, but I can't get my eyes to focus that far over. Especially because when she sets the plate and mugs on my bedside table, she unwraps the blanket and drops it.

Avery lifts the edge of the blanket on my bed and asks, "Okay?"

"Please!"

She slides in next to me—very next to me. Her bare thigh is warm against mine. I'm in sleep shorts and a big night shirt. Our torsos are far enough apart that she can hand me a mug of coffee and pick up the other mug, both of us sipping without banging our elbows together much. She puts the plate in her lap; it's pastries and cookies that Duke made and left in my fridge.

"How do you feel?" she asks.

"That knee and about half my muscles hurt, but not too bad considering. Are you going to get in trouble for staying?"

"I told my grandparents you got hurt and your house is all torn up and you'd need help and they were cool with it. Nadiya's acting mad about her car but it's not like she had anywhere to go today." She wiggles her toes under the blanket, rotates one ankle then the other. "I'm sorry that I have a girlfriend and you fell in a pit."

That cracks me up and she joins my laughter. "Yeah, me too."

"Do you know what you want?" she asks. "I mean, about that first part, what do you want to do?"

I want to kiss her again, but I should put some of my thoughts on loudspeaker first to make sure we're at least in the same universe about what we're doing. "I like you. I mean, I always have but now, I guess, I like you again but different. And I wish you could stay but you're going back to New York. I guess you'd kind of be an asshole if you broke up with your New York girlfriend when you guys set up to have a break. You really did that? Why would you do that?"

Avery tugs on her hair, as if that's going to jump start her brain. "She's a year older and has dated more than me. She wanted me to have more experiences, as long as I wanted that too."

"That makes us both look like assholes now."

"I know. Trust me. I know so much. I keep trying to have conversations with her in my head but also I don't want to get all mononormative and think that because I like you that means I have to stop liking her."

"What?"

"As if monogamy is the gold standard of all relationships and everything else is delusional," she says. "Like on TV when someone falls in love and suddenly it wipes out everything about their other relationship. Like you can't be in love with two people when you totally can."

I'm blinking at her, trying to process that I saw her mouth form the word "love" twice in the last few sentences. The unhelpful part of my brain is informing me that I definitely love Kinz—and not only in a friend way—but seem to be falling in love with Avery, so she's clearly got a point here.

If Kinz were single, would I be cooler about Avery going back to her girlfriend after this summer? Yep, sure would. So I guess I have to be that cool now.

"We've got five weeks," I say. "Do you want to hang out as much as possible? I mean not only hang out. Or in a way that includes kissing, if that's hanging out."

"Absolutely!"

My coffee mug is empty and I've eaten a pastry and a half from the plate in Avery's lap.

"Would you put this over there?" I ask, extending the mug toward the bedside table. Reaching leans me into Avery, my arm crossing in front of her. She moves the plate, takes the mug out of my hand and replaces it with her other hand. She stares at our fingers. I dip my face under the line of her hair and kiss her cheek.

She giggles. "Like we're kids again?"

"Not quite." I take my glasses off and hold them out. "Put these over there too?"

As she does, I kiss under her ear, down her neck. She slides an arm around me and shifts closer. I have kissed one other girl and that was all on-the-lips "are we doing this right?" carefulness. Since I saw Avery in the woods, I've been wanting to kiss her neck and throat, kiss along her collarbones, down one side and up the other, kiss her eyelids and between her eyes and the tip of her nose.

Her lips chase mine and catch them after I've planted that tiny kiss on her nose. The tip of her tongue circles mine and then she's kissing my chin and down my throat while her hand slips up the back of my shirt. Mine's on top of the tank top but I can feel the details of her ribs under it.

I kiss next to her ear and then, because I can't figure out how to kiss her ear itself, I run the tip of my tongue over its tiny ridges. She gasps and shivers against me. My hand edges upward to the curve of her breast.

"Hey Em, Mom wants to know if you're—" Mac's words cut off with a barked laugh. "Yeah you're okay. She's okay Mom, she's totally fine. I'll put her on in a sec but first I want you look at this thing in the kitchen."

Avery and I untangle, breathing fast and unevenly. I'm staring into her eyes from inches away and I never want to stop, but I have to or I'll kiss her again.

"Can I have my glasses?" I ask, chuckling when I hear my breathless self.

"Sure." She presses them into my hands and kisses me quick on the lips. "Should I go somewhere?"

"Nah, my mom will worry less if you're here."

"In your bed?" Her tone is rich with disbelief.

Mac walks back into the room with the phone still pointing at his face, saying, "She's right here. She's fine, I swear. Em... Synclair, tell Mom you're fine."

I take the phone and turn it, holding it far away enough that Mom can see Avery next to me. Mom's sitting on a white-edged patio in bright afternoon sun and I can't see her eyes because of her sunglasses, but I do see her eyebrows go way up.

"Oh, good morning," she says.

"You remember Avery," I tell her, because she has to.

It takes her a second to connect the girl she's seeing—in my bed, which I'll give her a bit more time to process—to my childhood best friend. "Avery? Oh my goodness, you're grown up!"

"Hi Mrs. Sinclair." Avery waves at the phone.

I say, "Mac's right, I'm in good shape. I banged up one knee a bunch, but that's it."

"You still need to see a doctor," Mom says. "Tell Mac he has to take you in. Concussions are serious. Even if the EMT says you didn't have one, I want you to get completely checked out."

"I can take her," Avery offers. "I'll make sure she goes this afternoon."

"Thank you." Mom compresses a lot of feeling into those two words, like she's still getting over that there's an actual girl in my bed—to be honest, so am I—and is also kind of happy about it, but not a weird amount of happy. Plus, if I were to guess, she's having feelings 'cause I'm the baby of the family and she knows intellectually that I'm old enough to be making out with girls, but maybe it didn't sink in until now, especially since I spent all of junior year pining over Kinz and not kissing anyone.

"I'll call you again when I've seen the doctor," I tell her. "Unless it's really late there and then I'll text with all the details. Mac is waving, I'm handing you back to him."

Mac gets his phone and walks out of my room talking about the pit and the construction in general. Yeah, Mom is so not going to worry about me and Avery when she's got that to think about. And the skeleton, when Mac breaks that news.

Avery hands me my phone from my desk. "You should call and get an appointment."

I do that while Avery gets me a fresh cup of coffee and goes to take a shower. When I'm off the phone, Mac walks into my room and sits backward in my desk chair, facing me in the bed. He must've gone to bed super late and slept on his face until Mom's call woke him. Pillow grooves ripple across one cheek and his short, light brown hair stands up all to the left. He's in cut-off sweatpants and a T-shirt so worn that one of the sleeves is tearing off at the shoulder.

"Synclair, I have to tell you something. Don't lose it, okay?"

I wrap both hands around my warm second cup of coffee and nod.

"The cops found a second body. When they were marking off the crime scene and stuff, they saw another skull in the dirt, so definitely two. Now they're waiting for some forensic expert."

"There are *two* bodies buried in our backyard?"

"Looks like it. Unless they find more. They're bringing out ground-penetrating radar."

Fear and disgust leapfrog up my back. "Oh shit. I am never using that hot tub. Are we moving?"

"Don't know. Depends on the skeletons, I guess. I didn't tell Mom. I told her the contractors found some old pipes. I don't want our folks thinking they have to fly home yet. It'll be better when the cops know more."

"Two bodies," I repeat. Two skeletons in the backyard is scrambled up with Avery having both me and a girlfriend— making each set of facts feel worse than they already did.

"You okay?" Mac asks. "You're all pasty like a toaster waffle."

I listen to make sure the shower's still running before I say, "Avery has a girlfriend."

"Then why's she all over you?" he asks, shaking his head.

"They're on a break for the summer."

"Sounds like they're breaking up," he says. "You're into her, you should go for it. It's kosher by her rules. And then if they are breaking up, you're right there; you're already in."

"Wow, that's decent big brother advice. Thanks."

"Brat." He grins at me. "I learned some things at college. Mostly about girls, but hey that turns out to be applicable for you, so our folks spent their money wisely after all."

"Is it cool if I stay somewhere else tonight?" I ask. "Kinz's or Duke's or anyplace without skeletons?"

"Sure, but let me know where you are. No more weird-ass parties in the middle of nowhere."

"I'm not planning on it," I tell him. But I haven't planned most of this summer so far, unless it counts as a plan to ask God to give me a summer of mysticism.

CHAPTER ELEVEN

The doctor confirms that I do *not* have a concussion and didn't break anything. Being oblivious that I was falling into a hole prevented my body from tensing up and getting hurt worse. My bad knee has a bone bruise. I get crutches and ACE bandages and a lot of instructions.

By the time I join up with Avery in the waiting room, Kinz has invited everyone to meet for lunch at the Thai place in the old downtown. Jay has to work, but Kinz, Camden, and Duke are sitting at a big table near the front when we arrive. I've got space to extend my leg and prop up my crutches. Duke brought his cane to see if I wanted to try it instead of a crutch. He nestles it in with my crutches and we grin at each other, comrades in physical complications.

Camden has her laptop open on the table and spent the morning Googling. She's in a pink T-shirt with little scallops and is wearing her gold-frame, round glasses with her braids wound into a dense bun. Duke is sporting another button-up short-sleeved shirt, this one a patchwork of blue patterns: dense diamonds, light speckles, stripes. If we turn into the Culinary & Fashion Club, I'm going to have issues. At least Kinz is wearing a gray hoodie that looks like she tore the sleeves off by hand.

Camden says, "I found the ownership records for your house going back about forty years. Three years ago your folks bought it from a professor and her husband. I'm not sure what he did. He's got a really common name. So I guess he could be the killer. They owned it for about twelve years and the people before had it for over twenty, so depending on the age of the bones, it could be them."

"Unless someone else buried the body," Duke points out. "What if there was a groundskeeper?"

"Like in a classic British mystery?" I ask, doubtful. "This is my backyard we're talking about."

"Could've been a neighbor or anyone who'd know if the residents were away. How old did the skull look?" Duke asks.

"I'm not sure, I was busy screaming."

"Not that old," Camden says. "Not bunches of decades. It didn't have tons of cracks or anything. I thought about that: what if the body had been there before the house was even built? What if it was a burial ground?"

"Bodies," I say reluctantly. They'll find out the minute they take me home—not that I plan on going home any time soon—so I might as well get this over with. "Mac says they found a second skull. I am never, ever using that hot tub."

"Your folks will move it," Kinz tells me. "Side of the house, maybe, or down the lawn. Or the next suburb over."

"Nobody wants the death feature," I grumble. "Kinz, can I move in with you?"

"Of course. But you might have to wear a dress on Sundays and go to church."

"Do I get to pick the dress?"

"Probably. Depends how into it my mom gets and if we're going to my folks' church or Camden's. Do you want me to ask? You really can spend the rest of the summer at my house. It might even make my dad less crazy."

The rest of the summer would be way too long to spend around Kinz's dad, but a week seems very doable. "Let's see how bad this turns out to be," I say. "But, yeah, would you see if I can sleep over a few nights."

Avery has been eating noodles quietly. Is she waiting to see if I'm going to tell the group about the whole girlfriend situation? But now she asks, "Do you think they knew each other before they died? Maybe they were lovers."

Duke shakes his head. "Does that make it better or worse?"

"They could've been really old," Camden says. "We don't know. Maybe they were married for fifty years and then someone didn't have the money for a funeral."

"Cool idea," I tell her. "But how did they die at the same time?"

"They don't have to. If it was long ago and one of their kids owned the house, or grandkids, and grandpop dies, they bury him in the backyard, they know he's there, so maybe grandmom lives a few more years and then they make sure they bury her with him so they can stay together."

"Do they know they're together?" Avery asks. "Like in the cultures that buried people together so they'd stay together in the afterlife?"

"The way I see things, they do," Camden says.

"In *heaven*?" Kinz asks, a hint of a growl in her voice. "What if they weren't Christian, or were sinners, or were any of the billions of people my dad says aren't going to heaven?"

Duke pulls a dish of snow peas closer and spoons more onto his plate. "Then they went to one of the other heavens."

"How many heavens do you have?" I ask.

"Depends who you ask. Reform Jews—and some of the mystical ones—get to adapt our worldviews. In Kabbalah there are four levels of worlds, so I'm going to say there could be at least four heavens."

"But what if you go to one heaven and the people you love go to another. Is there visiting?" Avery asks, taking the snow peas when he offers. "Isn't reincarnation easier?"

"Yeah." Duke chuckles. "Jews have reincarnation too, actually. My dad's not kidding when he says we have everything. Heaven seems boring, and I know someone's going to say it can't be because it's heaven, but I don't think we're really meant to be unchanging forever. It sounds like a drag."

Camden taps her plate with the tips of her chopsticks. "You can have both. In my theology, we're in a created world that has time and change, but there's also the eternal God who participates in everything that happens and then perfects it. It's like—take this metaphor really loosely—we're sitting here talking and someone's recording us, but recording everything, our thoughts, our feelings. And then they edit it to highlight all the best in us and after we die, we can experience it any time we want, any part of our lives or any other, edited to focus on what's great and to remove what's evil."

"Then why bother to be good now?" Kinz asks. She's tearing pieces off her napkin, making a pile of faux snow by her plate.

"First off because you weren't doing good in order to look good. And because there's still a film that's being edited and who do you want to be on that film? What do you want your life to be about?"

"Tell my dad that," Duke says. "He will love that. He says something like that—about how what we do in life, even the really small things, is echoed in heaven."

Avery is shaking her head slowly, which runs dark waves through her hair. "If you're always thinking about heaven, you're missing out on right now. I don't want to feel that I'm living for reasons other than the here and now. So much damage has come from the idea that all the big Sacred stuff happens somewhere other than this world. It's all here, with us."

Kinz nods, not entirely frowning. "Take out the religious stuff and I agree with you. We've got to keep people focused on this world, right now, because otherwise they're going to keep trashing it."

"We're on the same side," Avery says and grins at Kinz. "Hey, I've got to head back to my grandparents' and change and get ready for babysitting later. Synclair, are you all set?"

"Yeah, I'll go over to Kinz's."

Avery leans over and kisses me and I'm so surprised—so not used to being kissed in my group of friends—that I almost don't kiss her back.

After she's gone out the door and past the front window, Duke waggles his eyebrows at me and says, "She stayed over. How good did *that* go?"

"Really good but also she has a girlfriend."

"What?!" Duke and Kinz say at the same time while Camden turns to stare at me, eyebrows high.

I explain, "They're on a break because they haven't dated a lot of other people and Avery didn't think she'd see me and it is all very confusing." Then I have to rewind and tell more of the story, as much as I can remember about what Avery said.

"Get as much action as you can," is Duke's vote.

"Don't get too involved. You'll get your heart broken," Kinz says. "I don't like that this girl is perfectly set up to mess with you."

Kinz has always been protective of me, because she's bigger and a few months older—or maybe because she's protective of all her friends—but we've never had an opportunity for her to be protective about a girl and my heart. I like it. But I don't like *how much* I like it.

"Tie breaker?" I ask Camden.

"I can't answer for you because I'm not you," she says.

"What if it were you?" Kinz asks Camden. "What if I were seeing someone or wanted a break to kiss other people?"

"What other people?" Camden asks, quickly. "You have some other people in mind?"

"Hypothetically." Kinz raises her hands along with a shrug.

Camden swirls her tea in her cup and takes a sip, looking into the depths as if she's reading the leaves. "On the plus side, you could kiss this hypothetical girl and decide you like me more. Downside, maybe she's a better kisser. So if that's fifty-fifty, I have to trust, have faith, let it work out. Except that I'd be super distracted the whole time and I have things I want to work on this summer so let's not do that right now, okay?"

Kinz puts an arm around her and kisses the side of her face. "I wasn't really asking and I'd be pissed if you were kissing someone else, so don't worry."

Does Avery's girlfriend feel that way? Do I care? Shit, Camden was right about how distracting this can get. I have goals for this summer too! I reach into my shoulder bag and touch the card I got from Miri at the garden center. I found Tree of Life Meditation Center online and wrote the times of some classes on the back of the card. I should go soon, if I don't end up naked at another party or falling into a random pit.

Was it random? My summer has been littered with distractions. Maybe I'm supposed to surmount them to show my spiritual dedication. I'm going to get on that as soon as I've had an after-lunch nap and some time to get over the death feature.

* * *

Kinz drives us over to her place. I lie in her bed while she updates her parents and makes sure it's okay for me to stay. I don't sleep, just take off my glasses and let the world go fuzzy while all the moments of the last day whirl around in my head.

I return to last night and the feeling of presence with me, the warmth and love, being carried—why don't I have more words for this? I could say "God," but that means too much and too little all at once. Is Avery showing up in my life right now some kind of sign? What is God trying to tell me?

Kinz tells me we're invited over to Jay's for the night. I half don't want to go, not having known Jay that long. I've been over there once for a movie night, but Kinz's house is familiar, even cozy when her dad's busy. But we can't hang out with Duke here the way we can at Jay's. Even though Kinz has said that she's lesbian about a thousand times, her parents still have a "no boys after 9 p.m." rule.

Jay's mom is single—though she prefers to say "solo" because she's very *not* looking for someone—and doesn't mind us taking over the first floor of the house as long as we stay out of her upstairs. She's so single that last year she got a brown tabby cat that she named "Boyfriend" so that she could tell people who keep asking if she's dating that yes, she has a Boyfriend.

Jay's mom wants our teen gossip and of course gets the whole story about me and Avery from Kinz and Jay. They tell her about the bodies too, but she's more into the fraught romance. I guess she wants the experience vicariously at a distance, without having to go through the drama herself, and I feel weirdly useful despite my bruised body and even more bruised ego.

"What do you think I should do?" I ask after I've spun out the whole story in front of her.

"Have fun," she says, her kind, squinting eyes a mirror of Jay's. "It's summer. Can you enjoy Avery without getting too caught up?"

"Probably not."

"Well, you're young, you'll mend."

"I'm not sure how much of me I want mending at any given time," I say. "I'm already about thirty percent mending."

"Fair enough. Up to you," she tells me and goes to order us pizzas as if all of this is not the hugest deal in my life. Maybe someday I'll be that calm. Does she meditate?

After the pizzas arrive, she tells us not to bug her unless it's at least a mild emergency and takes her pizza upstairs.

We take over the living room, putting our pizzas on the long coffee table. Kinz and Camden are on the couch, sitting super close, with Jay on Camden's other side at a reasonable distance. Duke offers me the good armchair, but I shake my head and sit on the floor against the beanbag chair, leaning back into its cushiness. Duke tosses a throw pillow at me and I shove it under my bad knee and calf the way he wants me to.

"I've been wondering, did you see the second skull?" Jay asks.

"No."

"How do you know your brother is telling the truth? Because I've been wondering how the contractors didn't see the bones in the hot tub hole."

"Kinz kicked the dirt off the first skull when she came down to save me and the cops uncovered the other one when they were examining the first," I explain.

"But what if your brother put them there to freak us out and then told you there's another one and there isn't."

"He looked scared," Duke says.

I text Mac: *Are there really two bodies? Are you making this up?*

He sends back a photo of our yard torn up, crime scene tape, a second skull visible in the trench the cops dug down toward the first skull. I hand my phone to Jay who passes it around to everyone.

"They look together," Camden says. "I bet it was a couple."

"Speaking of—and despite this girlfriend business—when are we seeing Avery again?" Duke asks, leaning toward the coffee table and pulling two slices of the gluten-free, tomato-free, cheese-free pizza onto his plate.

I've already got my plate of pizza. I pick the olives off and eat them first. "I don't know. She hasn't texted since lunch but I think she had to drive her grandmom around a bunch."

"Have you texted her?"

"No. I don't know what to say. Kissing her this morning was great. But also: girlfriend. And furthermore: skeletons!"

"Give me your phone," he says.

I roll my eyes and hand it to Kinz, who passes it down the couch to Jay, who gives it to him. He knows my code and thumbs through my messages.

"Aw, you two are cute." He starts typing.

"Duke, what are you saying to her?"

He reads aloud as he types, "Hi, I'm checking on you. Scary night, huh? My knee's feeling way better and I want to make sure you're okay too." He hits send and asks, "Do I sound like a girl who's smitten?"

"You're making me sound ditzy."

"Actually it's pretty good," Kinz tells him.

My phone pings. "Oooh," Duke says and reads the reply in a breathy falsetto, "I'm still sorry! For everything! I'm glad you're feeling better!—she's using lots of exclamation marks here and emoji: downcast face, woozy face, teddy bear, really?"

"More reading, less opinion please, gay Siri," I tell him.

"I'm bi-to-the-gay-side Siri, thank you very much," he says. "I have not ruled out women completely, they simply have to be spectacular because men are so much easier. Avery's asking a bunch of questions, hang on." He types for a while, muttering,

"I'm telling her about the forensic team and how much your boobs long for her touch."

"You'd better not be."

"How do you spell areola?" he asks in the direction of the couch, without glancing up.

"A-R-E-O-L-A," Camden tells him.

I rest my head against the beanbag chair and practice some meditative breathing. Nope, not working.

Boyfriend trots across the room carrying one of his million cat toys, hops onto the coffee table and drops it on the pepperoni pizza.

"Ugh, sorry." Jay grabs him and puts him on the floor, then removes the besmirched piece of pizza. She tosses his toy across the room and he bounds after it. "Kitten energy. Everything is a toy to him. We can't let him outside anymore or he gets mice and brings them into Mom's bedroom."

"Amazingly gross," Camden tells her.

"Right! Imagine getting out of bed and stepping on a dead mouse in your bare feet. And when it's still alive—my mom can really scream."

"Okaaay," Duke says, drawing out the word. "Thank you for that charming image. Synclair, how much do you want to see Avery tonight?"

"Way more than I should," I tell him.

He types, waits, types, then says, "Good because she's coming over. She's borrowing her cousin's car for a babysitting gig and can swing by here on her way."

"When? I should bathe."

"You've got about thirty minutes."

Kinz practically carries me into the bathroom. Is she that relieved that I finally have someone to kiss? Have I been super obvious? Why do I still love it when she touches me?

CHAPTER TWELVE

I take a quick bath, keeping my bad knee out of the too-hot water, and then change into some of Kinz's clothes. We didn't want to go back to my house, so she grabbed extra for me when we were at hers. She mostly wears jeans and cargo shorts—and uses all the pockets. I'm in her old gray cargo shorts, which are too big but at least I can belt them tighter. She wears her T-shirts tight, so that's not a bad fit, but I have to roll up the sleeves of her sweatshirt. I hope the compression bandage around my knee makes me look somewhat badass despite the whole borrowing-my-big-sister's-clothes effect.

Kinz settles me on the couch with my leg extended across pillows on the coffee table, so Avery can sit next to me. Then she heads for the front porch; nobody else is in the room.

"Wait, you're leaving me?"

"Do you want moral support or do you want to make out with her?" she asks. "Priorities, okay?"

"What are you guys going to do?" I ask.

"Gossip about you and try to listen in and then, if you two get boring, we're going to all cram onto the front porch couch and watch a movie."

"Thanks, you're a true friend."

"I'm there for you, buddy," Kinz says. She gives me a cheesy grin and two big thumbs up.

"Company!" Duke yells from the front porch.

Avery pauses inside the living room doorway. She's wearing serious pajama bottoms—a very dark gray with golden pinstripe rectangles—and a light tan and black sweater over a cream-colored V-neck shirt. Babysitter Avery could watch me every day of the week and that would be just fine.

"How are you feeling?" she asks.

"Better now that you're here."

Her grin deepens as she joins me on the couch. She's got her contacts in so both her eyes are brown, one a hint lighter than the other. I guess that's to not weird out the kids she's babysitting, though they're missing out on life's full coolness. I flash to the dream of being in the forest with her, how dark her eyes looked. I still haven't told her all of it.

"Do you want me to come back tonight?" she asks. "The parents get home around midnight or one. Will you be up?"

"I'll try to be. I've been really sleepy since that whole falling into a pit situation, so if I don't text back, I will in the morning, okay?"

She nods and leans closer. Her fingers touch my jaw beside the bruise. "I'm sorry you got hurt."

"Thanks."

Our faces keep getting closer, all slow like in a movie, so I pull off my glasses and rest them on the back of the couch. From behind the couch, Boyfriend reaches a paw up to snag the frame. I keep one hand over them and ignore him. I'd ask Jay to come get him, but Avery's fingers are sliding around behind my head and pulling me closer to her.

As we kiss, I block out the part about her having a girlfriend, and then it's easy to forget about everything else except her being here now and that I get more weeks of this. She brushes her cheek against mine and kisses by my ear. I nuzzle under her hair and kiss the side of her neck. Our mouths come together for a long, perfect time. Not mashed together, but making little movements so we can keep feeling each other's lips.

She pulls away, checks her phone and says, "Oh good, eight more minutes."

I open my mouth to promise I'll stay up if she'll come back, but Boyfriend pounces into our laps. He turns in a victorious circle, a white tail dangling from his mouth. Avery yelps and scoots to the far side of the couch. I can't jump away with my leg propped up, but I raise my arms and pray he's not about to drop a mouse in my lap.

He turns toward the spot where Avery was, decides that's not good enough, spins for my lap and opens his mouth. Something fuzzy and bloody drops onto my thigh, rolls off, hits the cushion and lands on the floor. Boyfriend leaps down toward it and bats it a few times, into the middle of the carpet, then decides with inscrutable cat logic that he's done. He retreats to the side of the room to view his kill and clean his paws.

"He has a thing with mice," I tell Avery, who's staring at the mass on the carpet.

"That's not a mouse," she says.

I unfold my glasses, put them on and wish I hadn't because it is obviously a tampon.

"I'm starting to feel cursed," I say. "We meditated together on the beach and suddenly my life is all: getting naked at a party, dead bodies, cat with tampon."

"The world works in mysterious ways?"

"What if I did something wrong?" I ask, thinking back over the chain of events that includes everything I just said plus Avery having a girlfriend, though I'm not sure I should include that one. "I wanted answers and a spiritual journey. And now I feel like there's all this power, these strange things happening in my life, and I don't know what to do with it. What if it's dangerous for me to not figure it out faster? I wrote down a bunch of intentions at lunch with Kinz and then I met this woman who's magic at the plant store. Maybe I should go talk to her."

"Roll back there. What intentions?"

I drag my backpack over and pull the folded menu out of the pocket where I'd stuffed it days ago.

Avery turns it so she can read my writing and asks, "Why does it say 'someone takes their pants off' next to 'Avery's goddesses?'"

"Kinz was making a joke."

"From anyone else, that might be funny. From her, it's mean."

"Kinz isn't mean," I insist.

"She's mean about religion," Avery says. "Because her dad is super mean to her. I get it, but this is not okay."

The center of my back heats up, streaming fire into my fists. Am I pissed at Avery or at Kinz's dad?

She stands and gets halfway to the door before turning. I'm still steadying myself on a crutch so I can get across the living room without stressing my knee. Duke's agility with these is ninja-like. I'm starting to get how layered his situation is: having to walk with a crutch can suck—because of the pain, the way buildings aren't set up for it, the way people act—but also the crutch becomes more and more useful as I get used to it.

Avery takes my other arm in a way that isn't helpful but I like it anyway, and we make slow progress to the front door. We round the corner to the porch. Kinz and Camden are sitting with their arms around each other. At least they're not making out. From the set of Camden's mouth and the way Kinz has one hand making a fist in her lap, they're having A Talk.

"Where's Jay?" I ask.

"Kitchen with Duke, making dessert," Kinz says. "What's that face for?"

"She should maybe clean up the mess Boyfriend left in the living room."

"I'll tell her," Camden says and scoots past us, headed for the kitchen.

"Also." Avery holds up the scribbled on page and waves it in Kinz's direction. I hold my breath. She says, "I need more respect for my spirituality than this."

"We were joking." Kinz has her hands up, palms toward us, warding. "And none of it's real anyway."

I can't help but jump in. "I did end up with my pants off at the fireworks party."

From behind us, returning from the kitchen, Camden says, "That could have been the power of psychological suggestion. But I'm not saying that makes it not real."

"Plus suggestion only goes so far," I tell her. "Even if writing down intentions and asking various gods for them made it psychologically more likely that I'd take my pants off, that doesn't explain how I got invited to a game that gets people naked."

I step to the side so Camden can return to her spot on the porch. She sits on the couch a little farther away from Kinz than before, since Kinz is now positioned sideways and in full defensive mode. She's scared too. Maybe a lot more than I am. The way Kinz was raised, other people's gods are all devils.

"Can we go talk to someone about this together?" I ask Kinz. "A minister or spiritual teacher?"

"Me? Why? I'm fine," Kinz grumbles. "This is poo and what do you care? However it worked, you got Avery."

Avery's fingers on my arm tighten, sending warm tingles into my shoulder. I want to take her back into the living room and make out more, which reminds me that she has to go so she can come back later.

"Babysitting," I tell her.

"This does kind of feel like that—oh, you're right. I've got to go. I'll text you!"

She kisses me on the cheek and then, when I turn toward her, quickly on the lips. The menu page is folded into my hand. She waves bye to Camden and maybe Kinz, then runs across the lawn to her car.

Camden pushes off the couch, moves to the far end and nudges Kinz, who scoots into the middle. Kinz pats the open space next to her and I join them.

"Witches are so touchy," Kinz grumbles. "I'm sorry but I'm glad she's only here for the summer."

"They did get persecuted for hundreds of years," I point out, because I've been reading up about witches since I met Avery again a few weeks ago. "Mostly by that religion you don't believe in."

"Sometimes I want to believe. I want the safe bet," Kinz admits. "Pascal-style. Make sure I've followed the rules close enough that if there is a heaven, I get to go."

In a near whisper, Camden says, "It doesn't work that way."

"How do you *know*?" Kinz asks, fast and angry, turning to face Camden.

"You won't let me tell you." Camden puts her hand on Kinz's upper chest to stop her from saying more. "And I'm not going to try because I see your face when I say things like 'kingdom of heaven.'" To me, she says, "I think you should go talk to whoever you want. You don't need to be scared."

"That's all some religions are," Kinz mutters. "Fear and trembling and hellfire." She shoves off the couch and heads for the kitchen.

Camden pulls out her phone and thumbs through screens, scowling. Her mouth takes on a sculpted elegance when she scowls, which I am noticing for purely aesthetic reasons. Kinz is my best friend and I should go after her, but it doesn't feel right to leave Camden alone out here, so I sit on the far side of the couch, the part that's still warm from Kinz's butt. I stare at my phone without unlocking it, trying to figure out what cute message I could send Avery, waiting for Camden to talk if she wants.

"Awe isn't fear," she says softly. "But her dad." Like she's reminding herself.

"Yeah." Because she doesn't have to say more than that. We both know how awful Kinz's dad can get.

"He's taking her away from God. Cruelty on top of cruelty. Both hurting her and removing the ways she could heal herself."

"Not that simple," I say and Camden peers up from her phone, staring a question at me. I try to voice a thought I haven't put into words yet. "Mac's spatial intelligence is way better than mine—to the point where it's like we live in two different houses. He thinks it's ridiculous when I get lost in the piles in our basement. But they're really big piles and our basement is huge and I don't have a three-dimensional map in my head the way he does."

"Okay?" Camden rests back against the couch.

"I've been wondering if there's a spiritual intelligence or spiritual capacity and some people have it more than others. The same way some people get art and others don't, and some get math, and so on."

"And Kinz doesn't have it? So even if her dad wasn't abusive, religion wouldn't be a path of wholeness for her?"

"She has less than we do," I say. "And her spiritual intelligence is oriented toward animals, so she thinks church shouldn't be a big deal for anyone because she doesn't know what it's like to have that hunger." My voice catches on the last word and I focus on my phone, trying to cram all the ideas and feelings back into my body before they spill out in front of Camden.

"You have it," she says.

"Yeah. It's like when my parents say I shouldn't be religious, like they're asking me not to listen to music—ever. But I've already heard it and when it's not there, I miss it."

"I'm sorry," she says gently. "You should get to have all the religion and spirituality and wonder you want. And I appreciate that idea about spiritual intelligence. I should get Kinz to work out some natural world metaphors with me when she's not mad. If she's not mad."

I kind of want to hug Camden. Maybe we can be friends now that I'm not all twisted around that she's dating Kinz.

"She'll get there," I say, but neither of us goes into the house.

CHAPTER THIRTEEN

Duke goes home around midnight and the rest of us trend in a sleep-ward direction. Avery texts that the people she's babysitting for are running late but she's still game to stop by after one a.m. The only problem with this is that Jay's house isn't very big, so we're all sleeping in the living room. Except Jay, she has a bedroom, but out of deference to her straightness, none of us asked to sleep in there, not even on the floor.

We're also strongly avoiding the middle of the living room as the scene of Boyfriend's recent tampon kill. Kinz and Camden unroll sleeping bags—Jay has had a lot of sleepovers so there are a half-dozen in the hall closet—on the side of the living room by the kitchen. This leaves me the side by the hallway, bathroom and back door, which should work if Avery is going to slip back in. I very much want her to come back and cuddle up with me and kiss more. I want that enough that I'm willing to not feel weird if I make out with her across the room from where Kinz is sleeping.

It's like I have a girlfriend for five weeks. Does it work that way? I should ask her if she can have a girlfriend while on a break with another girlfriend. Nah, I'm going with it. I have a girlfriend!

Can we both fit in this sleeping bag? I'm reconsidering the plan where I have sex in college. I mean, not tonight, but we have five weeks and there isn't a more perfect person to have it with than Avery. Is it possible God's message includes that I should be having sex? If so, I am very on board with that God or Goddess.

I text her that I'm going to leave the back door unlocked, that I'll be to her left when she comes in. We'll have to be quiet—not that Kinz and Camden always give me that same courtesy—because although Kinz is a pretty deep sleeper, I'm not sure about Camden.

I wait until I hear Kinz snore. It's hard to keep my eyes open, already nearly one a.m.; last night and today took weeks to live through. I hobble to the bathroom and then, before returning to my sleeping bag, I unlock the back door.

I'm still sore and I don't know how easy it would be for Avery to get into a sleeping bag with me. I snag the throw blanket from the couch and lie down on top of my sleeping bag. Being on the floor with air-conditioning going, I'm chilly, so I pull up the sweatshirt hood and tug the sleeves down over my hands. I text Avery to wake me up when she gets here and let myself fall asleep.

* * *

An arm slips around my waist, a body curls against my back, bringing me half awake. I press into her. Her hand finds the sweatshirt hood, travels to its edge and touches my cheek with warm, dry fingertips. I shimmy onto my back without moving away from her. We're in the darkest part of the night. The living room is black figures in shadow. With my glasses off, I couldn't see much anyway, but I wish I could see her eyes.

I turn toward her, putting one hand on her hip, feeling soft pajama material slide over her skin. Her fingers tuck under the sweatshirt hood and cup my cheek. She kisses me.

The kundalini energy thing is definitely working. Maybe it's the few times I've tried to meditate on it or being kissed suddenly in the dark, but I get what Avery meant about the bubble tea straw up my spine. It's drawing heavy, golden energy right up to my heart, which expands as it soaks in that liquid sunlight.

Except…these are not Avery's lips. And I haven't had nearly enough time with Avery's tongue, but I don't think this is it.

As I touch the side of her face, braids brush my fingers. Kinzey? I move my hand from her hip to her back. This body in my arms is bigger and softer than Avery. But why is Kinz kissing me in the middle of the night—with her girlfriend across the room—and kissing me this nicely?

Of all the strange things happening this summer, this is the one I want to argue with *least*. Maybe she's jealous and making a move. If Avery can have a girlfriend in New York, I can at least kiss my best friend, right? From no girls to two? Maybe I am blessed. I return the kiss, curious about her mouth, her tongue.

I need to do more tongue with Avery, this is fun. See, I'm learning, this is good for all of us.

She pulls me closer and I smell sweet ginger and woodsy vanilla, feel more than three braids sift across my cheek.

I jerk back. "Camden?"

"What? Sync, how?"

"I'm wearing Kinz's sweatshirt," I say, part explanation and part apology. I grab her arm so she won't get up too fast and nail her head on the side table. I'd dragged it over from the couch to hold my glasses and phone.

I'm about to tell her about the table when the light flicks on. From the middle of the room, Kinz says, "Babe, where— JESUS!" She's not swearing, she's definitely praying.

"Table!" I yell, fast enough that Camden does not concuss herself as she jumps to her feet, away from my sleeping bag.

"I thought she was you. I don't have my glasses on and she's in your sweatshirt!" Camden explains, hands wide.

"She's half my size!"

"Nearly four-fifths," I protest.

"I left the lights off when I went to the bathroom because I didn't want to wake you two and I got turned around," Camden says.

Kinz is in mouth-open shock. Her eyes are wet and I feel like three kinds of stupid and four kinds of trash. Camden reaches for her hands, but Kinz turns and stomps down the hall to the back door. Camden runs after her.

I put my glasses on and get my phone. It's five in the morning. Avery didn't come over. Her babysitting people didn't return until after two. She texted but I must've been so asleep the buzz of the phone didn't wake me. When I didn't answer her texts, she figured she should go home.

I drag my sleeping bag onto the four-season porch and toss it across the weathered couch. The couch isn't long enough for any of us to sleep comfortably, but I'm supposed to keep my legs elevated anyway, so I pile cushions on the leg and prop them up. I focus on the morning conversation of the birds and try not to think about kissing Camden, which is the only thing I can think about other than how mad Kinz is at me.

After a while, footsteps approach and Kinz gazes down on me from the doorway. I close my eyes. I don't want to see the pain or blame in her face. When I open my eyes, she's gone.

I doze until about six thirty and then I text Duke: *You up?*

Sure am. ::sun emoji:: Why are you?

Girl trouble. Will you come get me?

Even if I don't get all the details, I am on my way. But I want details.

I sneak into the living room, which is not easy with one knee that won't bend, and get my shoes and bag. Kinz and Camden are dozing under an unzipped sleeping bag, their arms tightly around each other, and for a half second I hate them.

I'm waiting on the front steps with all my things when Duke pulls in the driveway. I get in the car and tell him, "Everyone else is asleep. I could eat."

It feels weird to leave. I didn't do anything wrong, but I can't look at Kinz right now, or Camden. I really can't look at

Camden. I can still remember her tongue in my mouth. And how much I liked it.

Duke says, "Dad's cooking."

"Cool."

Trees slip by in reverse as we pull out of the driveway. There's techno-Europop playing the perfect surreal soundtrack to this morning. Duke drives his mom's car, a Volvo that always smells like sugar. It has hand controls installed so that Duke or his mom can choose to hit pedals with their feet or switch it so they can drive only using their hands. Duke's got it set to hands-only.

"How's your ankle?" I ask.

"Mostly better, just sore," he says, then seeing that I'm watching his hands, he adds, "Pushing the pedals is a bad angle for it, makes it worse. Plus I just got used to these again."

I nod, wishing I could rewind the last few hours, maybe up to the point where Boyfriend appeared. "Can I stay at your house tonight if I don't want to sleep at home?"

"Of course. What the schnitzel happened?"

I wait until he turns onto a long, even stretch of road and then tell him, "Camden kissed me."

"On purpose?"

"She mistook me for Kinz. We were sleeping on opposite sides of the living room because—did you know Jay's cat killed a tampon?"

"Yeah. Apropos of that, I'm gayer now. Go on."

I shrug. "It was dark. I'm wearing Kinz's clothes. Camden got turned around coming back from the bathroom, so she cuddled up to me and kissed me. Kinz turned on the light and was rightfully upset."

"Why's it a big deal?" Duke asks. "One kiss, oops, mistake! You're like, 'hey, it's me,' we all laugh it off."

"I kissed her back. It wasn't exactly one kiss."

"Wait, wait, wait, are you saying you made out with Camden?" he asks, voice rising. "By accident? How?"

"Where's the line between a few kisses and making out?"

"Tongue?" he suggests.

"Oh, okay, then yes."

"Why?!"

"I thought she was Kinz," I say.

"You're still dying to make out with Kinz. Right. But weren't you *just* kissing Avery earlier tonight? You are a ho!"

"I've wanted to kiss Kinz for two and a half years." My voice sounds super small and Duke turns his music off.

"You thought she was making a move on you because now you've got Avery. That Kinz got jealous?"

"Yeah. I was asleep and then someone's kissing me. I didn't have a lot of think time. So when I realized it wasn't Avery, my brain was all, 'this must be Kinz,' I went with it."

"Who's a better kisser: Camden or Avery?"

"I don't know."

He makes the sound effect of a car pulling up fast, even though we're driving steadily, and glances at me. "Exqueeze me? How can you not know?"

"I can't make that call. They're both different."

"And if Cam thought you were Kinz, she'd go for it. Wow 'clair, have you had Cam's tongue in your mouth more than Avery's? You're batting two hundred."

"That's terrible, right? It feels…" I was about to say "terrible," but Camden is a really good kisser. Plus that whole energy rising effect was unlike anything else I've felt. Now I'm blushing and looking out the window, hoping Duke won't see.

"Say it," Duke insists. "Would you now rather be kissing Camden, your nemesis, than Avery?"

"She's not my nemesis. I like her. I just hate that she got to Kinz first. And no, I would rather kiss Avery."

"But you would not kick Camden out of Jay's living room for eating crackers. You lesbians are intense."

We pull into the garage at Duke's house and head to the kitchen. Duke's house is almost the same layout as the one I lived in before my parents got a bunch of money, so it's both disorienting and comforting to walk in. The rooms are all in the same place but furnished very differently. My folks' décor is super modern and crisp, Duke's folks prefer warm and bookish.

Duke's dad stands at the stove, frying chicken-apple sausage, wearing a worn brown T-shirt over tan hiking shorts. He's got a thick head of black hair and a matching beard that goes all the way down to his collarbones. It would be a big beard anyway, but it verges on huge because he's a slender guy. Most of his muscle is in his legs; his calves are as big around as my thighs.

I smell maple syrup and coffee so strong that I want to put my face in it and let it absorb right to my brain. We'd hang out here all the time, but Duke's mom has the same genetic disorder he does and she gets a lot more fatigue, so we tend to only visit often enough for his parents to know we dig them.

"Everyone okay?" Duke's dad asks. "I understand girl trouble can be quite serious."

I turn on Duke. "You told him."

"It's the furry butt-crack of dawn. How else is he going to understand my need to rescue you?"

I tell Duke's dad, "It's too embarrassing to explain, but I'm all right." He pours me a cup of coffee and slides the half & half carton toward me. I add, "Now I'm more all right. Thanks."

I take my coffee to the kitchen table and sit on the far side, facing the stove. Duke rummages in the fridge.

"Have you heard anything more from the police?" Duke's dad asks.

"No and Mac hasn't texted."

I've been too caught up in the Avery situation—which is now the Avery-not-Camden-no-really situation—to hound Mac for answers. And I'm not sure I want to know. I send him a quick: *What's up? I'm at Duke's. Any news?*

"He's probably asleep," I say. "The forensic people were coming over yesterday afternoon. I don't know if they've told him anything."

"Should at least have some info about the bodies," Duke says. He puts a plate of caramel rolls in front of me and sits to my right, in his usual spot.

Bodies. Ugh, my life.

"Does Judaism have ways to lift curses?" I ask Duke's dad. "Because I'm getting worried."

"Of course. We have everything. Eat and then tell me about this."

Duke's dad has taken classes at their temple about topics that include Jewish meditation and Kabbalah. I didn't know Jews even had meditation, but then I wouldn't know about Christmas trees either if friends hadn't told me. My parents are hardcore about not doing anything religious at home.

I delicately wolf down chicken apple sausage and eggs, leftover roasted veggies that have retained their amazingness, and most of a caramel roll that Duke baked, which is literally heaven. Duke does most of the cooking but his dad learned some things to bond with him. The father-son cooking picked up once they started watching competitions. It's sweet of the world to be treating cooking like a sport now, so Duke's dad can understand it.

"What curse?" Duke asks.

"That's probably the wrong word. But a lot of strange things have been happening since I started trying to figure out my spiritual path. I did write down my intentions. And Kinz joked that I should ask different gods to fulfill them, to see who was real, so I wrote that down too."

Duke's dad snorts and then chokes because he inhaled bits of egg. He puts a napkin over his mouth until he stops coughing and then has to pick egg pieces out of his beard.

"Does this happen often?" he asks when he can talk again.

"Never," I say. "Except I ran into this girl who was my best friend before she moved away six years ago, and now she's a witch, or Wiccan, along with some other stuff, like Buddhist meditation, and Kinz was kidding around, but she's also still really freaked out about everything religious."

"Well it's normal for kids your age to experiment with spirituality and even, at times, the occult," Duke's dad says.

"Really?" I ask, because that does not sound normal.

"More or less. Back in my day, we scared the daylights out of each other with Ouija boards. What makes you think your spiritual exploration went awry?"

"I fell into that hole in my backyard and there was an actual skeleton and then there was a gross thing with Jay's cat, but that could simply be cat behavior I guess, but then I—"

"She kissed her best friend's girlfriend by accident," Duke says.

"You kids impress me. All I did was explode things in the backyard."

"You still do that," Duke points out.

"Grill fires and rockets don't count; they're not supposed to explode. Now, Synclair, we have a few options for dealing with this situation."

I'm watching his light brown eyes for signs that he's humoring me. They're bright with amusement, but not in a "laughing at" way. And it's awesome to see an adult taking spirituality seriously. And God. I'm so used to my parents brushing off everything about that. Like if you can't see it and touch it, it's not real—when so much of human life is about everything we can't see and touch, like love and future goals and whatever force makes bad pop songs top the music charts.

Duke's dad says, "A straightforward option is simply to wear a piece of jewelry inscribed with the names of God and to contemplate this any time you're afraid."

"And you have these lying around?"

"No, but I know people." He waggles his thick eyebrows mysteriously. "The other choice, and you can do both of these at once, is to accept that now is a time when you're wrestling with difficult things, the way Jacob wrestled with the angel. Know that spirituality wasn't meant to be easy. And keep wrestling until the angel blesses you."

"Is that metaphorical, mythological, or psychological?" I ask.

"You pick."

"All of the above. God jewelry sounds amazing and I'll look out for this meta-psycho-mythological angel."

"I'm up for God jewelry too," Duke says and his dad grins. "You never know, I might need to back Synclair up on her spiritual journey."

"I'll put in a double order. Are you doing dishes?"

"Sure."

I offer to help, but there isn't room for two in the kitchen and Duke likes the feel of the hot water on his hands. I sit at the table nibbling the last of my caramel roll and read the story of Jacob and the angel on my phone. It's not really my thing. Maybe from hearing Kinz complain about Bible stories she had to learn, or because I'm not that into history, and also not into wrestling.

Mac hasn't texted back yet, but it's not even ten and he is capable of sleeping until noon if he has the chance. But I do have one text. When I see Camden's name, I get cold and hot inside.

Camden: *Can we talk about last night?*

Synclair: *It's okay. Just a mix up.*

Camden: *You kissed me back kind of a lot.*

Synclair: *I'm sorry?*

While I'm waiting for her reply, I get a text from Kinz. Are they sitting on a couch together both texting me?

Kinz: *Did you have a good time last night?*

Synclair: *Yeah, your girlfriend's the hotness. No, I feel like crap.*

Kinz: *Okay cool. I worried.*

Synclair: *I thought she was Avery!*

Then Kinz starts a group chat with me and Camden, so I guess they're not still over at Jay's.

Kinz: *She thought you were Avery.*

Camden: *Obv. except Avery doesn't have braids.*

I'm about to protest that I didn't feel her braids until after, except I did in the middle and started kissing her more intensely and that's hard to justify. Does she think I figured out it was her and then got really into it? I can't let her go on with that idea.

Synclair: *I thought they were Kinz's.*

Camden: *You thought you were kissing Kinz like THAT?*

Kinzey: *LIKE WHAT?*

Camden: *No seriously, answer the question Synclair*

"I'm moving to New York," I tell Duke.

He comes to the table, wiping his hands on his pants, and I give him my phone. After reading, he says, "Synclair if you're wrestling an angel, she is kicking you in the balls. Can I?"

I shrug and wave my hand like: *do whatever you want, my life is over.*

Synclair (courtesy of Duke): *I have a question for YOU: are you honestly saying you didn't figure out you weren't kissing Kinzey? Haven't you two kissed enough that it would be obvious I wasn't her? How much kissing do you need to get the "this is not my girlfriend's mouth" vibe?*

Kinz: *Cam? How much did you two kiss?*

Camden: *Not *that* much. Some.*

Kinz: *And you didn't know it wasn't me?*

Camden: *She was in your sweatshirt, which smells like you because that's the one that'd been in your car all week, and when she started kissing back, I just figured...*

Kinz: *Her mouth is totally different from mine.*

Camden: *Hey, have you kissed her? How would you know?*

Kinz: *I find it super unlikely that somehow, magically, Synclair kisses the same as me?*

Camden: *It was late! And dark! You think I wanted to be making out with Synclair?*

Synclair: *Hey! I'm a catch, jerks You're lucky to have gotten the chance!*

Kinz: *Duke, give Synclair back her phone.*

Duke-Synclair: *You two take your lovers spat off this chat and work it out. She's having a hard week, she doesn't need your crap.*

That doesn't get a reply. I guess they took their chat private. It's late enough in the morning that I can text Avery without being obnoxious, so I send her a good morning. My phone pings a minute later, but it's Mac.

Mac: *Hey, didn't you get my message?*

Synclair: *What message?*

Mac: *I gave Kinz's parents the whole update so ask them. Long story short: it's safe to come home.*

Synclair: *Oh cool. I'll be there in a bit.*

He doesn't know I didn't spend the night at Kinz's and I can't ask her parents what he told them. On any normal day, I'd call Kinz and ask her to ask her parents—but she and Camden are probably still arguing or making up.

I want to get out of Kinz's clothes and back into mine. The weight of the sweatshirt hood behind my neck keeps reminding me of Camden reaching past it to touch my cheek and kiss me. I'm assuming that "safe" means the cops have cleared out and taken any creepy skeletons with them.

"Mac says I can come home," I tell Duke. "I mean, not that he told me to leave, but apparently it's safe now. Can you drive me over?"

"Sure. You going to stay or come back here?"

"Can I decide when we get there?"

"Yeah. I'm going to go see if Mom's had breakfast, cool if we go in about thirty?"

"Great."

My phone pings again and now it is Avery asking, *How'd you sleep?*

Synclair: *I had to wrestle an angel.*

Avery: *Did she bless you?*

Synclair: *I don't think we're done wrestling. Also angel-wrestling is not my sport. What are you doing today?*

Avery: *Whatever you suggest. I can borrow the car, you want to go somewhere?*

Synclair: *Yeah, I'm going back to my house to change and catch up with Mac. Meet me there in about an hour?*

That should give me time to change, clean up and brush my teeth however many times you're supposed to between kissing your best friend's girlfriend and kissing your summer girlfriend.

CHAPTER FOURTEEN

When we drive up to my house, Kinz is sitting on the front steps with a white bakery box in her lap. Her damp hair hangs heavy around her shoulders and she's changed into gray cargo shorts and a sleeveless hoodie. I peek down at the shorts I've borrowed from her. We almost look alike, if I weren't so much smaller with way shorter hair.

Duke gets out of the car and says, "I love you. Dump all your other girlfriends and go out with me."

"I only have one girlfriend," Kinz grumbles, standing up.

She holds the box out to me. I'd swapped my crutch for one of Duke's canes and I'm steady enough that I can tuck the cane under one arm and take the box. It's small but very heavy. I lift the lid. Yes! Four brownies drip with nuts and caramel: the very decadent seven-layer grain-free brownies from the bakery in the new downtown. I hand it to Duke so he can appreciate the wonder. He's been working on duplicating these for me.

"I figured Duke would need one," Kinz says. "And Mac and then you and Avery." She pauses and stares at Duke until he walks back to his car and leans on it, gazing innocently into the box of brownies, pretending he's not close enough to overhear us while thoroughly eavesdropping.

Kinz steps closer to me. "You thought I was kissing you?"

I touch her three braids—the ends down by her collarbone—and shrug. "It made sense at the time."

"How?"

"I was half asleep; it made sense."

"You've got Avery," she says. "Why me?"

Her question holds curiosity, bewilderment. I contemplate her long face, her strong nose, the features that she thinks of as average that are handsome and comforting and better than all the other girls at our school. With Avery around, does she think I only like skinny, pretty girls? Does she really not know?

Now is not the time to tell her about my massive, multi-year crush on her. I have to come up with a cover story. But I've never been able to look Kinz in the eyes and lie to her. Glancing down doesn't work; apparently I can't look at her boobs and lie to her either. Also they're obviously big, but notably smaller than Camden's. How did I think that was Kinz last night?

I say, "I need to find Mac and get the update on the skeletons and whether my house is livable. And Avery is on her way."

"Sure," Kinz says, but her voice is flat.

"We can talk about it later if you need to," I offer.

"Fine." One-word answers from her are a bad sign.

Why is she mad? Just because I won't say why I thought—hoped—that it was her kissing me? Because I won't spill all my secrets? More likely she's still mad that I kissed Camden. Or that Camden kept kissing me. But she expected Kinz and I was in Kinz's sweatshirt, which still smelled like her. Maybe Kinz is mad about all of that mashed together and I absolutely don't know how to fix that.

What I want is a double date with me and Avery, Kinz and Camden, all having a great time together. I spent a lot of this spring at school watching Kinz and Camden while wishing we had a fourth girl, somebody for me, so we could all hang out on equal footing. The original foursome had been me and Kinz, plus Duke and cooking. That worked. We'd each dated other people, but not seriously—Kinz tended to like long-distance relationships—and not in a way that upset the friend group.

If we double dated, would it settle us into a regular pattern again? Now is *not* the time to ask. Will there be a right time in the five weeks I have left with Avery?

Using the cane to help keep my knee steady, I walk around Kinz and across the patch of bare ground that will be the new porch. During the construction of the last month, my front door has been moved fifteen feet from where it used to be. I unlock it and step into the new foyer in what was half of the old den. This makes my life seem even more backward. Maybe I kissed Camden because my house is being remodeled. That's what I should tell Kinz.

The foyer opens to the new great room (used to be the living room), which remains bare except for the TV and gaming console—and a legless lawn chair with a skeleton in it. The skeleton is wearing Mac's shorts and shirt. A white bony shoulder shows through the ripped sleeve.

I'm frozen, the inside of my body filled with static.

How could Mac have died and turned into a skeleton? He texted me this morning. Did I cross over into that world of dreams and visions? How do I get back?

I turn to the door but my legs are too leaden to run. Kinz stands there, confused by my stricken face, and I'm surprised she's still real—if I'm in the world of visions, how did she get here? Or all of this is horribly, physically real and she hasn't seen the skeleton yet.

I glance back at the skeleton in the living room. The skull and hand from the pit rest on the floor next to it. There's another hand and part of a pelvis, stretched out with the hands on a game controller, as if the full skeleton is playing against the partial one.

Who jokes with dead people? Serial killers, that's who. What if Mac is the killer and these are his victims and I'm next? If the bodies are recent, he could've buried them when he was home for the holidays. Except I'd have seen him digging in the yard, or at least spotted disturbed dirt, plus the fact that my brother is so not a killer.

But that means there could be a real killer. Is Mac already a victim? I limp for the door. I'm not going to be fast enough. Kinz's hands catch my upper arms and steady me. If we're both about to die, she should know some things.

"I have a crush on you," I tell her. "A huge one. I have since ninth grade and I was going to ask you out but Camden beat me to it. I thought you got jealous about Avery and kissed me 'cause maybe you felt the same way. That's why I was kissing back. But now we're going to die because a serial killer put skeletons in my living room so we should run."

She takes a step back out of the doorway, which leaves enough room for me to grab her hand and drag her toward her car. There's a third car in the driveway now, blocking Kinz's car. Duke is still standing by his car, texting. Avery comes toward us from the newest car.

"Skeletons!" I try to warn her. "In the living room."

"Why?" she asks.

I'm too scrambled to say more than, "Playing video games."

"Alone or with Mac?"

"He's gone. What if he's one of them?"

Avery shakes her head and walks past me into the house. I pull Kinz another step in the direction of the cars, but she plants her feet.

"You have a crush on me?" Kinz asks, voice thick with disbelief.

"How do you not know this? All those times I slept over or you slept over, you know I barely slept. Or were you too asleep to notice?"

"Too awake," she says. "Trying really hard to pretend I was sleeping so you wouldn't know that I was awake because I was thinking about you."

I want this moment to be a Moment, but I have used up my quota this week and there are dead people in my living room. Plus Avery just heard me say I have a crush on Kinz. My heart is beating double, super fast, about Kinz and Avery and the skeletons. I can't feel all that at same time. Kinz was thinking about me? Why are there skeletons when I need to be figuring out Kinz?

I tell her, "Hold on to that thought. If you're not going to run, we should call the cops." I fumble my phone out of my pocket and drop it. Kinz bends down to get it.

When she hands it back to me, her hand stays over mine. I switch my phone to my left hand so I can hold her hand, but then it's almost impossible to hit numbers with my left thumb.

Avery steps out of my house holding a skeletal hand. I yelp and jump away from her, knocking into Kinz, both of us tumbling in a pile in the dirt.

"You don't have to be afraid," Avery says. "Look."

She bends one of the fingers and points between the white bones at thin, dark wires. Murdered skeletons don't get wired up, as far as I know.

"You're still holding a dead hand," Kinz points out. "Which is super gross." She gets up and helps me stand.

"I'm sure they sterilize the bones before they wire them together," Avery says as we all head into the house. She's obviously less afraid of death than Kinz.

Mac ambles in from the backyard in too-short cut-offs and a tight T-shirt smudged with dirt. He's got his super smug pranking smirk on because of course he had to be the one to put the bones here. "Hey, messy shorts, you look like you're going to pee yourself."

"You fart-ass shitball!" I cross the living room and kick him in the shin like I'm five. Luckily, because of the mending knee, it has about that much force too.

"Ow, crap, what'd I do to you?" he asks, putting his hands up and stepping back.

I point to the skeletons.

"Yeah, isn't it awesome?" he asks.

"To have dead people in the living room?"

He shakes his head. "Didn't Kinz's parents tell you?"

"Tell me what? We stayed at Jay's."

"That's what you get for not updating your brother about your whereabouts," he says, as if he's Dad now.

Mac steps around me to the display, lifts one skeletal arm and waves it at me. Avery waves back with the hand she's holding and glides across the living room to put it back on the game controller.

Duke walks in while Mac is waving the skeletal hand. Paler than usual, Duke watches Mac set the hand back on the controller, then asks, "Fake?"

"Yeah, resin," Mac says.

"If they're fake, why all the cops?" I ask.

"They're super expensive life-like fakes that the university uses in their forensics classes," Mac explains. "They looked real to the cops, but the forensic people figured it out right away. We've got about four thousand dollars in skeletons. The professor who lived here buried them so they'd be the right kind of dirty for the next body lab, but then she forgot to tell anyone when she moved. The forensics people had a really good laugh yesterday. I told all this to Kinz's folks and asked them to tell you."

"We'd already left for Jay's," I say.

"Serves you right, then," Mac replies.

I glance at Avery and she flashes me a smile. She doesn't know about the part of the night where I was kissing Camden. She's in light blue pajama pants today with thin navy stripes down them and a flowing sleeveless yoga shirt, pale gray, making her hair stark where it falls across her shoulders. Her eyes are intense, the blue one looking very sapphire under the sweep of her black hair.

I step over to Mac's side and shake the skeleton's hand. "Nice to meet you. Have you named them yet?"

"Nah, was waiting for you," he says and throws an arm around my shoulders for a sideways hug.

Duke walks over to the skeletons and slowly around them, nodding to himself. "These are great."

"I'm with Synclair that you're a donkey's butt, including the hole in it," Kinz says to Mac. "You could've texted. Wouldn't have taken that long. And this is super creepy." She's still in the doorway, arms crossed, not coming any closer.

Her face is set, humorless. I start to get why she didn't figure out my crush. I can almost see what she thinks when she looks at herself through the wrong lenses: the way her nose is heavy enough to dominate her face, weighted by her solid cheekbones, making her eyes look too close together, except they're a warm, light brown and I want to kiss her and brush my thumbs over her cheeks and tell her that she's perfect. We've lived long enough through high school to get away from these skinny girl beauty contests. She's always been my ideal with the thick hips and an ass she thinks is too big, with her belly and her big hands and her bigger laugh.

Except…I look at Avery. How could I know she'd turn out skinny and classically beautiful?

"You all work out your kissing issues?" Duke asks, still staring at the skeletons. Then he gets what he said and claps a hand over his mouth, glancing at me with "oh shit" wide eyes.

"What issues?" Avery asks, because Duke's reaction gives away the fact that he's obviously not talking about Avery and me.

"Camden accidentally kissed me this morning, thinking I was Kinz. She got turned around in the dark and I was wearing Kinz's sweatshirt. I thought she was you and we stopped when we figured it out."

Avery's mouth hangs half open. She blinks at me and then at Kinz. She has a girlfriend. She cannot be mad that I kissed someone else by accident.

"You might be right about something strange going on," Avery says. "How much kissing did you include on that list of intentions?"

Kinz blows out a breath and leaves the doorway for the front yard. "Move your car, Avery," she yells.

"Back in a sec," Avery tells me and follows Kinz. I want to go with her and ask Kinz to come back inside, but we can't talk, not with Avery here. I'll text her later when I have chance to figure out what I can say. How do I tell her how amazing she is without sounding like I'm trying to split up her and Camden? And should I say any of that in the same twenty-four hours that I was kissing Camden?

On my phone, I type to Kinz: *text me later.* I stare at the words. Erase them and retype them. Hit send.

"Do you have to give the skeletons back to the university?" Duke asks Mac.

"Yeah, but I figured we'd drop them off when the fall semester starts." He turns to me and adds, "How much do you want to set these up for Mom and Dad's return? They know they're fakes, I already told them, but do you think they'll remember that if they walk in and see them in our clothes?"

"I can't tell exactly how terrible you are," I say.

"The right amount," he insists.

"You could've told me about these."

"I did! Or close enough. Blame it on Kinz's folks."

"In the meantime," Duke says. "Can I play with them?"

"Sure," Mac tells him.

"No one is going to watch a cooking show with skeletons," I insist.

"Oh, wait and see."

They're really cool now that I know they're fake, but also I've seen too much of them. Even resin skeletons are creepy, especially knowing that they're lifelike. They're only one step away from actual dead people. We're still all going to end up like this someday and I'm not anywhere closer to finding out what happens then. That's part of the questions about God and the Sacred, isn't it? Knowing the context we're in, knowing what happens or at least having a future we can trust. I see how hard it is for Kinz to feel safe in the world when she's worried that there's a hell waiting for her.

I shake my head and get the box of brownies from the foyer closet, brushing by Avery as she comes back into the house. She follows me onto the patio, where I put the brownies in the outdoor fridge.

"What do you want to do today?" she asks.

"I don't know yet."

I have this whole open day and a beautiful girl to spend it with—and I still want to run after Kinz and talk about our crushes. She was awake too back then? She was thinking about me? Why didn't she make a move? Same reason I didn't or some other set of doubts?

Focus, Synclair! You've only got a few weeks with Avery and then a whole year to figure out things with Kinz. Try thinking about one girl at a time for once. I focus on Avery for a whole three seconds as she drags two chairs side by side between the table and the kitchen.

"How long have you had a crush on Kinz?" Avery asks as she brings over an outdoor ottoman for me to rest my leg on. "Why haven't you two dated? Did you try?"

I sit and prop up my leg. She settles in the chair next to me as I try to explain. "I was friends with Duke and he brought her into our friend group in eighth grade and I didn't realize I had a crush on her until after the first year of high school."

"That's a long time ago." Avery takes my hand and plays with the tips of my fingers.

"It took me about a year to get up the guts to ask her out, but then she was dating someone, and then I met this girl at camp who I was maybe going to date and Kinz broke up and found someone else and I did date a girl for four months—our timelines never matched up for long enough."

"What happens when I leave?" Avery asks.

"I wish I knew. I really like Camden. I don't want to break them up."

"They've been fighting the entire month I've known them," she points out.

"I think that's one of their things, maybe," I say, though I'm even less sure of that than I sound. "Do you think I should be with Kinz?"

She has the hand not touching mine pressed between her knees and stares at the ball of her thumb. "I wish I could make two of me and one would stay here."

I should say that I want that too, but right now I can't be sure.

* * *

Avery and I have lunch at the house, which is much easier to do now that I know we have fake skeletons. She assembles sandwiches and we split a brownie. Then she wants a tour of my suburb, so I give directions while she drives around the new downtown and then the old one.

"The old one is cuter," she says. "But the new one has some good stores. Anywhere you want to stop?"

I open my shoulder bag and pull out the card that I got in the garden center days ago. "Do you want to check this out? They teach meditation."

Tree of Life Meditation Center is a storefront at the end of a row of shops, across the lawn from a church. There are yoga posters in the front window and fliers about meditation classes. When we walk in the front door, Jo is sitting behind a counter, tapping on a battered laptop. She is the same woman who gave me a ride home from the bonfire: stout, short graying hair, warm smile. Avery recognizes her.

"Hi! You organized the fire," Avery says.

"As much as anyone can organize a fire," Jo replies with a smirk.

A thick curtain hanging over a doorway on the far side of the room parts and Miri steps through, holding a small blue laundry basket. She's in a different collection of flowing colors, but the effect is the same: intelligent, bright eyes in a long face framed by curly brown hair, and then a waterfall of colorful fabrics.

"Hi," I tell her. "I'm Synclair, this is Avery. We thought we'd come learn more about meditation."

"Very good." She grins and walks over, tipping the laundry basket toward me so I can see inside. It's full of toys: squishy gel balls, nubby ones, action figures, stretchy bands, blocks. "Meditation for kids is on Saturdays. The oldest kid who attends is eighty. But most are in their teens."

"Cool, I'll check that out." I glance over at Avery who is no way going to a kids' meditation class. I'd feel weird coming without her, but I might anyway. "You get to meditate with toys? I thought we were supposed to sit still."

"There are many ways to meditate," she says. "Sitting meditation is one of the classics but there's walking, standing, eating, toys. It's about the quality of your attention, not how still you can keep your body." She shifts the box closer to me. "Take one if you want."

There's a cube with switches and dials and bumps on its various sides. The cube itself is dark purple and the switches and buttons are very pink. It looks super gay. I pick it up and turn it in my fingers, flick a switch on and off.

"It's yours," she says.

"I can bring it back."

"If you like." Miri puts the box in a double-doored closet to the right of the counter.

While we were talking, Avery filled out the signup list for both of us and paid the fee. Jo waves us into the meditation room where two people are already sitting quietly on cushions on the floor.

I ask, "Do I sit like that and stick out my leg?"

"If that's easy for you. Or I can get you a chair," Jo says. "If you want to sit on a low cushion, we'll fold a blanket under your leg to help support your knee."

The hard part of this is getting to the floor without bending my leg, but with a lot of help from Avery, I manage it. Then it's not that different from sitting cross-legged, except one leg is bent in front of me and the other is sticking out while being cuddled by a thick blanket so it doesn't bend or rotate outward.

Miri enters the room and collects a low chair from the back of the room, putting it in the back-last row, near me. I'm on the right, so my leg can stick out away from the main group of cushions, with Avery next to me in the middle of the row. Miri takes the spot on the far side of Avery. She ties a yoga strap around her thighs and sits forward enough that her back isn't touching the straight back of the chair.

She notices me watching and mouths the words, "Knees," while patting one with her palm. Then grins and closes her eyes.

Three more people have joined the group while we settled in. From the front of the room, Jo reminds us to follow our breath and, when we get distracted by our thoughts, because of course we will, to return to the flow of the breath in and out of our nostrils. She rings the gong and we get started sitting and doing nothing.

EMANATION FIVE:

Discipline

I'm pretty sure I'm meditating wrong. First I think I'm sitting wrong, but I feel the memory of fire in a line up my spine and that helps me understand how to relax my body while sitting up. Then I worry about Kinz. She can be so tough at school, strong for her wounded animals, but not so much around skeletons. Maybe I should've caught on that she was into me when she jumped into the pit after I fell. Not everyone will jump into a pit for you.

Come on, brain, focus! Back to breathing.

I wonder if Camden would like meditation. Is there Christian meditation? I guess if there's Jewish meditation, there's probably a Christian kind too. I should ask Duke's dad about the Jewish kind first. And get that necklace from him. I'll text Duke after this and find out when I can come over, that is when he can come pick me up. Would Avery want to go? She could take me if I can invite her to come along. Okay so after meditating, first ask Avery if she's interested in running by Duke's for some stuff and then text Duke, or, wait, text him first.

I'm supposed to be attending to my breath. I sigh and peek at the clock. All that only took four minutes. Today's meditation is going to take forever—the longest twenty-five minutes in the world.

Is Avery as bored as I am? I peek at her out of the corner of my eye. She's super still. Rockstar meditator. She looks like Jo in front of the room, very upright, chin slightly down, eyes serenely closed. What about Miri? Can she sit that way in a chair? I turn my head enough to see. Jo's got her eyes closed, so who's going to catch me?

Miri sits differently. Not only because her legs aren't crossed, it's her whole body. She's moving and not moving at the same time. Her belly expands slowly as she inhales and her shoulders rest on the rising breath, relaxed in a way that Jo's aren't. I double check. Jo looks stiff compared to Miri. Miri's hands, palm down on her thighs, are casual, lightly resting. Jo's hands have the fingers close together, tense. Her body and Avery's seem to have rods in their backs and shoulders, necks and fingers. Miri's body is filled from the inside with breath and life, her arms, shoulders, neck soft and easy around that energy, like she sat down casually and found her posture from the inside out. Her slightly open mouth quirks up on the side with a tiny smile.

I return my attention to my body and breathe into my belly, letting everything expand and then relax on the out breath. My shoulders drop their tension and that looseness rolls down my arms to my fingers. The energy inside of me is wider than a bubble tea straw and hazily defined, a soft stream flowing from the very base of my seat up to the back of my head. Dark and light at the same time, full of sparks and presence. I shift in my seat and feel when I'm off-center of the stream. This makes it easy to line my body up, keeping kinks out of that steady flow of energy.

Is this the energy of two goddesses, like Avery said, connecting inside of me? I focus on the energy low in my pelvis, where it rises from underneath me, where I'm sitting on the cushion. It has a dense, warm, dark quality, bringing comfort and safety, but also openness, an invitation. I follow it up to my head, which feels bright and sparkly, full of ideas and words. Where do these energies mix in my body? If I'm only these energies, who am I?

I'm still trying to figure that out when Jo rings the gong to end the meditation part of the class. That went fast. I peek at Avery, who stretches up and rolls her shoulders. I don't feel that I need to move yet, but I do the same anyway.

Avery looks amazing on a meditation cushion, with the flowing wave of her hair and the drape of the soft fabrics of her shirt and pants over her body. But I keep thinking about Kinz and how surprised she was when I said I had a crush on her. I'm not paying any attention to the question and answer session because I'm trying so hard to remember-the-expression on Kinz's face.

Jo tells everyone there are refreshments in the front room and she'll be around to answer more questions. Avery helps me up and we get cups of spicy licorice tea, then wander over by the register where Miri is organizing the top shelf of the books for sale.

Avery says, "When Synclair told me about meeting you in the garden store, she said you know queer magic. Can you show us some?"

Miri makes a soft "hmmm," and looks around the room. "Let me get set up," she says. She walks to the table where the other meditators are standing, talking with Jo. There's a tea dispenser, cups, teabags, a plate of sugar cookies and coconut macaroons. Miri pours a small amount of water into a cup and picks up a macaroon. When she gets back to us, she shows us the bit of water in her cup and holds up the macaroon.

She puts the macaroon in her mouth, chews, swallows, washes it down with the water and shows us both the empty cup and her other empty hand. "There, it has disappeared. It's magic."

"But you ate it," Avery says.

"I was hungry," Miri tells her and turns her sparkling eyes to me. "Synclair?"

From Avery's tone, she thinks Miri is teasing us, but I have that feeling of pressure behind my skin, of something vast opening under or behind me.

"I don't understand," I tell her.

"Good. You're learning."

She might've been ready to say more, but Jo calls, "Miri, hon," from across the room and Miri goes to confusingly answer someone else's question.

I could get used to confusing answers. They remind me of being in my dream world and seeing Avery with her mouth full of light. Maybe I even like these answers.

CHAPTER FIFTEEN

When we get back to my house, I'm a mix of tired and relaxed. Going over to Duke's can wait for another day. After some lazy, wonderful cuddling and making out in my bed, Avery heads back to her grandparents' house.

Kinz still hasn't texted me. I admire the skeletons because they do look badass in the living room now that I know they're fake. Then I flop down on my bed and text Kinz.

I ask: *You okay?*

She writes back: *yeah, I'm fine.*

Synclair: *Do you want to talk about things?*

Kinz: *No.*

It's impossible to tell from texts if she's upset because I kissed her girlfriend or because I thought I was kissing her. Or because I have a crush on her. Or that she didn't know, or maybe just skeletons playing video games and hell and all that.

In case her upset is about me kissing Camden, I type: *I had a good time with Avery. I'm not trying to move in on you or Camden or whatever.*

Kinz: *Great.*

Synclair: *You don't sound okay. Can we talk about it?*

Kinz: *Cam's mad at me because you two made out. What's there to talk about?*

That made no sense at all. I ask: *What'd you say to her?*

Kinz: *Are you blaming me for this? You?!*

Synclair: *No, just asking.*

Kinz: *Don't be a twit. You're not just asking. You're on her side. You think I'm being ridiculous over nothing. You don't get what it's like and you should stay out of it. Both of you.*

Synclair: *Both…me and Camden? We're not together in anything.*

Kinz: *You're getting to be as bad as my folks, all self-righteous with your religion crap.*

Synclair: *How did we get from kissing to religion?*

Kinz: *Ask the witch Avery. She says I started it all by asking you to write down what you want.*

Synclair: *She only said that because she thought you were mocking her.*

Kinz: *I was. It's ridiculous. Grow up!*

Synclair: *It is not! Billions of people have religion! Why can't I have that? You don't get to tell me what I can believe or do. You? Of everyone? Why are you being like this? I didn't kiss Camden on purpose. I'm having a great time with Avery. Why can't you be happy for me? I was happy for you all the last crapton of months when you've been all over Camden and now that I have a girlfriend, you can't suck it up and be on my team for the next few weeks?*

Kinz: *I'd better get right on appreciating you two since you've had to suck it up all this time with me and Cam. You two are awesome! The flooding awesomest! I hope you have the most mind-blowing spiritual time. Oh wait, I'd better stop before I accidentally cause you to be literally blown because I'm so super powerful like that in other people's lives.*

Synclair: *You could write down what you want for <u>your</u> life.*

Kinz: *Why bother? You know how it's going to be for the next year.*

Synclair: *Yeah, you'll have a shitty life at home and be making out with Camden in my bed. Double standard much?*

Kinz: *Cam is part of our group. Avery isn't.*

Synclair: *She's part of our group because you made her part of it. Don't I get to bring someone in?*

Kinz: *Probably doesn't matter. I'm not coming over if Duke's going to cook with a gross skeleton sitting around.*

Synclair: *It's fake.*

Kinz: *Whatever. It's symbolic. I've got to go.*

I read back over the conversation. Camden's mad at her—why? There must've been a whole fight she's not telling me about. How did we get here from everything we said about crushes this afternoon? Did Kinz tell Camden what I said about the crush?

I could see how Camden would find that threatening; Kinz and I have been friends for years, while the two of them have only been dating since February. We'd seen Camden around school, but she and Kinz didn't start talking until last winter when Kinz showed up at the copy place where Camden works weekends. Kinz had a bunch of lesbian fliers to print and Camden asked if she could keep one. I thought that was super smooth after I got over being mad about it.

Camden knows that Avery is going back to New York in a few weeks. Maybe she's afraid that when I'm available again, Kinz is going to dump her for me? Like she ever would. Would she?

I laugh at my phone and at my bedroom and all its symbolism of me. Or, to be more accurate, all the hobbies I've copied from other people. I have a few model horses because Kinz likes those, and a framed painting of Arabian horses galloping in the desert. I have a stack of cooking magazines that Duke wanted me to look through and help him decide what to make next.

There's a viola case in the corner that I haven't opened in years, from the time in seventh grade when I was crushing on a girl in the school orchestra. I have a framed drawing of a building that Mac drew as part of his senior project in college and a big collage of family photos. I have a bunch of gay books, schoolbooks, dog training books—no, we don't own a dog, they're from Kinz—and regular fantasy books out on my shelves. But in my closet there's a whole shelf of books about meditation, theology, history of myth, cross-cultural shamanism. I never put them out on my shelves. I don't want my parents to see them every time they come into my room. They wouldn't be able to stop themselves from making little comments about primitive cultures and weak-minded people.

Sometimes I wish I were a normal kid who hid porn in my closet. Okay, honestly none of my friends do that. The ones who want it figured out how to look it up online on any device a parent isn't monitoring, and then most of the time—at least from what I'd heard—they'd regretted it.

But the point was: half the stuff in my room had to do with Kinz. I wasn't even into most of it, just into her. So if she *was* jealous and waiting for Avery to leave town and did dump Camden, would I go out with her? Yeah, in a flooding heartbeat. If she drove over here tonight and asked me out, I'd probably dump Avery for her.

Should I still feel that way? Last night when I thought I was kissing Kinz and my whole body lit up—I can't ignore that. I'm so happy hanging out with Avery, but not on fire. The fire seems pretty important.

I get the list of intentions out of my bag and spread it open on my thighs. Come to think of it, Kinz was in the room the night of the party when I ended up naked and stepping into an initiation. Maybe the intention wasn't for Avery to take my pants off, maybe it's that Kinz would.

Does that also explain the fire licking up the inside of my spine? Because Avery is the one I dream about, the one who showed up today to save me, she's the one who should be evoking that kind of reaction. Also, if I'm being precise, I felt this fire kissing Camden, I only thought I was kissing Kinz.

It's possible that I'm bad at girls. Or bad at spirituality. What I really hope is that I'm not terrible at either and they're interacting in a super strange way right now.

"God, I have questions. Can we get some answers here without pits or nudity or any other mishaps?"

My phone pings and I jump, but it's my music service telling me about some new, hot gospel music. Whatever divine presence is looking out for me, at least they're funny.

CHAPTER SIXTEEN

Avery has more babysitting shifts lined up for this week, but I don't want us to spend that much time apart. I tell her that my folks are giving me an allowance to help with the work on the house and if she helps too, I'll split it with her. That's mostly true: I get an allowance anyway and it's more than I need for food out with friends.

I want to hang out with her as much as possible. And Kinz is not super available right now. Or even a little. I text her over the weekend and she barely replies, but that's not too weird for a weekend, especially with her having to go church on Sunday. Sometimes she wants to complain for hours about what her dad put in his sermon but if she goes to church with Camden, I don't hear from her for the rest of the day. This is one of those times and I don't mind because Avery is over to start on the basement with me—and it's much easier to spend time with Avery than figure out what's going on with me and Kinz.

Yesterday, Mac made up a list of jobs for us to do in the storage room. He's keeping us away from his part of the basement, which is easy to do since our basement is huge. It's the same size as the first floor, which has two regular bedrooms and a master suite, plus kitchen, big living room and den. The basement has fewer rooms, so the space that's living room, kitchen and master suite upstairs is one vast room that now holds all the house's furniture except what's in my bedroom.

Mac laid claim to the part of the basement that includes two guest bedrooms and a bathroom. Mac's staying in one of the guest bedrooms and the other is stacked with boxes. He's doing the new tile work in the basement bathroom because he wanted to try out a cool pattern in the tub surround and if he screws it up, the contractors can fix it.

When I bring Avery down the stairs, between the walls of boxes, to the laundry room and through it to the storage room, she has the same thought that I did: "We're really far away from everywhere else."

"Yep," I say, beaming. I could've taken us into my bedroom and locked the door, but it's right next to a bunch of construction. Sitting on my bed together and hearing guys talk about joists and plaster and electrical does not feel private. It is not conducive to Avery's hand going up under my shirt, which I'd like to feel in the near future.

Avery walks back through the laundry room, into the labyrinth of boxes and furniture in the main room. "What's that way?" She points to the archway to our left as we face the stairs.

"A hall with two bedrooms and a bathroom off it. Mac has the far bedroom and the near one is jammed full of more stuff. He's tiling the bathroom so we have to use the one upstairs by my bedroom."

"If we're going to sort through boxes, we need a place to put them," she points out.

I'd thought our main basement room was huge. It easily housed two ellipticals and a weight bench, plus rows of bookcases laden with Dad's extensive plastic tote storage system. But filling it with the contents of the other two floors of the house has maxed its capacity. There isn't anywhere to put another box. I wish we could use the dining room table, but it's upside down on other furniture in the middle of the room. I can see its legs poking up behind the wall of boxes.

"We also need a bigger path to the laundry room or we'll never get trash out," I say. We'd climbed over an armchair to get in, which was especially awkward with my knee still wrapped and sore.

"What if we flip that armchair onto that table?" she asks. "And maybe move the boxes off that couch so we have a place to sit when we want?"

"Let's do it!"

This turns into a four-dimensional puzzle because furniture from the past and future keeps showing up as we move things around. Our house has a lot of furniture. More than could easily fit in the basement bedroom and workout room, but Mac and the contractors brought it down here anyway, piling it as high as they could. We'd had to box up all the books and knickknacks and carry them down here, plus side tables, lamps, etc. The piles of furniture had piles of boxes on top—since Mac and I had brought the boxes down after the contractors moved the furniture and we weren't as careful about where we put things.

By day two, Avery and I had the couch clear, a path to the laundry room, and an end table set up next to the dryer. That gave us both the table and dryer to put boxes on and look through them. One of the first boxes we opened held old family photos. We sat on the couch together, going through them and talking about when we were kids together.

Day three, we realized that the couch was too close to the stairs and so we made a cozy corner in the laundry room with a sleeping bag stretched out over an old bed topper. Avery's hands spent a lot of time under my shirt and mine under hers.

Day four of the week of "wow this is what it's like to kind of have a girlfriend!" we went to Tree of Life for a meditation class. Still super difficult to focus with Avery sitting next to me, but it got easier every time I looked over and saw how still she sat. Not that I could pay attention to my breath in my lower belly for any longer than before, but now when my mind wandered and I got frustrated, I could stay sitting and get another shot at following my breath for a few seconds.

"Meditation in the morning, boxes and stuff in the afternoons?" Avery asks over lunch.

"Absolutely," I tell her.

This is exactly the summer I wanted, but it doesn't feel right. After our second meditation class together, we're having sandwiches in the little coffee shop in old downtown, plus cookies good enough to remind me of Duke. He's been helping out around his house a bunch this week because his dad's working and his mom's having a flareup of her hypermobile Ehlers-Danlos Syndrome. He keeps sending me photos of everything he's baking and I reply with encouraging notes about how great it must taste. I want to ask if he's heard anything substantial from Kinz or Camden, but if he hasn't then he'll worry too.

Jay is off at basketball camp and isn't allowed to use her phone except for talking to her parents. The camp is super serious about team bonding; otherwise I'd have texted her to find out how Camden was doing.

I could text Camden, but that feels weird, like I'm going behind Kinz's back, especially since Camden and I kissed. What's she going to think if I message her? And if Kinz told her about the crush thing and I ask about Kinz, how ultimately weird is that? Way too.

I realize I haven't said anything to Avery in a while. She's been sipping her coffee and watching me turn my phone facedown, then faceup, then facedown, up, down, up, down.

"I'm worried about Kinz," I tell her. "We've been super close for years and now she's not talking to me much. I mean, little things, pics of her dogs, but nothing real."

"And you kissed her girlfriend," Avery points out.

"Yeah, and…said some stuff trying to make that better and made it worse. I think she's also mad that you're here, as if you're going to take me away, but that might be me reading into it and maybe it's the religion stuff. She keeps trying to get away from it and now you and I are going to meditation classes. I get how she could feel surrounded."

"Her dad sounds awful. Can she leave? Move out?" Avery watches me as she asks, half a cookie in her fingers, resting on her plate, not approaching her mouth.

"Not yet. And, you know, college, money."

"Therapy?" Avery suggests.

"Maybe. If they didn't make her go to a fundamentalist therapist."

"Wow. Suck. Yeah we should definitely not talk about spiritual topics around her. Should you bring her food or something?"

"Duke usually does that. We could see if he's got food we could pick up and take over to her place."

"We should. It's bad to feel alone," Avery says. She lifts the half cookie and sets it back down.

I reach my hand across the table, palm up, and she releases the cookie and slides her fingers into mine. I text Duke one-handed and confirm that Duke has some brownies. His "failed" batch of trying to copy the bakery brownies is still going to be amazing.

When we get to Duke's, he has a third of a pan bagged up and ready to go. But when we get to Kinz's, her dad meets us at the door and says she can't talk now. We leave the brownies and all the way back to my house, Avery is silent.

"Does he remind you of your dad?" I ask when we pull into my driveway.

She nodded. "Kind of. Close enough, I guess. I'm sorry for her having to live with that."

"She turns eighteen this fall. I've been thinking about asking my folks if she could live here. We have plenty of room."

"You should," Avery tells me. "Really, sooner rather than later. Even if she doesn't take you up on it, let her know she's got options, that she can get away. Though, I suppose, if you're dating her...are you ready for that?"

"Uh, no, but we'd be on different floors, other sides of the house. We'd figure it out. If I was dating her. Which I won't be, because she's with Camden."

* * *

Kinz and my texts keep slipping by each other, like people at a crowded party who can't quite meet up. I need to talk to someone about Avery and about Kinz. Someone other than Mac, who would listen to me for only a few minutes before rolling his eyes or making a gagging sound and going back to his tile project or games or friends or friends-playing-games. He has a girlfriend in Chicago that he Skypes every other night, but he doesn't talk about her—evidence of his lackluster talking-about-girls skills.

By Monday evening, swallowing my pride, I text Camden. She and Kinz would've gone to church together yesterday, so she should have a decent read on the situation.

Synclair: *Hey, can I ask you how Kinz is? She's not telling me.*

Camden: *Oh hi to you too, I'm glad you're worried about how I'm doing.*

Synclair: *That too! How are you?*

Camden: *Been better. You?*

Synclair: *Good-ish. How was church?*

Camden: *Kinz didn't go. Good sermon, though. The younger minister is on the ball. Postmodern womanist theology is the absolute best.*

Synclair: *She didn't go?*

Camden: *You're pretty one-track, you know.*

Synclair: *Ugh, sorry, I'm worried about her. Every time I text, she sends me pics of her dogs. Unasked, that's a good sign. But not when she won't answer with anything else. Her dad didn't even let me in to say hi to her last week.*

Camden: *Yeah, she's a mess and her folks are furious about church. She's grounded.*

Synclair: *Why? What happened?*

Camden: *The Sunday before this, her dad did a "wages of sin" sermon that included homosexuality and she walked out. She says she's sick of hearing all that. Sick of talking about it. Told her dad the world would be better without religion. I disagree, but I get where she's coming from.*

No wonder she was grounded. To Kinz's dad, that would be worse than all the swear words jammed together into an uber-swear.

Synclair: *How grounded is she?*

Camden: *Limited phone. She can still come over to my place because they don't know, but she can't hang out with non-Christian friends until she agrees to go back to church. I'm working on her. And Mom's being great—even looked up how to make tamales since they're Kinz's fave. They didn't hold together but they tasted good, and Kinz laughed about it.*

Sinclair: *Is it working? Do you think she's going to feel better and do enough to get her dad off her case?*

Camden: *Church-wise, I've escalated to the point where I'm prepping a very steamy reading of the Song of Songs, hoping that will do it.*

Sinclair: *Hot Bible readings are a thing?*

Camden: *They are now. Next is Ruth as an alternate universe coffeeshop fanfic and if that doesn't work, I'll see what I can do with Esther. I believe there's heat between her and Vashti.*

I am jealous? Envious?…Of what? It's not like I want smutty Bible stories. Maybe it's the effort that Camden is putting into this, if it's that much effort. Does she know all this off the top of her head?

Sinclair: *How do you know all this?*

Camden: *Might want to be a minister when I grow up. If my not-insignificant lip-sync battle skills don't earn me internet millions.*

She's not kidding. Her lip-sync videos are extremely on point. She can be totally into a song and at the same time delivering a political parody about both Washington DC and the power structure of our school. She did one of the *Les Mis* songs "On My Own," the Nikki James version, under a framed portrait of Obama, while pacing in front of a mock-up White House with a tangerine on its front steps. The lines "I love him" were sung to Obama, but "without me, his world will go on turning," went to the tangerine, which had a puff of cornhusk hair. It got more likes than our school's cheerleading squad videos.

Somehow Camden manages to be cool and unapologetically real. On good days, I wonder if those two go together and how I could make that work.

Sinclair: *You could be a lip-syncing internet pastor and make millions.*

Camden: *That's a genius idea! I need to make a list of song sermons. How versed are you in Christian rock?*

Synclair: *Zero percent, but I can learn.*

Camden: *I'll send you links, tell me what you like best.*

Two hours and more respect for Christian rock later, I messaged her:

Synclair: *Nichole Nordeman & Amy Grant: "I'm With You"— hands down. That duet is so gay. I love it!*

Camden: *Nichole also has a cover of "Gotta Serve Somebody," I've been thinking about mixing that with Beyoncé's "Irreplaceable."*

Synclair: *How do those go together?*

Camden: *Trust me. God made all of it.*

Synclair: *Music, sure, but...Kinz's point about the Dumpster fire of the world. Did God make that too?*

Camden: *No, it's part of the system of the world. You can't have a universe that has time and change without having loss and you can't have free will without having people who can do evil. Do you really want me to say all this? What do you think?*

Synclair: *Don't know. I feel God or Goddesses or the Sacred, as a presence, and it seems rude and foolish not to pursue that, figure it out, at least how to have it more in my life. What you said about God calling to us, that makes sense to me, but what's it for?*

Camden: *For us to live our best lives. God offers us possibilities for a better future, with more love and justice, art and adventure. But we have to make it happen.*

Synclair: *Is that womanist theology? What is that?*

Camden: *Theology based in the wholeness of an entire people and centering the experiences of Black women, because intersectionality. You know what that is, right?*

Synclair: *Yeah, how when you have multiple oppressions working, like sexism and racism and homophobia, it's distinctly worse than any one of them alone.*

Camden: *Nice! Now, how much womanist theology are you up for learning about?*

Synclair: *Start with the most amazing parts and go until I fall asleep?*

Camden: *You're on!*

In between getting amazing texted paragraphs from Camden, I text Kinz. I tell her that I heard about her getting grounded and I'm sorry and to let me know if I can drop off more brownies. She doesn't reply, but she might not have her phone. I'm a shivery combination of super worried and chill about this, because I've been through about ten groundings a year with Kinz since I met her. Her dad can't ground her from taking care of the pets they have and never tells her not to go to the wildlife rescue center where she volunteers, so I know her animals are going to keep her sane, I'm just worried about how sane.

I watch more of Camden's videos from last spring that I'd been ignoring because I was mad about her being with Kinz. She is so good and I want to help her come up with video sermons. But how could I have a fall semester where I fiercely want to be dating Kinz and also deeply want to help Camden?

EMANATION SIX:

Beauty

I copy my favorite paragraphs from Camden out of the text stream and put them in a separate document, so I can think about what she said. She wrote:

Our world makes change possible. We exist in time and have free(ish) will (more on this in a bit). A world with time and change—even changes that are great—means that there will be loss and pain. It means we can grow up and be amazing and fall in love, but it also means that people die and we lose people we love. Loss and pain are part of the system of this universe and because of that, there can be suffering.

God calls to us with possibilities that work toward individual and community wholeness, well-being, justice, aliveness. But we also have everything that happened in the past creating our current conditions and we've got our own free will.

Example: me and Kinz right now. God calls to me with possibilities and love and energy to support Kinz. And God calls to Kinz's dad, but he can choose to ignore that calling, or maybe because of his past and the context he's in, he can't fully receive it.

How do we know he's not right? Because his actions don't lead to a situation in which everyone is as whole as possible. For his way to work, Kinz would have to give up who she is.

Evil involves destruction and suffering, which go beyond the regular loss and pain that are going to happen anyway. Because God is pulling for the best in all situations and the best in us, when people go against the best, that's evil. And it can be murky—there are situations in which there are many best ways or the best isn't clear—but this at least gives me a guide for my life. A lot of times I can see some of what's best and if I don't fight for that, I'm not doing what's good.

God is both within the entire universe and beyond it. That beyondness of God is what we could call heaven. Because God is in the world, God perceives everything and it's echoed in the beyondness, in heaven—but in heaven the contrasts are changed. In heaven Kinz's dad…well that's a bad example. I was going to say that his love for her is highlighted, but I don't see him loving her at all. I'm going to say that in heaven Kinz's mom's love for her is highlighted and her inability to stop Kinz's dad is pushed to the periphery. It's not denied, we still know it happened, but the contrast is turned way down so we're not staring at it, we're seeing that love. In heaven, everything Kinz is doing now to keep herself sane is brightened and lifted up and celebrated.

We're seen and we're celebrated, all the time, even for the smallest actions. This doesn't mean that we're supposed to wait for some "kingdom of heaven" after we die and not resist now. It means resist more, fight for our best possibilities now in this world, because they're echoed in heaven now—because we're seen and known and loved.

And our faults, our mistakes, "sin" if you want to call it that, these are forgiven, which means they're understood by God, they're held gently in God's heart.

Racism, sexism, heterosexism, classism, homophobia, transphobia all divide people. They destroy the wholeness of individuals and groups of people. We live in a beautiful, diverse world full of adventure, which is the direction of God's calling. And God also calls us to justice and healing, so we can all have a future with more love, connection, and beauty.

CHAPTER SEVENTEEN

On Saturday, Mac goes off with his friends. I invite Avery over again. I'm low-key freaking out because we're definitely going to hang out in my bedroom and I still haven't resolved if I want to have sex with her. I chicken out and text Duke to see if his mom is feeling better and if we can come over for lunch.

He says yes! He also says, "We're baking for Kinz." I'm not sure who "we" includes. Jay got back from two weeks of camp last weekend, so it could be her and Camden. Or it could be Duke's dad and brother. But I'm hoping for Camden. I have a lot to talk to her about.

Duke meets us at the door to his house holding an avocado-green bowl under one arm, two forks in hand, and says, "Try this. It's a seafood salad. Avery, you okay with shellfish?"

"Thoroughly," she says and takes one of the forks.

I use the other. It's creamy but not soaked with mayo and has the woodsy green of tarragon in it. "Love it," I tell Duke. "Who's here?"

"Camden and Jay. They're entertaining me while I bake and helping me think through my video series. We have pages of notes! They might make sense to no one but us, but it's progress."

We follow him into the kitchen. Camden and Jay sit at the table, a notepad between them with sketches on it: lots of squares with stick figures inside of them. Storyboarding?

Jay's in knee-length light blue denim shorts, impeccable mostly white high-top sneakers and a sleeveless T-shirt that has suspenders printed on it. I feel this shouldn't work as a look, which is probably why it works. Camden is in one of those breezy summer dresses with sandals and I envy how easily she wears it. I'm in lightweight jeans because I tried Avery's pajama-bottoms style and couldn't handle how flowy they felt.

"Hey," Camden says to me, grinning. Her gold-frame round glasses have slipped down a half inch and she pushes them up. Jay gives me a squinting-into-the-sun smile and a nod.

Camden's grin fades to half brightness as she sees Avery behind me, but she does a passable job of not appearing disappointed. Is she still mad about Avery arguing with Kinz on Jay's porch? That was almost three weeks ago. But yeah, I would be too if I were dating Kinz.

Avery sits at the table across from Jay, and I get us drinks and plates for the seafood salad. There are also chopped fresh veggies with dip and a loaf of sweet, braided bread to break chunks off.

"We're down to two ideas," Duke says. "Either The Cooking Dead, which is like *The Walking Dead* but with much better food and nobody gets shot."

"Or the Blair Witch Cooking Project," Camden says.

"Because the witch is always the bad guy, right?" Avery snarks.

"In our version the witch is the chef," Camden tells her. "She's trying to make a bunch of food for her coven and these crazy kids keep bursting in on her, so she puts the skeleton up to keep them away. It's a cross between *Tucker and Dale vs. Evil* and *Get Out*, upending the usual horror tropes to make viewers question their own unconscious habits of vilification."

"Oh, that's amazing," Avery says.

"What'd you expect?" Jay asks and turns to Camden. "Has she not seen our videos? Why haven't you linked her our videos?"

Camden and Jay tell her about their long, shared video-making history while I eat salad and swap smiles with Duke. He comes around the counter and joins us, taking the empty chair next to me. There's blue KT tape on his ankle but nothing else. Under the line of his shorts, his quads look thick, but not quite as dense as his shoulders. The more muscle he has, the better his joints are protected, and he said he was going to lift heavy this summer, so clearly that's working.

I pat my shoulder, nod at his, and tell him, "Looks good. Mac's going to be keeping up with you soon."

"Pshaw, never," he replies, but his broad grin contradicts his casual tone. "What else did I miss last week? What did you two do?" He points at me and Avery.

"Sorted boxes in my basement and went to meditation classes," I say.

"Did you get all the answers to the mystery of life?" he asks. We'd been having a side conversation but of course this is the moment when Avery, Camden, and Jay fall quiet, so they all hear Duke's question and turn to me.

I should have an absolutely slick and mystical answer, but all I can think about are the quotes Camden's been sending me.

"Meditation is starting to feel less crazy," I say. "And Miri showed us some magic I haven't figured out yet. But answers-wise, Camden's texts are pulling ahead."

"Whoa!" Duke says. "Share with the class!"

I have no idea how to explain that Miri ate a cookie and it was magic because I can't replicate her smile or her eyes, so I ask, "Share the texts? Camden, do you want to?"

Camden pushes her glasses up again and leans forward on her elbows. "There is something you all could help me with. If I explain this theology to you, can you make a secular version? Kinz and I have been going around in circles and I need a way to say some things without getting into a fight."

"How much have you been fighting?" I ask before I think about it.

Camden shakes her head without speaking. She usually has words for everything. How much have they been fighting? Breakup amounts?

"Hold up, what?" Jay asks. "How are you fighting so much about that?"

Tears gather in Camden's eyes. I get up and step around Avery, kneel next to Camden. Almost like I'm watching myself except there's still a me in my body, but she's the version of me from the sacred world. All she sees—I see—is that this bright, mystical friend of ours hurts and I want to take away the suffering. Regular, everyday me is freaking out because I'm never the first one to do a thing; I'm not a person who's this bare and emotional. But I put a hand on Camden's wrist, open my arms to her. She takes off her glasses and folds down to me. She's not full-on crying, just pressing her face against my shoulder so she won't lose it. I hold on to her. She smells of vanilla and coconut, familiar, and I remember kissing her, though I'm trying not to. I don't let go until she pulls away.

"I'm okay," she says, glasses in one hand, wiping her eyes clear of the tears that didn't fall. "It's a lot to have her be so hurt and upset. All the things I used to be able to say to help her feel better only piss her off."

"So you need a secular version." Avery nods, her eyes intensely dark and light as she watches us.

"We got you," Jay says. She has a hand on Camden's back.

Camden cleans her glasses with the edge of her skirt. I get back into my seat as she nods at me and says, "You start."

"Test time? I haven't made flashcards yet, but okay. So there's God and there's the universe. The universe could be seen as a second God or Goddess, for Avery's worldview, which I like, but if we go with a two Goddess model, let's call one God and one the universe for now. And God is in the universe but also way beyond it and eternal, but not unchanging. God includes all the best possibilities for everything."

"Hold up," Jay says. "I was reading a thing." She gets out her phone and scrolls through screens. "Emergence? That's when a complex system is different from what its parts can do. Being a person is an emergent property of our bodies. And I've been reading some Carl Jung, he's the European psychiatrist from the early 1900s who wasn't a hot mess. He writes about humans having a collective unconscious. What if that emerges as a system from groups of individual people?"

Avery leans toward her, resting one hand on the table next to her empty salad bowl. "You're saying emergence lets you use the collective unconscious in place of an external Sacred Something?"

"Yeah," Jay tells her. "And still have a force that pulls us toward our highest possibilities."

I'm making sense of that as Camden asks me, "Do you think that would work for Kinz?"

"You're going to get more traction with emergence than collective unconscious," I say. "She's not a fan of psychological stuff. Sorry, Jay."

"No worries. Some of that archetype stuff can be racist AF," Jay says. "But it's also a sweet way to include ancestors without a bunch of…" She trails off, wiggling her fingers to indicate ethereal, spiritual whatnot.

"How?" Avery asks.

"If there's a field of energy that emerges from lots of conscious humans over time, then humans in the past have contributed to that—there's a shared humanness at a fundamental level that we're all in. But you can also get to honoring ancestors through genes and epigenetics, so Kinz won't be missing out."

"I don't think she's going to want to honor her biological ancestors," I point out. "Her dad is the product of a few generations of abuse."

Duke taps the table. "If Kinz can handle thinking about fields of energy, she could tap into the power of her queer and trans ancestors."

"The what?" Camden asks. "We can do that?"

Duke nods, fingers tapping a faster pattern. "Why not? With all the queer and trans folk who've existed throughout history, a bunch of them must've made wishes for future people like them and put energy into the world for us. We don't have to be locked into biology. The collective unconscious sounds mega queer to me."

"I could see Kinz liking that," I tell him. "But the more physical we keep it for now, the happier she's going to be about it."

Camden nods. "Straight up empiricism then: the physical universe as a whole is a system with emergent properties that I call God and Kinz can call emergence?"

"But God calls to us," I say, because I love that part. "To be our best selves and create a better world. Does emergence do that?"

Duke, Jay, and Camden glance at each other and shrug.

"Imagination," Avery suggests. "Or maybe imagination and the collective unconscious together. We can imagine better futures, best selves and maybe when there's billions of us imagining that, it's way more than what any one person can imagine. Maybe it's so strong that our collective imagination— our collective desire to live good lives—calls to us."

"Thank you," Camden says to Avery with the barest hint of surprise in her voice.

"I like collective imagination," Jay says. "Can I use that?"

"Sure."

"Personally, I prefer when there's a God. Actually, the two Goddesses in love with each other," I say. "But this works too. I really like that we're—that you're—coming up with a way to give Kinz better possibilities, to give her a future worth living into."

Camden watches me from across the table, her eyes deep behind her glasses, her soul seeing mine. I want to be a better person for her, but is that imagination or emergence or is it my soul getting seen by hers? She's the one person in all of this who gets that part of me, even more than Avery does. Or maybe

Avery and I haven't talked about the right stuff yet, since she also loves the two Goddesses version of the world.

"Emergent collective imagination it is," Duke says. He hops off his chair and walks around the counter. "Prepare to be amazed by the emergent properties of flour, sugar, and water! These cookies are much greater than the sum of their parts."

"And they're definitely calling to us," I say.

During a course of warm chocolate chip cookies and weird-but-not-bad coconut milk ice cream, the talk circles back through the video project and returns to Kinz and spirituality.

"Is emergence going to be enough for Kinz?" Jay asks Camden.

"I don't know how to tell Kinz that the little things she does matter. That her taking care of herself makes a difference beyond just her."

"Well that sounds good by itself," Avery points out.

Jay says, "And it fits into emergence, because she's in the system, so she's part of improving the totality of it."

"But the littlest things," Camden says. "The teaching that our actions flow back to God and are made fully good within God. I need her to know she matters. All the time."

"Raising holy sparks," Duke's dad says from the doorway behind me. I jump and turn in my chair as he asks, "When did you kids start a Kabbalah study group?"

"Five minutes ago," Duke tells him.

"This is postmodern womanist theology," Camden says. "But some of it comes from process theology, is that in Kabbalah?"

"I have no idea. But what you said is very much what I've been taught." Duke's dad pulls a folding chair from against the wall and unfolds it. "May I join?"

We look around at each other and nod. Duke brings him a plate of hot cookies. Then his dad has to get up and make some coffee, so we keep eating and telling Duke how amazingly, emergently great this new cookie recipe is.

"Explain the sparks," Duke tells his dad when he's back at the table.

"A core teaching of Kabbalah is that the holiness of God is contained in every bit of physical matter, as holy sparks, and each action we take has the potential to liberate those sparks. Because God is a perfection that is continuously perfecting, we become part of the perfecting process."

"Yes!" Camden almost hops out of her chair with excitement. "Our actions flow back into God, who holds all time as a living memory that emphasizes the good and moves evil to the periphery. That's heaven."

"Kabbalah has a lot of heavens," Duke's dad says. "But also teaches that what we do on earth is mirrored in and influences the heavens."

"How …" Camden falters, unable to formulate the question, but I think I know what she's trying to say.

"How can two different theologies from such different times and parts of the world have such similar concepts?" I ask.

Duke's dad grins, his teeth extra bright in the darkness of his beard. "Maybe human beings are on to something."

"We could say we're looking at the same Sacredness, but seeing it in slightly different ways, or we're looking at Emergence," Jay says. "But you could also say that it's similar because human brains are similar, which is probably what you should say to Kinz, Cam."

"The Eternal can't be fully known; we can point toward it, but never really comprehend it," Duke's dad agrees. "I'll cast my vote with the similarity of human brains."

We break into smaller conversations after that and Duke's dad goes upstairs to change into a T-shirt and dad shorts—the kind that have zippers at the bottom because they can also be full-length hiking pants. He brings down a square black box and slides it across the table to me.

Camden, Jay, and Avery are storyboarding the Blair Witch Cooking Project and peripherally watching this exchange. Duke scoots his chair back to watch over my shoulder. I open the box and see two necklaces resting on dark gray foam.

Duke tells me, "Dad didn't know which you'd prefer, since you don't read Hebrew. He says I get your leftovers."

"Which one did you want?" I ask Duke.

"I like them both, you pick."

One is a small silver square with Hebrew engraved on it. When I touch it, Duke's dad tells me, "It says: 'God will guard your going and coming from now and forever,' from the psalms."

"That's beautiful," Camden says across the table.

The other is a geometric design of silver lines with tiny gemstones at the intersections. I lift that one from the box and hold it in my palm.

"The tree of life," Duke's dad tells me.

"It feels familiar," I say.

"There's art of it at temple," Duke reminds me. "You've seen it a bunch of times."

"Or you remember it from the creation of the universe and because it's in all of us," his dad says, the gleam in his eyes only partly mischief.

"Oh well if that's where I know it from then, yes, thank you."

He gets up so he can put it on me and clasp it behind my neck.

"And this will protect me from curses or weirdly messed up spiritual energy?" I ask.

"It's not a formal charm for that, but it'll keep you focused on what's what. And if you're particularly worried, when you kids get up to casting your intentions, or whatever passes for teen trouble these days, this clear golden stone in the middle is Tifereth. It corresponds with your heart. Touch that and it will clear up any magic-related problems you're having."

He returns to his chair and Avery touches my shoulder to get me to face her. Her fingers brush my skin as they trace a line up the pendant. "Like the kundalini energy," she says. "You have to have an open heart."

"Perhaps. I wouldn't know," Duke's dad says. "You ascend the tree in a zigzag pattern, but an open heart is recommended in all ways."

"Run in a serpentine pattern to approach the divine throne?" Duke asks and Camden laughs, so it's got to be a movie reference.

"I suspect it's more like lightning," his dad says. "But I only took two classes in this, so we're at the point where we'd have to ask the Rabbi."

"I'll put that on the list next time I come with you," I say. "Thanks very much, this is great."

CHAPTER EIGHTEEN

The question of sex doesn't come up for the next few days because the contractors start working on the pipes. This is extremely loud and makes the whole house vibrate, but not in a fun way. On Tuesday, Avery has to drive her grandmom around, so I go to meditation class on my own. My knee feels good enough that I can bike over; the old downtown is less than a mile from my house via the bike trails.

I still sit to meditate with that leg stretched out, no point in putting more stress on the knee when I just asked it to pedal a bike. Plus I'm used to this way of sitting and today is not the day to switch things up. With Avery absent, I'm thinking more rather than less. Kinz is getting ungrounded because she agreed to go to church a few times. I need to see her and talk about everything. But also I've been in the group chat planning the Blair Witch Cooking Project with Duke, Jay, and Camden, and I really like Camden. I'm afraid Kinz is going to sense that and get upset about the kiss again.

And on top of all that, the make out sessions with Avery have gone from shyly taking our shirts off midway to starting with them off. How do I figure out if I want to have sex with her, especially when she's leaving in less than two weeks? Do I want my first time to be with someone I might barely see? Which brings me back to Kinz and how much I don't want to do anything that would hurt Camden.

Meditation is not working today.

"Restless?" Miri asks when everyone is gathered in the front room after the session.

"Yeah."

"Let's walk." She holds the front door open for me.

We walk to the corner and cross to the church on the next block. "Is it weird being so close to a church?" I ask.

"Not at all. Jo is a minister there. It's a very affirming church."

"Do you go?"

"Only when Jo's giving the sermon. She speaks a lot about how the purpose of our lives is to spread love and about the power of our community. You might enjoy attending; there are many LGBTQ elders."

"I'd love that."

We turn the corner and she says, "Slow your steps and feel your feet as they touch the ground, that will help settle you. You can meditate while walking, either at your regular pace, noticing everything your senses take in, or you can slow down and let the sensation of the steps be the meditation."

I try this for a block. Walking past the neatly trimmed lawn of the church makes it easier—it's not weird to be walking introspectively by a church. I feel the sole of each foot as it touches the ground and spreads, balances, holds me up. Walking has way more moving parts than I thought: balance, momentum, breathing, joints, muscles, probably some ligaments.

"I'm trying to figure out—" I interrupt myself because I'm not going to say: *if I should have sex with Avery*. "I had a dream about Avery—or someone who looked like her but wasn't. Someone magic and sacred. Twice. Except the first time it wasn't a dream because I was awake. Do you ever have that happen when you're awake but you're dreaming?"

"Do you mean a trance?" she asks.

"Is that what it is?"

"Are you simultaneously awake and in a different state in which you're having a vision that's similar to a dream but mostly lucid, except you're not controlling all of it?"

With anybody else, I wouldn't be honest. But nobody else would ask the question that way. I feel like I've known Miri much longer than the few weeks since I met her.

"Yes," I tell her.

"Do you get into that world through a portal or passage, maybe a tunnel or by flying?"

"Yes!"

"That sounds like trance to me. Some people call it shamanic journeying or simply journeying. Who taught you?"

I shake my head. My cheeks ache with the broadness of my grin. It's so good to have someone to talk to about this! "I started doing it as a kid. As an extension of daydreaming, imagining stories, and then I figured out that if I held a part of my mind open, if I relaxed and made a space for things to happen, then it wasn't only me making up a story. A presence showed up for me and would calm me down if I was scared. I wanted to learn to meditate and figure out religion so I'll know where else I can meet that presence."

We've turned two corners and we're walking along the back side of the church, with the parking lot and trees. It feels like we've walked into one of my dreams, my trance journeys.

Miri laughs, a dry, soft sound. "That's beautiful, Synclair. I think you know you can meet that presence anywhere because She is everywhere. But also I think you're looking for how to experience her in your body. How to call on Her."

"Yes! I want to feel Her with me."

"And *within* you?"

I stop and stare at her. "That's what the cookie is about?"

She pauses, lips pursed with delight, her hair a mane of brown curls the sun shines through. "Your body is a microcosm of the whole universe, of the Sacred. And I ate that cookie because I knew I was hungry."

We start walking again. Her words have the shape of a regular answer, but they're not. She didn't say "because I was hungry," she'd said "because I knew."

I talk my way through my next thought. "You knew because you know your body and if your body is the universe, then knowing your body is a way of knowing God."

"I think walking meditation suits you," Miri says with a round joyfulness in her voice.

One mystery answered, for now, I'm ready for the next. "In the dream, I was asking the person who wasn't really Avery an important question and she said she couldn't tell me the answer. I might have been asking what happens when we die."

Miri says, "That you are guaranteed to find out someday. You won't be disappointed."

"Very funny. Why can't anyone answer the big questions?"

"Many realities can't be said in words—any answer you can be told isn't the real answer. There's a story a friend of mine tells about how he was sitting on his back porch with his dog and there was a huge, beautiful harvest moon on the horizon. So he pointed to the moon and his dog looked up and licked his finger. There are a lot of mystical stories in which people realize that a reflection of the moon isn't the real moon, but I like this version best. I couldn't have told you and Avery an answer to the question about what magic is that would approach the truth of the answer I gave you. But talking about eating a cookie is not the same as eating it."

"And licking a finger isn't the moon," I grumble because I don't know how to apply these answers. And, hearing myself, I laugh. "Wait, is Avery the finger in this analogy?"

"She's not the moon," Miri says.

We walk quietly past the front of the church again. Normally I'd feel conspicuous walking around a church in the middle of the day, especially more than once, but with Miri in her flowing lavender and teal and orange, we couldn't be more obvious already, so it works.

"If all the real answers are experiential, how do I tell other people?" I ask. "Like Kinz. She acts tough, but she's so scared so much of the time, scared she's wrong and going to hell, scared she's right and doesn't know what to do about all the people in the world being awful to each other. She has such a huge heart.

I want to reassure her. I want to figure out all the mystical stuff so I can make life easier for her and for me and for everyone."

"You can't walk her journey for her. But you can love her and walk your journey."

"Ugh, love." I sigh and shake my head and she's chuckling, but not at me. I say, "I'm in love with two or maybe three girls and I'm not sure how into me any of them are. And I keep thinking that Avery is so everything, but if she's not the moon then maybe she's just the normal kind of great. Can I get one easy answer here?"

"Oh, you want a really big answer for everything? Okay, how's this: don't be mean."

"What?"

"That's from Kate Bornstein, a Buddhist, and trans, like me, but nonbinary, unlike me. I think Kate's statement is a strong modern translation of Hillel: 'what is hateful to you, don't do to others.'"

"I thought it started with 'do unto others…'"

"This way is more practical. Don't be mean. The rest is commentary. Go live it."

I'm working out the smartass answer she deserves and thinking that I like a God with more instructions. I prefer Avery's view of two Goddesses in love with each other and with plenty of love left over for me. And Camden's view that God is the best that's possible and is always calling to me, always there. But now I can also feel God in my body—all the trillions of cells and processes that make me possible, that go on without my conscious effort.

EMANATION SEVEN:

Victory

After I get home, I want to do that trance thing again and find my Miriam in the giant forest and see what she can tell me. My leg aches from biking, the muscles not used to stiff-knee riding, so I start the tub. I pour in Epsom salts and essential oils that Avery and I picked up at the natural foods store. The smells remind me of the incense Avery's mom used to burn at her house. I read the tiny oil bottles: frankincense, sandalwood, and cedar. Together they're sweet and musky with a clean, bitter note. Did Avery know what she was buying? Or are these the cleansing scents and her mom was all the time trying to cleanse the energy of their house?

I'd ask, but I don't think she wants to talk about it. She'd bring it up if she did.

I rest my head against the back of the tub and close my eyes. I visualize a photograph from the album on my desk. I'd been showing Avery the album yesterday and breezed past the photos of me in sixth grade, but came back to look at them after she left. This one photo was the worst of the lot. As I tried to smile, my face was breaking from the inside.

I want to go back in time and get that girl and bring her here. If my body is magic can I enter that awake-dreaming, trance world from anywhere? How would I enter it? Can I simply call on Miriam, my dream guide, and have her help me? I mouth the words, "Miriam, can you make this happen?"

I receive a feeling that means "of course," followed by the sensation of riding a flying lion. Sweet of her to change my ride! I hope the dream symbolism is better than it was for the winged horse.

Winged lion, not easier to ride. Next time I'm asking for some kind of saddle. As I focus on the feeling of flying, I see the sky behind my eyelids and then a familiar landscape. We're above my old neighborhood. We circle the elementary school where I'd first met Avery, and where I'd had to keep attending classes and sitting alone at recess after she'd left. The lion sets down in the playground.

I walk up to a window and peer inside. The desks seem so small now, but still arranged in a circle like I remember from sixth grade history. History is my worst subject and I hated that class. I love the future and find the past hard to remember, especially the dates and all the guys we're supposed to think are important who did stupid crap.

I should be able to pass through the wall, dream-self and all, but end up walking around until I find an unlatched window. As if all of this is real. It does feel a kind of real that might be more real than my torn-up house and everyday life.

I push the window open and shimmy through. This classroom smells like stale citrus floor cleanser, staler perfume, shattered social aspirations and the clean wood pulp of paper.

The hall is shorter than I remember and the lockers reach only to my shoulder. Have I grown that much? I pass the closed cafeteria doors and the scent of beef cooked for years, then on down toward the gym where the acidic plastic smell gave way years ago to sweat and the odor of fruit snacks. I find the history classroom and stand in the doorway. I used to sit over there and, in the first year without Avery, there'd been days where I cried silently over my history book.

I go to an empty desk in that part of the classroom and kneel beside it. The ghostly memory of myself fills in the seat.

"Hi, little Synclair, it's me. That is, you, only older. I've come back so our memory doesn't have to stay here. We found Avery again and a lot of other friends and magic and one or more gods."

"You came back," she whispers. How many times, sitting here, had I believed someone would come for me. Was I right—remembering the future?

She puts her feather-light arms around my neck and I lift her out of the chair. I feel immensely foolish carrying a ghost of myself out of the school, but having started this piece of theater, it carries me. I take Synclair-at-eleven back down the hall to the science class and climb through the window, then wait and catch her as she comes through.

She doesn't snuggle into my arms the way she did as I carried her to the window. She pulls away and stares across the playground. There's another one of us standing there, even more transparent than this younger, visioned me. She's also eleven, also me, but nothing like the kid beside me: wild hair, wilder grin, wearing layers of costume and clothing. I think she has wings, but they're part of a fairy costume she has on over a warrior costume.

"Am I supposed to bring you back too?" I ask.

She waves at us. Little me waves back, wistfully.

That's the part of me that wouldn't walk up to Avery's house and return the Hecate statue. That's the part of me that stayed to comfort Avery. This part of my soul started spending more and more time apart from the everyday me. What has she been doing this whole time while I went to school and did all the mundane things? Is she the part of me who hears God's call? The part of me held by the Goddesses?

I take a step toward her but little me grabs my hand. "You don't have room for both of us," she says. "Not yet."

"How do I—?"

A tapping on the door brings me back to the tub, the cooling water, the sound of Mac saying, "Hey you've got the only working shower, when are you done?"

"Minutes," I tell him.

I close my eyes again but the vision is gone. "Take care of her," I whisper to God/desses and have the responding feeling that this is of course what will happen.

While Mac is singing loudly in the shower, I get the intention sheet from my bag and take it to the back patio. I open the grill, put the page on it and light it on fire. I don't need this list and the confusion it has generated. I need to keep making space for the divine in my life. Maybe also in my body? If that wild, sacred aspect of myself was in the schoolyard at age eleven, where is she now?

CHAPTER NINETEEN

We're going to spend the whole weekend at my house. This is the last weekend that we can all get away from family and back-to-school obligations before my parents return. Jay brought the sleeping bags from her house and most of the rooms are finished enough that people can have their pick of where they sleep.

I've been obsessing about inviting Avery to sleep in my bed. She has to go back to New York mid-next week and I so much don't want to dwell on that. She knows I don't want to go "all the lesbian way" and seems cool with it. I said "no" up front because that would be easier to change my mind. I love the idea of sleeping snuggled up with her and maybe I want a lot more? I guess I'll get there and find out.

Kinz went back to church last weekend. For this weekend, she's got her parents convinced that she's on a church retreat with Camden and Jay, hosted by Camden's church. Camden's folks conspired with Jay's mom on this because everyone is on Team Kinz.

Mac invited his friends Gnocchi and Risotto over. They're planning to take the metal firepit down by the woods after dinner. I strongly believe this is so they can smoke weed away from the rest of us, but they're saying it's so the neighbors don't see a fire and call the police. There's a limit to how many times we can have the police at our house this summer without our parents losing all trust in us—and that limit is one—even if it wasn't our fault.

Duke makes us dinner that we all eat sitting at the back patio tables. The new kitchen is hooked up and our new oven is, according to Duke, the very best. He wants to bake his dessert pies in that, so we go in to figure out how to make that happen. Through the open window I hear Avery and Camden talking about movies—and laughing. This is the double date I wanted. It's all working.

Duke makes two pies, one berry and one apple. He figures out that he can convect them if the apple one goes on top. Then he works out how the new timer operates, while I rearrange drinks in the fridge so they're easier to grab. As I'm doing this, my folks call.

"Hey," I answer. "Isn't it the middle of the night there?"

They've got video on, so I can see them sitting on a patio under a dark night sky.

"We were partying. And I wanted to say good night to my babies," Mom says in the voice she uses when she's pretending that she and Dad know how to misbehave. Spoiler: they don't. Though in truth, neither do I, so I'm not judging.

"Mac's outside with his friends, hang on."

I walk onto the back patio and look for Mac. He's standing at the grill with tongs. Oh crap! There are burgers and hot dogs on the grill. I hope nobody can taste the paper I burned. Apropos of that: what happens if people eat burnt intention-making but also religion-mocking paper? It's normal paper right?

I want to tell him to stop, take everything off the grill, let me clean it, to be safe, but already Gnocchi and Risotto are eating hot dogs. They look fine; their pants are still on. I'm overreacting for sure. Plus I can't say any of this in front of

Mom. This has to look like a normal, casual kids cookout that's going to end at a reasonable hour with absolutely no magic or spirituality or, heaven-forbid, religion. Of the things I can't say to my parents, the fact that I've spent the bulk of this summer learning about magic and meditation and mysticism is higher on the list than drinking and way higher than kissing girls (which they're annoyingly excited about).

I step next to Mac, holding out the phone so he can wave from in front of the grill.

"House looks great," he tells them. Mom takes up most of the frame, but Dad crams in behind her as they both wave back.

"Did they get the microwave hooked up?" Mom asks.

"There's an issue with the circuits drawing too much power, they're going to add another circuit on Monday. It should be in when you get home. Everything looks great here. You're going to love it."

"We won't need the microwave if you're still grilling," Dad says.

"Yeah you might not say that if you saw how bad I'm burning these burgers. Love you, gotta go!"

"Who else is there?" Mom asks, so I take my phone around the patio.

Kinz says hi and that she wants to see all their photos when they get back. She introduces Camden, who they kind of already know but haven't seen a lot of. I introduce Avery, who they remember, and spend five minutes talking about how she's grown up and how beautiful she is and how much they're looking forward to seeing her again. They won't actually get to, not in person, because she's leaving a few days before they get back, but I'm still not thinking about that.

By the time I get off the call with them, most of the burgers and hot dogs have been distributed. I touch my new necklace, tell myself I'm being ridiculous, and get a hot dog.

After pie, Mac and his friends carry the firepit into the woods. We watch the dancing orange of their small flame through the trees.

"I hope they don't light anything on fire," Avery says.

"Supposed to rain in a bit," Camden tells her, pointing at the dark clouds scudding in fast from the west. "It'll be okay."

"Are we watching a movie or setting up to start filming the show?" I ask.

Duke is sitting across the table from me, next to Jay. He steals the pie crust off her plate and says, "Let's half set up, then watch the movie. I want to film tomorrow when it's light. But I wouldn't mind playing around with the staging. Where did Mac put the skeletons?"

"That's a really good question." I get up to look for them, but pause in the doorway to watch Camden and Kinz talking with their heads close, Duke, Jay and Avery using cutlery to talk about skeleton staging. Why do I still feel something missing?

I check the master suite first. Knowing Mac, he's going to rig the full skeleton to whip down a zip line at our folks when they walk into their new bedroom. But the rooms are empty except for closed paint cans, tool boxes, painting trays and drop cloths. They smell like construction and the crispness of it all, a new beginning.

From the patio door, I call to Duke, "No skellies in my folks' room. He must've put them in the basement."

A shadow darkens the house. Clouds came up fast, the dark green kind that herald a quick, hard summer thunderstorm. Mac should be back in a minute with his friends and I can ask him where the skeletons are.

"Rain's starting." Kinz points at the dark spots on the patio tile. "Better get the rest of the food in."

We rush amid fat raindrops, gathering the last plates and glasses and napkins, closing the grill, grabbing the papers Camden and Duke were using to organize the show. Once we're inside, Camden and Duke move around the kitchen, planning. Jay helps by playing the role of the skeleton and standing where they ask her to. She is an unusually robust and cheerful skeleton.

Rain patters down steadily but not too hard. Mac and his friends might try to wait it out under the cover of the trees.

I can't see their fire anymore. The back door is open, the air blowing through feels hot and dense, one of those wild summer squalls. It might be over in minutes. But if it isn't, I don't think they've got flashlights other than their phones and I doubt they want to hold their phones in front of them in pouring rain.

The electrician had a big flashlight with her yesterday as she figured out the wiring issue with the new kitchen. Maybe she left it here. I go through the living room and into the master bedroom suite, turning on lights as I go, searching for a flashlight or toolbox. I find a heavy tarp that I could use in place of a raincoat and set that by the master suite door.

The heart of the storm comes closer. Lightning flashes and the thunder isn't far off. Isn't standing in a forest a terrible idea during a thunderstorm? I think as long as the lightning doesn't hit the tree you're under, you're fine. I hope Mac knows more about this than me; we both grew up in a neighborhood with far fewer trees than this one. We're lawn and sidewalk kids. So are his friends.

I open cupboards in the master bath, still searching for the flashlight. The smell of sawdust, plaster, and paint is strong in here. I wouldn't have liked it at the start of the summer, but now it reminds me of Avery and time by myself. A thunderstorm-darkened evening would be a perfect time to make out with her in my bed, if I can find her and if Kinz and Camden haven't had this idea first.

I can check upstairs for a flashlight, pick out an empty bedroom to shoo Kinz and Camden into, and keep an eye out for Avery while I do. She could help with my search and then we'll both end up in the same place.

As I step out of the upstairs bathroom, a massive boom sounds from down the block. The lights snap off. I didn't see lightning, but I guess something got hit. I turn on my phone flashlight, shining it toward the stairs. I descend slowly, listening hard but not hearing anyone on the first floor. There should be chatter or laughter or someone tripping over things in the dark and yelping.

They wouldn't have gone outside, but the great room is empty. I hurry toward the kitchen and look onto the back patio. Nobody in either of those places. Fear tells me they've all vanished into the storm. There's too much magic. I didn't learn enough. My friends are gone and I'm alone in the world. I want to curl up in a ball. I want to run wildly into the woods to find Mac.

I know what I'm feeling is irrational, but that doesn't matter. This is the problem—for me—with the way my parents removed all the deep stuff from our lives. I have no toolkit for dealing with existential panic.

EMANATION EIGHT:

Splendor

Closing my eyes, I focus on the energy inside my body. It's there, slow flowing and sparking. Out loud, I say, "Hey, I could use some help here. God, Goddesses, whoever's mine, could you do something?"

"God has no hands but ours," Camden says from behind me.

I spin around. She's got her phone-flashlight out too, shining down at our feet.

"Lights are off all down the block," she says.

"Where's everyone?"

"Looking for skeletons in your basement."

"Are they okay? Nobody knows the mess down there except Avery. And Mac's still in the woods."

In the dim light, Camden's eyes are darker than usual. How can I see a difference between dark brown and deep black? I don't know, but it's there. She's herself and more, as if there's a presence overlapping her, regarding me through her eyes. The same presence I saw in Avery in my dream. The same presence I've known all my life.

"You have a choice," she says. "Choose."

She is *not* talking about a choice between Mac and my friends. She's asking how I want to do this. Am I going to go alone, stumbling in a flat material world, or am I going to say yes to the presence in her and in myself?

I hold the tree of life necklace between my thumb and finger. If all ten of its stones overlapped, imbuing the same place with their light, they would have the infinite dark luminous quality of her eyes. I know my answer to all the questions she could be asking, the answer I'll choose again as often as asked.

"Yes."

Lightning flashes with immediate thunder. It would utterly count as a sign from God except that we're in the middle of a storm so lightning with thunder has been happening every few minutes.

CHAPTER TWENTY

In the shock of silence after the thunder, I hear a smaller crash from my basement and a yelp of pain. I run for the stairs and at the top step, my phone goes dark. No charge. Of all the times to forget to charge it. Okay, I forget pretty much every day, but still, it feels like there is a curse and we all ate it.

Good thing God's on my side, isn't She? I turn back to the kitchen and wait for the next blast of lightning, but I don't see Camden. Screw it, this is my house, I know my way around—or at least I used to before the remodel, but close enough. I feel my way down the first steps. My eyes adjust and there's a faint glow at the bottom. Beyond the last step, Avery stands in the small pool of light cast by her phone.

I reach her side and ask, "What happened?"

"Things fell, lots of things, over there across the room."

"We need to go see." I step into one of the narrow, deep valleys between the boxes.

Avery stays by the wall. "We could get trapped in there too. We moved all that stuff and we didn't put it in the best places. And Mac moved more of it. I don't remember how to get through it. We're no help if we're under a pile of boxes."

"Give me your phone," I tell her and grab it as her hand comes up toward me.

She sighs, still choosing between scared and curious, but she follows me. This part of the basement has no windows and without overhead lights it's very dark. Piles of furniture and boxes limit how far the phone's beam can reach. I move along this aisle, calling, "Kinz! Duke! Jay!"

"Over here!" Jay yells back.

"Where's here?"

"It's where my voice is coming from."

Sounds like she's two aisles over, partway down the back wall. I move in that direction, asking, "Are you hurt?"

"I'm stuck," she calls back. "There's—probably an armchair—upside down on top of me and it's got boxes wedging it down, I can't shove it off. At least not without more boxes coming down on me or you. And I don't want to break all your family china, or whatever, trying to get loose."

"Are the others with you?" I ask over the boxes.

"No, we split up to search the rooms," she says.

"Are you okay if I find them and come back? Avery's here, she'll stay with you." I glance back at Avery, who nods agreement. I give her back her phone.

"Find Duke," Jay insists. "I'll survive."

"See what you can do," I tell Avery, "I'll bring help."

"Got it," she says, holding her phone up toward the ceiling. "And I'll call for help as soon as I get a signal."

I give her a quick hug and kiss on the cheek, then move back down the aisle toward the stairs and basement hallway. Behind me, Avery talks softly with Jay.

My basement has never felt so huge. The fear is back, the one that told me all my friends had vanished, and now it's saying this basement is infinitely large and I'll never find everyone in time. Or I'll get lost down here in some room that didn't exist before tonight and they'll never find me.

I locate the stairs by hitting them with my shin. Okay, slow down, deep breaths, remember the layout of the basement. On the far side of the stairs is the long hallway with two bedrooms and the bathroom. Mac has been sleeping in the bedroom near the end of the hall, making that a logical place for Duke and Kinz to be searching for skeletons.

I feel my way around the stairs and into the hall. At least the bedrooms have windows; once I open the doors, I should be able to see. I open the door to the near bedroom and get very murky gray light that barely clarifies the bulks in the room.

"Kinz?" I ask. "Duke?"

No answer, so I move along the hall to Mac's summer bedroom. When I turn the knob, the door only opens a few inches. Outside the window, the storm has made everything so dark that I can't see anything other than the outline of the window. I try to force the door open and hear Duke grumble.

"Stop, it's me," he says.

"Can you move?"

"I don't want to."

"Are you hurt?"

"Yeah but I don't know how much. I fell over something. I might be fine." His voice breaks, with good reason. Sometimes he falls without getting injured, but most times what would be a little tumble for me is a serious injury for him. His body isn't held together as tightly as the rest of ours, so sprains and dislocations are much easier to come by.

"Duke, if you can roll away from the door, I can get in there."

"Why? If I'm injured, it's already happened," he says. "Go take care of someone else."

"You might only be bruised."

"Then I don't need your help, do I?" he asks, voice sharp.

"I'm not saying you need…I'm sorry, you know how to take care of yourself way better than I do."

He's crying, I can hear the soft wetness of his breath. "I hurt and I'm going to keep hurting. I'm sick of being everyone's optimist, Sinclair. I'm sick of putting on a good face and making everyone okay with me."

"You don't have to do that for me."

"Then go away," he tells me. "Let me figure this out without also having to make it okay for you."

I want to do what he says and I want to cram into the room and try to comfort him anyway. That's more about comforting myself, isn't it? He's had his body all his life and he's good at living in it. I've seen how people around him, strangers and some friends, try to take care of him as if he doesn't know how.

Lots of people get super uncomfortable when he's using his crutches. I would've been one of them if we didn't have cooking to talk about right away. But I learned and this isn't the time to forget all that.

He's right, I want to be able to help him so I'll feel better, not because it'll help him feel better. What I need to be doing is finding more light. And Kinz. She's got a phone and she's somewhere down here.

"I'm going," I tell him. "I'll be nearby if you need. And I'll come back. In a while, though. You've got this."

"Great pep talk," he says flatly. "Go get 'em."

I don't have a good reply to that, so I feel my way down the hall. This takes longer than it should, as if I'm in a labyrinth but with no turns because it doesn't need any, it just goes on forever.

I hate being alone in the dark. The little kid part of me wants to curl up and cry. Maybe I should go back and ask Duke if he can help me.

But I'm not alone, I tell myself. I'm never alone. Being alone is the illusion.

I keep shuffling slowly down the hall to the bathroom door at the far end. It's locked. Someone has to be inside.

"Kinz! Open the door!"

"How do I know you're really you?" she asks.

"I've been wondering that a lot myself lately," I tell her. "My middle name is Anne and I hate the fact that my parents picked two four-letter names from Jane Austen novels."

"The devil would know that," Kinz says.

The devil? That sounds one hundred percent like Kinz losing it.

"I never told him. I swear."

She doesn't answer.

Screw this, it's a flimsy interior door. I lean back, then ram it with my shoulder—and bruise my shoulder. I move away again and kick near the knob. The door swings wide and smacks the wall. I step into the doorway before it can swing shut again.

Kinz is sitting on the floor between the toilet and the sink. And there's the whole skeleton, sitting on the toilet in only a T-shirt, with a magazine open on his lap, like he's pooping but it's taking a while. The skull is on the vanity, one hand nearby holding a mascara brush.

The wall by the vanity is torn open and in the semi-darkness it resembles a narrow pit, one that could go down forever. Kinz must've come in here to pee right before the power went off and panicked at being alone in a bathroom with no lights, (fake!) skeletons and part of the house opening into nothingness.

I sit on the floor across from her because there's no space next to her. "Camden's upstairs. I can go get her in a minute and she'll come tell you no devil business is going on."

"We got hit by lightning," she says. "For being sinners."

She's rolled her shoulders in, making herself small. Kinz was not made to be small. It's a bad look on her. Her hair is forward, braids in front of her ear when they should be tucked behind it, braids and waves hiding half her face. I've seen her manage horses eight times her size without a hint of fear, seen her talk a scared thirteen-year-old into getting on a horse and having a decent time of it, because that thirteen-year-old was me. But her parents got to her when she was tiny and told her so many stories about hell and Satan that she's never managed to get out of her head.

Plus I've heard the way her dad talks to her even now, at seventeen, like she's small and disgusting. That's the part that burns, the real hellfire in her life, when her dad asks, "Why can't you be *normal?*" his voice filling that word with horrible power. He talks to her as if she's filthy and evil, like she picked the worst life possible to spite him, and he says it in such everyday words that she can never repeat it to anyone in a way that makes sense of the pain.

I wouldn't understand if I hadn't been over at her house enough for her dad to forget about me. I'm not sure even Camden has heard him talk that way. He's different around "guests." And I've only caught it a few times, but when I asked Kinz how often he's that way, she said, "All the time at home."

It'd be easy to think that any loving God would've hit Kinz's dad with lightning—except I guess loving Gods don't lightning people. Camden has been telling me about God being noncoercive.

And Christianity didn't set Kinz's dad up to act that way. There's so much about being loving in the Bible that her dad has to work to find verses he can make hateful. He doesn't hate Kinz because she's queer. He hates her because he's a mean person and he can't control her. The queer stuff is his excuse.

I wish I could get into Kinz's fears and shame—to demolish all of it. I want one big answer that will solve everything, but I'm starting to understand how that answer is life itself.

I tell Kinz, "We're in a big storm and the power is out. Probably a tree fell on the power lines."

She says, "Everywhere I go there are skeletons, like a warning. What if my parents are right? What if we're all going to hell? What if I am, because I'm awful?"

"Kinz, you're amazing."

"We're all horrible sinners and I love girls, I'm going to hell for sure and I'm going to burn forever for this, but I can't not love who I love. Why am I supposed to choose?"

I think of Camden upstairs, filled with presence, infinite eyes, asking me to choose—and I choose again, for me and for Kinz, I choose the love, power, divinity, and magic that gives us the lives we need to live.

"That's not the choice on the table," I tell her. But I don't know how to prove that to her. I need Camden.

I push off the floor and take the skull and hands from the sink, putting them in the bathtub. Then I lift the skeleton off the toilet, complete with his magazine, and settle him in the tub, facing the skull. Now they can comfort each other, in case Kinz's hellfire and brimstone talk is freaking them out too.

I pull the shower curtain across so Kinz won't see them when she stands up. The shower curtain features cats showing their butts; my mom finds this super funny. Hey, it's animals. Maybe that's part of God taking care of Kinz. Or making it possible for me to realize I should do this for her and block off the skeletons with cat butts. I like a God who can work with cat butts.

"You okay staying here?" I ask Kinz. "I'll be back soon."

"It doesn't matter where I am," she says. Her fingers twist together between her knees and she stares at the tile floor as if it's going to open up and drop her into a burning pit.

"Definitely back soon," I tell her.

CHAPTER TWENTY-ONE

I feel my way back along the short hall. With my eyes still adjusted to the light of Kinz's phone, I can't see. At least I remember where the boxes and furniture pieces are in this part of the basement. If I hold to the wall on my right, I'll get to the stairs without smacking into anything.

I round the corner toward the stairs and crash into someone, grabbing at them fast so neither of us goes down. They grab me too and our opposite momentums keep us standing, though we tip sideways and bump into the wall.

Braids brush the fingers of my right hand. I smell vanilla and coconut. "Cam?"

"Synclair? Thank God. Where—?"

"Kinz is in the bathroom freaking out but otherwise okay. Duke's in the bedroom, I think he's okay for now. Jay is stuck way across the big part of the basement and Avery is trying to help her."

Camden keeps her hands on my arms. I keep hold of her too. My eyes have adjusted and I still can't see anything because this windowless part of the basement is dark as midnight.

"Where's your phone?" I ask her. "My battery's out."

"I met Avery on the stairs, coming up. She couldn't get Jay out and was going to see if she could call for help, so I gave her mine too. We have different carriers. Maybe she can get a signal on mine if hers isn't connecting. All the cell towers can't be down, can they?"

She sounds afraid that this is the end of the world. Feels like it with thunder booming outside.

"Is Mac here?" I ask.

"I think they're stuck in the woods. It's started hailing. Safer under the trees than trying to run across the lawn."

"But not that safe," I say. "I found a tarp upstairs. Do you think we could get it to them?"

"I don't know how to triage this. How bad is Kinz? Who needs help first?"

"The skeletons were sitting in the bathroom and she's losing it, about the devil and how she's going to hell for loving girls. Er, a girl. Her dad…Cam, we need to talk about her dad after this, okay? I have to tell you about how he talks to her when you're not there."

Camden tugs on me and I move forward until we're holding each other again, tightly. Her body quivers in my arms. She's sobbing silently into my shoulder.

"Hey, it's okay," I say, but I hear the doubt in my voice. We both know Kinz isn't okay and that she needs a lot more than her parents are going to give her and maybe more than either of us can.

"There isn't a hell worse than the one her parents are putting her through," Camden whispers. "But I don't know how to save her. I'm trying. I can't say the right things, I can't find them, I can't…I make her angry or hurt or more scared. She wants me to tell her I don't believe, but I do."

"I know," I say. "I love that about you."

I bite my tongue, hard, on purpose and take deep breaths while she's crying on me. I like how she cries. And how she kisses. Which are not things I can be thinking right now when I need to not lose my own shit.

"I can't just be for her," she whispers. "Not all the time. Not with all of this. I'm trying so hard but hearing all that over and over, I can't."

I hug her tighter because although I don't get all of it, I get a lot of it. Camden loves her religion and is up for fighting to make it inclusive, but a version of that same religion is being used to break Kinz. Her choices seem a lot harder than mine.

Hail smacks against the distant windows like rifle shots. It's getting worse. Weeks ago we had a storm with hail the size of golf balls and this sounds as bad.

"We have got to move," I say. "I'll talk about this as much as you want later. You can tell me anything and I'll listen, but right now what would queer Jesus do?"

"I have no idea," she says.

"Then find the best possibility and remember that God has no hands but ours."

She sighs, relaxes against me. "Yes. God's calling. We need to help the others. Who first?"

I want to pull her down the hall to Kinz and see if we can help her together, but I'm worried that we can't. What if what she needs right now is someone to tell her that religion isn't real? Neither of us can pull that off convincingly.

I trail my hand down Camden's arm and wrap my fingers around the warm, soft strength of hers. Disentangling from our hug, I pull her toward the hall and the far bedroom door.

"Duke, I really need your help," I say through the door. "Are you able to help?"

"Leave me alone," he growls.

"He fell," I tell Camden. "And got hurt, but not badly, I think. It's a lot for him if we need him to take care of us too. But he knows how to talk to Kinz."

"Duke, where's God right now?" Camden asks through the door.

In the moments when the rain lets up, I hear him crying.

"That didn't help," I whisper to Camden.

"Give him a minute," she whispers back.

Thunder booms over the house and Duke is still crying, but he says, "Here." And then, louder, but not to us, "Here I am." After another minute he asks, "What do you need me to do?"

I tell him, "Kinz is losing it and we need someone to talk her down, or up, not sure."

His laugh is short and hard. "Why *me*?"

"Because you can do it without saying 'God.'"

His next laugh is looser. A small light goes on behind the door. He shuffles away from the far side. I push the door open. He's sitting on the floor, cradling his right hand to his chest.

"How bad?" I ask.

"Dislocated my thumb but it's back in, just aches. Probably sprained my wrist and I'm *pissed* that it's my right hand. If you'll use my phone and light the way, we'll see how I do."

"You want a hand up?" Camden asks.

"I really don't."

He drops his phone and slides it toward me, then goes back to holding his hand against his chest. I shine the phone in front of him. It takes him a minute to stand without using his hands because he's got to keep the one holding the other, but he climbs to his feet.

We progress down the short hall with me walking sideways so I can light the path for Duke and Camden. I open the bathroom door all the way and step inside. Kinz remains sitting against the wall, her arms wrapped around her legs. She stares in front of her, not looking at anything I can see.

Duke brushes past me and lowers down to sit against the side of the tub. Kinz's eyes slowly focus on him and she points at his cradled hand.

"Dislocated it saving my pretty face," he says. "You look dislocated too."

She nods and inches closer to him. He stretches out his legs and pats his thigh. Kinz rolls onto her side and lies down, resting her head there. He tucks his swelling hand against his belly and uses the other to stroke her hair.

"There's no hell, sweetie," he says. "It's a metaphor and you know that because there's no place to fit a hell in a universe that's evolving, emerging into greater amazingness. A hundred years from now when you die, someone's going to put you in the ground and plant trees in you, a whole bunch of trees and they're going to get huge and drop leaves in the backyards of Camden's and Synclair's grandkids."

"We're having grandkids?" Camden asks.

"Not together," Duke tells her. "You and Synclair are, like, neighbors."

"I want to be trees," Kinz says. "But how can people be so sure about hell?"

Duke says, "Same way they're sure about anything made up. The sun used to circle the Earth, right? Now, pick a topic: ice cream or pie."

"Yes," she answers.

"Okay, I'll name a pie, you tell me which flavor goes with it."

"Chocolate chocolate chip," Kinz says.

Duke chuckles. "With strawberry rhubarb? No way."

"Yes way."

"I suppose the tartness of the fruit would deepen the flavor of the chocolate. We could make a coulis. But what about blueberry?"

"Chocolate chocolate chip," Kinz insists.

"Only if there's ganache. Is there a ganache?"

"There's always a ganache when you need one," Kinz tells him. Her eyes have closed and her shoulders look less wooden.

I glance at Camden, who's starting to smile. She nods and tips her head toward the door. I wave Duke's phone at him, but he shakes his head. Kinz's phone shines brightly from the floor. We back out of the bathroom with his phone flashlight.

As we get back into the big room, I hear a shifting crash from the far side.

"Jay!"

I dart along an aisle between boxes, turn right at the wall and jump back as one box slides off another. Camden grabs my belt and pulls me back another step. The box hits the floor at my feet, spilling out books.

"You guys okay?" Jay yells over the box wall.

"Yeah, you?"

"My legs are cramping and I'm still stuck under an armchair and starting to panic. More like in the middle of panic."

"We can handle two of those problems," Camden tells her. "You need to handle the third. What's that breathing thing you told me about?"

"Box breathing?" Jay asks. "You want me to do box breathing under a pile of boxes? Hah, yeah. Fucking get me out of here!"

"How does it go?" Camden insists. "You know I'm stubborn, so tell me or we'll be here all night."

"Four counts of four," Jay says, her voice ragged. "In, hold, out, hold."

Camden starts counting to four, over and over. I'm worrying about Mac in the woods and the hail, about Avery not coming back—what if she went after him and got hurt? By lightning or hail or both?

Camden is still counting so I match her count with my breath: in, hold, out, hold. My heart stops speeding up.

"Jay, can you shine your phone up?" I ask.

With Jay's phone and Duke's we survey the problem. The massive armchair that my dad loves slipped sideways off a pile of boxes, must've knocked Jay over and then settled with its back and seat on either side of her torso. She's got one arm trapped at her side and her legs are bent up because of more boxes, so she can't get leverage any way other than pushing against the floor. But other boxes and part of a table are on the legs and seat of the armchair, so her last attempt at pushing up shifted a box into another stack of boxes. Lucky for her they fell toward us and not on top of her.

"We can get that box off, but then we've got to deal with this big table," Camden points. "The leg is pinning the armchair down. If we move those boxes…"

"I can go around and pull the table back," I finish the thought for her.

"But I'll have to hold it up on this side, otherwise it'll hook on the edge of the chair and wedge in more."

No wonder Avery couldn't get Jay out on her own. Where is she? Did she reach help or go to help Mac herself? What if they're all trapped in the woods?

What if I got all this wrong and I was supposed to make a choice about running into the woods to get Mac? If he were here, he'd get under the heavy table, Atlas-style, and heave it up so Jay could scramble out from under the chair. I take as slow a breath as I can manage and feel the energy in my body. Keep moving, keep doing until everyone is okay, not frantically, just steadily; life itself is an answer.

I take Duke's phone and retreat up the aisle to the next one over, where I can grab the back legs of the dining room table. It's super heavy because of the extra leaves underneath the top. I count to three and pull. Camden lifts and pushes. I stagger back and nearly get slammed into the wall by the weight of the table, but Camden has a hold on the other side. I hear her grunt with the effort of holding the sliding weight.

"Move," she says.

"Can't let go or it'll pin me," I tell her. I should've grabbed it from the edge, not the middle, but it's too late now.

There's a crash, a series of small thumps, and the weight of the table lessens. Camden is laughing, so I'm not as worried as I could be.

I slide out from behind the table and yell, "I'm clear."

It crashes into the wall. Jay yells back, "I'm out! From under the chair. Not any other kind!"

"I'm going for Mac!" I tell them and run for the stairs, the way lighted by Duke's phone. I feel like I've been in the basement for an age, but it can't have been that long because the storm is still overhead.

On the first floor I turn off the phone. There's enough light from the lightning and the last bit of sunlight behind the heavy clouds. Hail pelts the windows—not little pings, but hard hits, like a hundred stones fired from slingshots.

I grab the tarp from the bedroom doorway and put Duke's phone on the kitchen counter. I'm not going to risk getting it wet and ruining it. Unfolding the tarp to cover my head and shoulders, leaving it almost an inch thick, I wrap myself and shove out the back door. I have to pause on the patio and brace against the high wind whipping around me. That's why the hail is hitting so hard. If it weren't raining, I'd fear tornadoes. Wait, can you have a tornado in the rain? Maybe I should be afraid of them anyway.

But not right now. I'm making choices. If I can get this tarp to Mac and his friends, they can hold it over all of us as we run back. I sprint for the trees, thick raindrops and biting hail smacking against my knees and shins. One piece of hail makes it under the edge of the tarp and pings off my glasses frame. I squint my eyes as closed as I can while running, bend forward and run harder.

EMANATION NINE:

Foundation

Under the trees, water streams through the branches, but the canopy is thick enough to catch most of the hail. There's no fire to navigate toward, nor the glow of phones. If I were Mac and his friends I'd get into a thick stand of pines. I walk with the tarp over my head, keeping as much of the rain as I can off my glasses. Within minutes I have to stop and wipe my glasses, but even after I clean them, I can't see any sign of Mac or his friends.

Lightning flashes with thunder and I jump. The storm is right overhead. How tall are these trees? Am I going to get hit? I'm supposed to lie down in a ditch in a bad thunderstorm, but then I'll be pelted with hail.

Even though I don't see Mac, I feel that someone is here. I spin around but see only more trees and streams of water in the spaces where the leaves collect rain. I'm soaked and chilled and wondering how bad it is to be wet in an electrical storm. Maybe the feeling of being watched is my brain telling me how completely unsafe I am out here.

I stumble between the trees. How do I know which ones are taller?

Someone is definitely here with me. She takes my hand, a small hand in mine, maybe eleven years old, tugging me toward a grove of short pines. There's a thick, squat tree with heavy, branching roots. The curve of roots creates a concavity deep enough for me to sit half inside—for *all* of me to sit inside. That small, wild self climbs into my lap and sinks into my body.

The life in the tree draws me close and touches the life in me. I sense the roots and bark, trunk, branches going up, the leaves shaking with the wind—and the leaves above, from other trees, much taller. The roots talk to other roots, worried not about this grove but the one at the top of the hill, the one with the old oak who's been leaning, who's giving in to the wind, who's going to fall. Worried less for that oak, who is ready to fall, but for the saplings who will be fallen on.

I'm in branches and roots carrying information and care, a network of compassion and harshness, growth and life and decay, sacred and physical, two energies harmonized by a third or into a third body: divine and human meeting throughout this material world. I open to the mystery, magic, this jumbled, ancient, true language. Sitting in the bent and twisted roots, being in harmony with the creativity that moment by moment gives rise to all of this.

The world arises in the space between my soul and the divine. I'm made of the imagination that creates the world. As if this one tree is saying to me: My friend, Synclair, the Tree of Life and our Gods and Goddesses, our world and your soul are the same.

I lay my hands over the tree, my fingers smaller versions of these roots. Inside my fingers are the smaller fingers of my wild self who wouldn't be told what to do, who wouldn't let herself be collapsed into a two-dimensional world of things with no Sacredness, no emergence.

"I choose you," I tell her, myself. And then, much louder, to the world and the Sacred, "I choose you!"

"Where are you?" a voice yells below the thunder.

"Here!" I yell back. "I'm here!"

A bulky figure comes into my tiny clearing, saying, "I choose you too, Ash Ketchum."

That valiant but dated Pokemon reference can't come from anyone other than Duke's dad. Plus it's his voice.

He crouches in front of me, drenched despite his raincoat and heavy hat. "You okay?"

"Great. I have a tarp," I say, laughing because it sounds so ridiculous. "But I can't find Mac."

"Mac went to your neighbor's house and used the landline to call around to us grownups," he tells me.

Of course. I have a smart brother.

Duke's dad offers me a hand up. "Shall we?"

I offer him half the tarp and we put it over our heads and walk back. The bits of hail are fewer, spread out, smaller. Pinpoints of ice hit the ground, landing next to chunks the size of quarters.

The electricity still isn't on, but someone found the big flashlight because it's shining out the back door to guide us in. When we get close, I see that Kinz is holding it and fling myself at her, hugging super hard. Duke's dad takes the flashlight, shuts the door and leaves us.

"You okay?" we ask each other at the same time and laugh and grin and hug more.

"No really," I insist.

"You first."

"Soaked with hail bruises on my legs, but fine. Now you."

"I'm okay for now," she says. "Come on."

She pulls me farther into the great room. There are lights on the far side, mostly in the foyer, portable lanterns. Two EMTs have joined my friends, one wrapping Duke's hand and the other examining a bruise on Jay's ribs.

Kinz makes me sit down. My shins are bleeding in a few spots from the hail. One of the EMTs comes over when he's done with Duke and says a super-friendly "Hi!," which is when I realize he's one of the same EMTs who showed up when I fell into the skeleton pit.

"We're not like this all the time, I promise," I say.

He grins. "You're not my boring patients, that's for sure. Having a good summer?"

"Up and down, some chaos, but honestly, yes, it's amazing."

CHAPTER TWENTY-TWO

Duke's dad is going to stay the night with us in case the power doesn't come on and we have some other kind of teenaged emergency. (He doesn't know that almost all our teenaged emergencies involve using salt instead of sugar, kissing the wrong girl, and cats with tampons—not anything more dangerous.) He goes into the basement with Mac to clear off the bed in the empty guest room. I hear them yelling to each other as they move boxes around.

They've got the big flashlight, so me and Kinz and Camden and Duke are sitting in the living room with a small electric lantern that Duke's dad brought. We're passing a half-empty pie tin around, because most of us are hungry again.

"Where's Avery?" I ask Kinz. "I'm starting to wonder again if I made her up."

"Oh she's real," Kinz says. "When help got here, she offered to be the one to do car errands. She's taking Jay home and then driving within range of a working cell tower so she can call her grandparents and check on them, let them know she's okay too.

Jay's going to call my folks and Camden's so they know we're okay—my folks still think we're at a church event so she's going to tell them the storm didn't hit hard there. I hope Avery comes back with more food."

I lean around Kinz and look at Camden, raising my eyebrows. She offers me a small smile. Her braids are pulled back in a thick ponytail, which reminds me that they've been that way all night except when I saw her in the kitchen, in the dark, they were in a high bun. Was it really Camden I saw? I don't know how to ask her that: *hey were you possessed by the Divine at any point tonight?*

She's working on a question too, because she asks me, "How did you know to say that? When you said, 'God has no hands but ours.' I've been thinking about that a lot lately. How did you know?"

"You said it to me first," I tell her.

Kinz is deliberately ignoring us—from the moment Camden said "God,"—focusing on digging bits of crust out from around the pie tin.

"I did?" Camden asks.

"In the kitchen, right after the lights went out, when I was freaking out and you told me everyone was in the basement."

She watches me, her eyes deep brown and puzzled behind her glasses.

"And that I had a choice?" I offer.

She shakes her head. "What choice?"

"To choose my reality. The one within me. The way I relate with the world, full on sacredness and God stuff."

"I told you that?"

"You might've been not only you," I tell her.

"Who else would she be?" Kinz asks.

But I see waves of understanding crest in the depths of Camden's eyes and the way her smile stretches broadly.

"Where's the phrase from—God has no hands but ours?" I ask.

"Two places. In a sermon this week, the minister quoted Saint Teresa of Àvila: 'Christ has no body now on earth but yours; no hands but yours; no feet but yours. Yours are the eyes through which the compassion of Christ must look out on the world...Yours are the hands with which He is to bless His people.' Did you know that of the Orishas, the one associated with Saint Teresa is Oya, ruler of storms and wind and change?"

"I barely know thing one about Orishas," I admit. Pretty sure that's about to change. "Do you think...?" I don't have to finish the question, which is good because I don't know how.

Camden shrugs and gives me a knowing smile. "In the sermon, the minister gave us that same idea through a Sufi teaching story: A master is traveling with a student and that night he asks the student to take care of their camel. In the morning it's gone and he asks what happened. The student says: you always teach me to trust Allah, so I asked him to take care of the camel. And the teacher says: yes, you must trust Allah, but also tether the camel because Allah has no hands but yours—if he wants the camel tethered, the best and easiest way is to use your hands to do the work."

I chuckle and tell her, "That would be Mac's favorite spiritual story ever."

"Lots of ideas there, of course," she says. "Our minister talked about the wisdom of the world, how the creativity of the sacred comes through in many ways, how these possibilities come to us and make a way that fits our context. Here are these two very different people: Saint Teresa and a Sufi master, but they're saying very similar things. Like when my theology aligns with what Duke's dad says about Kabbalah."

"Jay would say that's because we all have similar brains," I point out. "But right now I'm going to think it's because we all have the same sacred world inside of us."

Kinz snorts. "Mac's going to hate that he missed the chance to make a poop joke right there."

While we're laughing, Kinz wraps her arms around Camden, who leans into her. I try to turn down the heat on my simmering envy. I'll eventually get used to this. At least I had a summer girlfriend.

"You know, this would be a perfect time to film a Blair Witch Cooking Project," I point out.

That gets Duke brainstorming with Camden again. Avery returns with bags full of chips and cookies and jerky and drinks, like we're going to be stranded in this one house with no power for a week. She's so relieved that everyone's all right that she volunteers to play the witch in the video if Duke will tell her what to do cooking-wise.

CHAPTER TWENTY-THREE

Avery leaves today, this afternoon. I want to be a grown-up about this but I know as soon as she's gone, I'm going to spend the rest of the day crying. Of course I want her to come over anyway.

She brings muffins and I make eggs. We take our plates onto the patio and stare out over the hot tub pit, the lawn, the trees where we first kissed.

"I thought there'd be a hot tub by now," she says.

"They're estimating another week at least. The fake skeletons delayed them a few days and then with that big storm, they figured they'd finish up inside first while it dries out."

"So next year when I come visit…"

I would one-hundred percent hang out in a hot tub with Avery, but I don't want to wait a year to have a girlfriend again. My words come out less enthusiastic than I want. "Yeah. Sure. And Duke says he wants to teach you to make spanakopita."

"I'd love that," she says, super quietly.

"What are you going to tell your girlfriend?"

"That I had a thousand times better summer than I expected," Avery says. We eat in silence for a bit and she adds, "I'll tell her all of it. Or most of it. The way I feel—I don't know how to talk about it yet."

"Maybe leave out the part where I fell in a pit, okay? And the cat-and-tampon story, well, that's up to you. But definitely not me getting naked in front of everyone in that ridiculous game. Don't tell her that."

She puts her plate down and pushes out of her chair with such determination that I set my plate on the table, ready to get up too. She sits in my lap and cups her hands around my face.

"You," she says, a whole universe in that word, and kisses me.

It's obvious we're not eating any more. We go into my bedroom and there's a lot more kissing and some crying, but mostly not by me. I hold Avery as she full-on sobs against my shoulder, feeling so lucky to have the friends I do, this year to look forward to, the support of this whole Sacred world.

When we're lying on my bed, contemplating our entwined fingers, sniffling, she says, "I brought you something. Do you want it?"

"Of course."

She retrieves her shoulder bag from the kitchen, sits on the foot of my bed and unzips it. Out comes a box wrapped in dark blue paper with stars that she hands to me.

It's heavy. I peel the paper off and open the rectangular white box. Nestled in lavender tissue paper, the young aspect of triple Hecate gazes up at me.

"Is this…can this be the same one?"

"I asked Mom to send it. It's the one I gave you six years ago," Avery says. "If you want."

"Yes. Absolutely yes! Thank you."

I lift the statue out of the box and turn it in my hands, grinning into each of the three faces. Then I hop out of bed, grab all the cooking books on the left side of my bookcase and put them on the floor. I set Hecate there so she can watch over me. I get Miriam and Tzipporah and Jesus out of my closet and arrange them next to her.

Avery has her phone out. "Hang on, stay there. Can I take a picture of you with them?"

I grin and try to keep from being too much of a lopsided smiling dork. When she's taken the photo, I fling myself back onto the bed next to her.

"Why are there three of Hecate if there are two goddesses?" I ask. "Right? There's the Sacredness that manifests the physical world—and She's who I feel reaching up when I meditate, cradling me in her palm—and then there's the Sacredness that's transcendent, that maybe I can never fully understand, who reaches down into reality to touch Her lover. That's two, so where's the third?"

Avery takes my hand and laces our fingers together again. "We are," she says. "We're the third face of God."

"Wow, I bet the first two faces have some strong opinions about that," I say. "Do you think it's proof of God that you came back, that we met this summer, all of this?"

"Of course," she says. She digs in the front pocket of her bag and pulls out a piece of paper that she unfolds and hands me.

It has her and her mom's address and home phone number, her grandparents' address and phone, even Nadiya's contact info.

"I never want to lose you again," she says.

So I have to kiss her, the paper crushed between us. And the kissing continues until her phone chimes to tell her she'd better move her butt or miss her plane.

When she's gone, after I've watched her drive away, waving and starting to cry again, I take the rest of the books off the top of my bookshelf. A few I want to keep, but a bunch are going into a donation pile.

I get the box out of my closet and unpack all my religion and spirituality books. They go next to Hecate, Miriam, Tzipporah, and Jesus. And then I take Jesus out of his box. I put him with Miriam and Tzipporah. I have to remember to show this to Camden, to explain how God/Goddess made the world—that will be Tzipporah—and reaches into the world from beyond—that's Miriam since she's the prophet—and lives within us.

I'm pretty sure she'll say that's the point of Jesus but my real question for her is whether she can communicate all that in a lip-sync music video.

CHAPTER TWENTY-FOUR

Before I can decide if I want to spend the rest of the afternoon alone or text Kinz and Camden, Kinz pounces on me via an actual phone call.

"I'm coming to get you," she says. "Where do you want to go?"

This is my usual Kinz: a fine blend of bluster, boldness, and consideration. She knew when Avery was leaving and gave me one hour to get my head together.

My folks are coming back in two days and then it's a week and a half until school starts, most of which will be my folks wanting to spend time with me and Mac and then getting ready for school. We only have a few more days of real summer left.

"That little beach by the lake?" I suggest.

"You're asking to go outside? What kind of transformation happened to you?"

"Maybe I got hit by lightning."

"You didn't, did you?"

"Not literally. Mythologically. Also on the way we have to get food. Donuts! I could eat some donuts. And invite the others if they're around."

"About that," she says. "Duke and Jay are busy, so it would only be Cam. Is that cool?"

I try to figure out what Duke and Jay could be doing together. Editing the Blair Witch Cooking Project? Trying new recipes? But Duke would want us there for that.

"What are Duke and Jay doing?" I ask.

"Movie date. He asked her out."

"Exqueeze me? I thought he was ninety percent gay."

"The other ten percent is sweet on Jay," Kinz tells me.

"Why didn't he tell me?" I feel way more betrayed than I probably should.

"Because he's afraid of how it's going to be for you if he's with Jay and I'm with Cam—"

"And I'm the only one in our group without someone? Maybe I'll date God."

I can hear Kinz wince, but she doesn't challenge me.

"Maybe you'll meet someone at this beach again," she says. "It's been good luck for you so far."

She picks me up and we stop for drinks and donuts on the way to the beach where Avery first taught me to meditate. There are a few people out walking and a group sunning at the far end of the beach. On the other side of the very short pier, we stroll onto the jut of rocky sand that's empty and lay out the blanket from Kinz's car. It still smells of horses and a bit of vanilla.

We flop back on our elbows, the box of donuts between us. I grab one that's chocolate-frosted and caramel-filled. Kinz winces at how sweet that's going to be and picks a tart blackberry donut.

"Do you want Cam to join us—she can get a ride over—or only the two of us?" Kinz asks.

I grab Kinz's phone and text to Cam: *Don't say anything flirty, this is Synclair, and you're welcome to come to the beach with us.*

Cam replies: *Bummer, I just downloaded the great flirts of Saint Teresa of Àvila.*

I type back: *Oh like what?*

She doesn't reply right away, so I hand the phone back to Kinz who reads the message and raises her eyebrows at me. I shrug and lick salted caramel out of my donut.

When Kinz's phone pings again, she reads it and hands it to me. Cam has typed:

"The important thing is not to think much but to love much and so do that which best stirs you to love."

"To reach something good it is very useful to have gone astray, and thus acquire experience."

"Accustom yourself continually to make many acts of love, for they enkindle and melt the soul."

I am actually blushing because of Saint Teresa of Àvila. Okay not mostly. I'm blushing because Camden and remembering kissing her and this is really good flirting—and also that moment when I said "I love that about you" to her in the basement. There's a whole lot I love about Cam.

Kinz lifts the phone out of my hands. She's kneeling over my legs, examining my face. "You *do* like her." She doesn't sound angry, but I'm not going to risk a peek at her face to check.

I didn't think things could get worse than my hopeless crush on Kinz. But now I get to have two hopeless crushes on two people who are dating *each other*?

I scramble back so I'm not sitting under Kinz and say, "It'll pass. I'm walking. Be back." Then I run halfway down the beach.

When I get winded, I walk to the far side of the crescent of sand, near where Avery taught me to meditate. I sit most days now. Sometimes for only five minutes and I can be heavily distracted. I'm going to keep attending classes and maybe also take one at Duke's temple, about mysticism, plus take more walks with Miri, even if I only understand half of what she says.

I stare at the ripples of water on the lake. "God, you'll go out with me, right?"

Of course the answer is yes, and I get the impression that God is laughing…not at me, but definitely near me.

I slog back toward the blanket, figuring I'd better have more of a talk with Kinz *before* Camden gets here or this is going to be the second most awkward moment of my summer, right after being naked in a room full of girls. Which, come to think of it, also included Camden. That memory is almost enough to get me to turn around and cut through the woods back to my house. But I'm getting good at tough choices, so I keep going toward the blanket, even when I see that Camden is already there, sitting half in Kinz's lap, eating the other chocolate and salted caramel donut.

I settle on the far corner of the blanket and grab my water bottle.

"I'm sorry if I crossed a line," Camden says.

"No, it's cool. I mean, if you guys are cool, I'm cool," I babble, turning the bottle in my hands.

"Cool with what?" Camden asks.

I look at Kinz like: *You didn't tell her I'm officially crushing on her now too?*

And Kinz stares at me like: *Don't be silly, I tell her everything.*

I try to shoot her a look that asks: *Why aren't you freaking out?* But she only smiles at me, which is not an answer.

Camden pats the blanket closer to where she's sitting and I shake my head.

"You don't want to come over here?" she asks.

"I figure I shouldn't."

Camden slips her glasses off and polishes a lens. She's in a sleeveless white and gray striped top, with a black skirt that has two white stripes near the hem. Plus black and white sneakers and a cute white socks with little scalloped tops. Kinz is in her usual gray V-neck T-shirt and cargo shorts, so Camden is conspicuously cute compared to the two of us. Not that I'm noticing.

Camden puts her glasses back on and says, "I like you."

"Great, pals!" I declare and take a swig of the cold water, trying to burn less on the inside and my face.

She leans toward me, a hand planted on the blanket for balance. "No, Synclair, I *like* you. *Like* like you, or however many likes I need to say for that to register. I didn't mean to kiss you, but now I'd like to, on purpose."

Too fast, overlapping some of Camden's words, Kinz asks, "What would you think about dating us?"

Us?! I gasp-inhale. Water goes up the back of my nose and explodes through my sinuses, so I'm coughing and choking. Kinz takes the water bottle out of my hand and puts a napkin there. As I recover, take off my glasses and blow water out of my nose, her hand rests on my knee.

"There's no way your religion supports this," I mutter into my napkin.

"Hey, I'm an atheist, I converted," Kinz says. "Jay officially signed me up and we're going to a meeting later this week."

Camden adds, "And my mom's actually cool about teen poly stuff—though she doesn't call it that. She said when she was my age it wasn't weird to be dating two people sometimes. We're supposed to be trying out different relationships to see what we like. I'm not sure how she'll feel about me dating two people who are dating each other, but we'll get there when we get there."

Camden is intensely close to me. When Kinz scooted over to my right side to take the water bottle, Camden moved to my left. I've got my glasses off and when I look up, she's near enough that she's barely blurry.

I hold still and let her kiss me. Only the first second counts as "letting," since I start kissing back when her lips touch mine. This time is sweeter, softer. I can admit to myself that I'm kissing Cam—that I want to be kissing her, to keep kissing her, that I love how she kisses and how she thinks—at least for a second before I remember that Kinz is *right there* seeing me kiss Cam!

I pull back and pick up my glasses, unable to look at either of them. They're so close that I feel more than see them move toward each other. They're kissing and I don't want to see that, but also I do because it's different now. I compromise and look up without putting my glasses on, so they're fuzzy around the edges. They're kissing more intensely than me and Cam because they've had more practice. And all I can think is that Kinz is kissing lips that just touched mine so it's almost like she's kissing both of us.

I press my fingers against my lips. When the two of them break apart, Kinz wraps her hand around my wrist and pulls my fingers away. She leans close to me, pauses inches away. I slide forward and press my lips to hers.

If souls can sigh, mine does. I've only been waiting to do this forever, or at least two years and three months. I'm shaking with the intensity, so I turn my head and slide forward, into her arms. But also I reach to my left until Camden takes my hand because I don't want her to feel left out. She puts my hand on her side as she leans in and wraps her arms around both of us.

I can't think while snuggled in the middle of them, so I pull back and we all grin at each other from inches away. "You guys are really serious?" I ask.

Camden has her glasses off now too and she looks as amazing without them as with them.

"No, we're just—" Kinz starts a moment of sarcasm, but Camden shakes her head and Kinz presses her lips together, smirking.

"Yes," Camden tells me. "We talked about it a lot. We both really like you and it seemed that was mutual. I'm not coming out at school in the near future, so you and Kinz can go do all the official lesbian stuff as long as you're super sweet to me afterward."

"Of course," I say.

"And you and I can do all the 'woo-woo religious stuff' that we like," Camden says. "And Kinz has me for the activities that involve the outdoors."

"Hey, I liked that one tree," I protest. "Okay yeah, I am definitely not a forest monk. What if we get jealous?"

"We talk about it," Kinz says. "You know I'm crazy about you, when I'm not plain being crazy. When I was panicking in your basement because of Mac's pooping skeleton and all that shit about hell, the one clear thought I had was that I don't want to go to college without having dated you. And Cam and I didn't figure that was a decent reason for us to split up, not when the two of you are sparking all over the place."

"So, do we get, like, matching sweaters?" I ask.

"No," they say in unison.

"T-shirts?"

"Do you think the three of us are ever going to agree on the same T-shirt?" Camden asks while Kinz shakes her head.

"Who sits in the middle during movies?" I ask.

"Whoever wins theology trivia," Camden says.

Kinz snorts and rolls her eyes. "Horse trivia."

"Food trivia?" Camden offers and Kinz nods.

"I call dibs on the middle right now since I'm the newbie," I declare and dive between them, tackling them to the blanket. So many parts of this summer have felt like magic and ritual, but this is some of the best.

EMANATION TEN:

Indwelling

Since the start of the school year I've learned that three-way kissing is challenging and three-way movie viewing is amazing, especially when I'm in the middle. Kinz, Cam, and I have been hanging with the full Culinary Club now that school is on, but this Saturday it's only the five of us from the core group on my back patio again. We're double-dating with Duke and Jay, to celebrate the summer we made it through and the fact that we're seniors now.

Kinz grills fish while Camden and I chop up the salad pieces and Duke folds gluten-free pastry dough around fruit and chocolate fillings.

"Did you tell your mom that you came to church with me?" Camden asks as she pours bits of green pepper into the big salad bowl.

"Not yet. I said we went shopping," I admit.

"At least she's cool that you're dating two girls," Duke points out as he gets up to put the tray of mini-pastries in the oven.

"I think she's bragging about it at work," I say with a wince.

On his way back to his seat, Duke is blocked by Jay's arm. She tucks her fingers over his belt and pulls him into her lap while he laughs.

Kinz shakes her head. "Who knew you two would work?"

"We said the same thing about you three," Jay tells her.

Duke kisses Jay and then scoots back to his seat. He pulls over a spare cutting board and goes through mushrooms much faster than anything Camden or I could manage.

He asks, "Are you guys going to be okay when Kinz moves over here?"

"Six more weeks," Kinz says with a sigh.

She's been putting on her best act for her dad, going to church, not bringing up me and Camden—and all the while moving her favorite things from her house to mine, one backpack load at a time.

My parents and I talked about it after they got back from Greece and then included Kinz in the discussions. As soon as she turns eighteen, she's welcome over here for the rest of the school year and summer and after that if she wants, depending on where she goes to college. I'm not positive, but I think my folks are putting some money into her college fund.

"That'll make my life easier," Camden says. "Both my girlfriends in the same place."

"You won't get jealous that they're spending more time together?" Jay asks.

Camden laughs. "You know me, I absolutely will. But they'll make it up to me."

"We're going to be extra attentive for weeks," I say.

"Months," Kinz says. "This mahi mahi is ready, y'all better get over here and get some."

We fill plates with fish and the mango salsa that goes with it, salad, asparagus risotto and buttery gnocchi that Duke made to honor Mac and his friends. Dinner is all about the Blair Witch Cooking Project, which hasn't rivaled Camden and Jay's other video efforts but is building its base.

As we're clearing dishes, Duke says, "Speaking of upcoming birthdays, Synclair, we brought you stuff."

"I love stuff."

He waves to me to sit down and opens his backpack. Kinz goes out to her car and brings back a blue cloth grocery bag. She pulls out a big square box, then scoots over so Camden can get a long box out of the bag, followed by Jay tugging another wrapped gift from the bottom.

Duke puts his small, blue-and-white wrapped box on top of Jay's, so I open that first. It's a round silver ball with carvings of houses and fruit trees on the outside. There's a catch that opens it, revealing places fit the bases of two candles.

"Shabbat candle holder," he says. "In case you want to start lighting the candles but also because I remember how you like that stylized old Jerusalem cityscape. You can keep it as art if you want, if you're not lighting the candles."

"It's beautiful," I tell him.

I open Camden's gift next and it's a prayer candle—which would be strange since that's not something her church does, except of course it's St. Teresa. Along with that, there's a book about Orishas. I get up and hug her. She presses her lips to my cheek.

When I pick up the gift from Jay, I can tell it's an action figure. I rip off the paper and I'm looking at a gray-haired and mustached man in a dark gray suit with his glasses pushed up on his head. The box says: *Carl Jung action figure*. Tucked in with it is a magnet with a sketch of Jung and the quote, "Magic is a way of living."

"Wow, I need to read more Jung," I tell Jay.

"I have recommendations," she offers, her broad grin squinting her eyes even more than usual.

Kinz's gift is a tree made out of thick copper wires for the branches, trunk and intense root system, with little green wires looped for leaves. The twisted roots extend in two directions, not quite perpendicular, and then weave into a wooden base. Between the roots, there's enough room for a tiny person to sit against the trunk. I bend Carl Jung's legs out and seat him at the base of the tree.

"How did you know?" I ask Kinz, my voice thick with all the feelings.

She shrugs. "I know *you*."

I hug her a lot and then go into my room and get Jesus and Hecate, Tzipporah and Miriam. Tzipporah and Miriam obviously go with the Shabbat candle holder. Jesus stands under the tree next to Jung, which leaves Hecate contemplating the St. Teresa candle and Orishas book. We arrange them all at the head of the table while Duke gets his pastries out of the oven.

"Is the ice cream out here?" he asks.

"No, it's in the big freezer," I tell him and turn toward the patio doors.

My mom stands in the doorway staring at the display on the table. Her mouth is open, forehead crinkled. I watch her gaze flick to each item, scroll back across a few, try to compute them together. She frowns, lifts her eyebrows in a mini-shrug. The strangeness of it all is going to make it easy to dismiss.

"Mom, I have to tell you something," I say. "I'm religious. I've been going to church with Camden."

"And you, what, want me to know you believe in God?"

I glance around at my friends. Kinz and Jay share a worried look. Camden is on her feet, ready to come to my defense. And Duke is wide-open grinning at me like: *you've got this*.

"It's not about belief," I tell my mom. "It's about who I am and who I want to be and the fact that I need a relationship with the Sacred, who I call God."

"How many relationships are you going to be in?" she asks, her tone part joking but also really not joking.

"Three, right now. And please be as cool about this one as you are about my other two. Except you don't have to brag about it. Or, really any of them."

She turns to Kinz, because she knows that Camden's going to agree with me. "You're okay with this?"

"Sync's got to be herself," Kinz says. "I'm not cool with telling people how they can and can't be. If I've got the freedom to be an atheist, she's got to have freedom and support to have her relationship with God."

Mom surveys the tableau of action figures and other items and sighs. "Okay," she says and goes into the house shaking her head.

I turn back to the table as Camden's putting an arm around me. I lean into her and feel her lean back. My fingers travel across the tree roots to the magnet and I tap it. "Jung, you are not kidding about magic."

Bella Books, Inc.

Women. Books. Even Better Together.

P.O. Box 10543
Tallahassee, FL 32302

Phone: 800-729-4992
www.bellabooks.com